"The problem

He stopped.

Rachel waited fo~~ ~~ ~~ughts.~~ No
hurry. Besides, she was enjoying the electricity in
the air and the guy's low-key yet unmistakable
masculinity—a refreshing change from the
macho specimens she knew.

"Lauren's mother insists that she belongs in a
family," Russ explained. "She remembers me the
way I was five years ago, not remotely ready for
parenting."

"How did you change her mind?" This ought to
be interesting.

He cleared his throat. "I told her I was engaged."

That was weird. "To who?"

"Well...you."

Dear Reader,

The story of Russ and Rachel launches a new series about police officers and children. It actually began as two separate ideas.

First I pictured a woman who had survived a terrible car crash and was finally getting her life on track ten years later. She and her two closest friends volunteered at a homework center and became involved in the lives of needy children. At age thirty, they'd almost given up on love.

The second idea concerned three police officers (originally all male) who were reassessing their lives after narrowly escaping death. Each had to tackle an issue concerning children—perhaps a child given up for adoption, or a desire to have a child—now that life had given him a second chance.

These two ideas mingled in my mind until I realized that they belonged together. In the course of working out the stories, one of the officers became a woman—Rachel—and the man who'd given up a child for adoption became a doctor.

Subsequent stories concern Rachel's friend Connie and her next-door nemesis, Hale; and Marta—the accident survivor—and the department's Romeo, Derek. I hope you enjoy them!

Best,

Jacqueline Diamond

Jacqueline Diamond
THE DOCTOR'S LITTLE SECRET

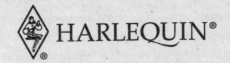

TORONTO • NEW YORK • LONDON
AMSTERDAM • PARIS • SYDNEY • HAMBURG
STOCKHOLM • ATHENS • TOKYO • MILAN • MADRID
PRAGUE • WARSAW • BUDAPEST • AUCKLAND

ISBN-13: 978-0-373-75153-2
ISBN-10: 0-373-75153-2

THE DOCTOR'S LITTLE SECRET

This edition published by arrangement with Harlequin Books S.A.

® and TM are trademarks of the publisher. Trademarks indicated with ® are registered in the United States Patent and Trademark Office, the Canadian Trade Marks Office and in other countries.

www.eHarlequin.com

Printed in U.S.A.

ABOUT THE AUTHOR

A former Associated Press reporter, Jacqueline Diamond has written more than sixty novels and received a Career Achievement Award from *Romantic Times BOOKreviews*. Jackie lives in Southern California with her husband, two sons and two cats. You can e-mail her at jdiamondfriends@aol.com or visit her Web site at www.jacquelinediamond.com.

Books by Jacqueline Diamond

HARLEQUIN AMERICAN ROMANCE

*Downhome Doctors

As always, for Kurt

Chapter One

Under other circumstances, Rachel Byers might have enjoyed being invited to a party by a couple of guys. Especially great-looking guys with guns.

Unfortunately, her buddies at the Villazon, California, police department thought of her as one of the boys, with maybe a few minor differences.

Take this request from Detective Hale Crandall, the beer-bash host: "Yo, Rache, how about bringing a DVD tomorrow night? A chick flick would be fine. Like the kind with mud wrestling."

Fine. As long as he didn't expect *her* to do the mud wrestling. Speaking of wrestling, she could pin Hale as often as not, and he knew it.

That might be, she supposed, part of her problem.

"Bring a couple of girlfriends, too," suggested Officer Derek Reed, a Brad Pitt clone whose womanizing reputation had earned him the nickname Sergeant Hit and Run from the nurses at the local hospital. "You know my type. Big blond hair, big—" he made a descriptive gesture with his hands "—you get the picture."

"If I had girlfriends like that, I wouldn't let them

anywhere near you clowns," Rachel returned. "Excuse me. Some of us have to patrol. We can't all work sissy desk jobs."

Hale snorted. Derek, who seemed less than thrilled about his recent assignment as head of community relations and public information, scowled.

Rachel would hate flying a desk. She loved wearing a uniform and a gun, and enjoyed a little physical action now and then to set the juices flowing.

Too bad she wasn't getting any physical action in her personal life. At five foot eleven, she either intimidated men or inspired them…to invite her to join their softball team. If she ever met Mr. Right, she'd have to arrest him to reach first base.

Wait. Scratch the reference to first base.

"I wish you wouldn't encourage them," muttered Elise Masterson, the other woman on the swing shift. "They're sexist enough as it is." She fell into step beside Rachel as they walked toward the back of the building.

"Were they being sexist?" Rachel had difficulty figuring out the finer points of political correctness.

She sympathized with Elise, whose efforts to skin back her blond hair in a bun did little to discourage the masculine attention she considered so annoying. Men had an amazing ability to detect curves even beneath a Kevlar vest.

"Never mind," Elise answered. "We have more important things to focus on. Finding that lost kid, for instance."

They'd been advised during briefing to watch for a three-year-old girl named Nina Franco who'd wandered away from her parents a few hours earlier. An intensive search was in progress around the park where she'd vanished.

With luck, some well-meaning civilian would bring Nina in before dark. The disappearance of a child was unusual in the Los Angeles suburb of Villazon. Although it had its share of burglaries and domestic assaults, by and large residents felt safe.

Outside, Elise strode off across the rain-dampened parking lot. A couple of male colleagues paused en route to their cars to study the sway of her butt, graceful despite the heavy lace-up boots.

In high school, Rachel had submitted to dance classes in an attempt to refine her own clunky strut. After she accidentally kicked a classmate and pulled the barre loose from the wall, the teacher had advised her to try the wrestling team. Good suggestion.

Glamour still evaded Rachel with a vengeance. A few months earlier, hoping to update her style, she'd dyed her brown hair to what was supposed to be auburn. It had emerged a brassy red that was still growing out.

Well, she had the right build and temperament for her dream job. What more could a girl ask?

The air smelled of wet asphalt, a testament to the February rains that had soaked Southern California for the past few weeks. Rachel tried not to think about the sodden slope behind her condominium or the risk of its collapsing. Out of her control, so why worry?

Her assigned car was a different matter. Rachel took nothing for granted. Before getting in, she checked the gas level and the tires, tested the lights and oil level, made a survey for any unreported dents and poked around the backseat to make sure some arrestee on an earlier shift hadn't stashed contraband.

Satisfied, she stowed a gear-filled bag in the trunk and, beside her, secured a metal box containing paperwork and forms. She didn't want stuff sent flying during a pursuit.

Then, strapping herself into the driver's seat and switching on the two-way radio and the small computer screen known as a mobile data terminal, she called dispatch to report that she was in service.

Rolling out on patrol provided the usual burst of energy. Rachel treasured the independence and the challenge. On the street, she became her own boss.

Her assigned patrol area today encompassed the central section of Villazon. There was nothing flashy about Rachel's hometown, she mused as she merged into the flow of traffic, her windows rolled down so she could monitor street noises. Despite its location within a dozen or so miles of Hollywood, movie stars never set foot here unless they got lost fleeing the paparazzi.

The community of fifty thousand offered a mix of shops and office buildings in its core area, along with blocks of Craftsman cottages dating back to the twenties and thirties. Cruising past yards filled with rosebushes and tricycles, Rachel enjoyed the town's old-fashioned feel. Even its special events had an endearing corniness, she reflected.

Each May, the Pickle Parade celebrated the town's former claim to fame as the site of a large pickling plant that had processed cucumbers from surrounding fields. The fields were gone, and the pickle factory survived as a farmer's market that imported most of its produce from either Imperial County, California, or Mexico. Rachel wasn't sentimental, though. She *liked* shopping for gifts at In a Pickle.

As she wove a random pattern through the neighborhoods and listened to the radio chatter, she kept watch for Nina. Three feet tall, twenty-five pounds, straight dark locks and brown eyes that smiled from the photo clipped to Rachel's visor. Last seen wearing blue pants and a pink top with a white bunny on the front.

The searchers near the park hadn't found her. One

witness reported a child of a similar description entering a car driven by a gray-haired man. As Rachel noted the information, her heart squeezed. Kids that age were so helpless and trusting. The possibility of someone harming a child aroused a deeper anger in her than any other crime.

Rachel didn't remember much from her own life at that age, and what she did recall, she preferred to forget. An alcoholic mother, absent father... Luckily she'd been adopted by a new family who provided as much love and support as a child could ask.

Nina's image stayed at the forefront of Rachel's thoughts. After pulling over and citing a gray-haired driver who'd run a red light, she visually inspected the car's interior and asked him to open his trunk. He complied willingly once she explained the reason, and revealed nothing more threatening than a bag of groceries.

Later, she backed up another officer checking on an elderly woman whose daughter couldn't reach her by phone. Rachel scanned the children who gathered outside to gawk at the squad car, but none resembled Nina. Indoors, they found the woman with a broken hip and requested an ambulance.

As Rachel returned to her car, early-winter twilight was closing in. On the radio, the exchanges about the search acquired a grim tone. With this lengthy an absence, the possibility of foul play increased.

Still, the story of the gray-haired motorist might be a red herring. If an older child had found Nina and invited her to play, perhaps they'd headed for a playground near the civic center.

Rachel checked out the nearest one, but the slides and climbing equipment stood empty. It was nearly six o'clock. If any children had been there earlier, they were long gone.

Frustrated, she cruised an alley behind the library, passed the post office and crossed the boulevard to the town's medical complex. This late on a Friday, the doctors' building beside the Mesa View Medical Center would be deserted, but she decided to make a circuit of the parking structure just the same. You never knew when you'd come across a stolen car listed on one of the hot sheets from briefing.

On the second level, past a support pillar, she glimpsed something that made her mouth go dry. A little girl, the bunny on her T-shirt smeared with dirt, sat on a car bumper while a man knelt on the concrete floor. He'd pulled up one leg of her blue pants and was holding her ankle.

All Rachel could observe of him was a tailored suit and powerful shoulders. Then, evidently hearing her approach, he glanced back. The flat overhead lighting showed nearly black hair graying around the temples.

As Rachel braked facing the suspect, adrenaline surged. She notified dispatch about the girl, the man and the location, and emerged ready for action.

First priority was to ensure the girl's safety. Second, to secure the suspect. Mr. Power Suit had an inch or two on her, and judging by his muscular frame, he'd be no slouch in a fight. He might also be armed.

Releasing his grip on the girl, the man rose to greet Rachel. He made no sudden moves, but she noted tear tracks on Nina's cheeks and a torn knee on her pants.

"Step away from the child, sir. Move to your right." Although she strongly considered reaching for her gun, several recent scandals and a tarnished public image had inspired a departmental policy urging caution when confronting citizens.

That kind of caution could get cops killed. Still, Rachel restrained the impulse.

The man shifted a couple of steps, but irritation flashed in his slate-blue eyes. "I found her wandering in the garage, Officer. She said she hurt her knee."

He gave the words a convincing, gruff inflection. The guy was attractive with a personable air. Well-dressed and accustomed to giving orders, not taking them, she judged.

To her, that made him all the more loathsome if he'd endangered the child.

"Sweetheart, come stand next to me," she told Nina.

"He gave me candy," the girl replied earnestly.

That didn't surprise Rachel. "Is that why you got in his car?"

"Wait a minute!" the suspect snapped. "She was never in my car." He glanced at child. "It's okay, honey. No one's going to hurt you."

The youngster eased toward him, holding out a hand. That was too much for Rachel. "Move away from him, Nina!"

"Oh, for Pete's sake, you're scaring her!"

The girl had drawn close enough to be grabbed. Despite the shrill of an approaching siren, Rachel couldn't wait for backup.

"On the ground!" she shouted. When the man failed to respond, she lunged forward, spun him around and slammed him against the vehicle. Before he could recover, she wrenched his arms back and reached for her cuffs.

With a shocked cry, the little girl retreated.

"You've upset her! Keep those things off me!" The man's twisting motion threw Rachel against the pillar and sent a jolt of pain through her hip.

Breathing hard, the suspect held his position. "I didn't mean to hurt you, Officer, but nobody pushes me around."

Rachel drew her gun. "Hands overhead. Face the car."

Reluctantly he complied. When he glanced over as the

screech of tires announced her backup's arrival, he didn't appear the least bit frightened.

Elise Masterson exited the cruiser. "Need help?"

"Officer, would you please talk sense to Ms. Byers?" The suspect must have read Rachel's nametag. "I was walking to my car when I found this little girl."

Nina merely stared at the three of them, eyes round as pepperoni slices. Rachel kept her weapon trained on the man. "He assaulted me."

"That's not true!" he answered tightly. "Besides, you had no business shoving me into the car."

The matter wasn't up for debate. "Hands behind your back!"

He looked to Elise, who produced her cuffs. "Do it," she confirmed.

Resentment darkened his gaze. Mr. Power Suit was definitely used to running the show, Rachel mused. He'd better recognize who was in charge. In one more second, two policewomen were going to take him down.

The rumble of another car reached her ears. Good.

Then she heard a whole bevy of car engines, until the structure echoed like the parking lot of the Villazon Doughnut Emporium during a two-for-one sale. Which reminded her of another unwelcome change in her turf— under the new chief's regime, officers were no longer allowed to accept free doughnuts.

As Elise clicked the cuffs into place, the cars bumped into view around a curve of the ramp. In the lead, Chief Willard Lyons halted his unmarked sedan. With the suspect under control, Rachel holstered her gun.

Behind the chief came a patrol unit, followed by a station wagon she recognized as belonging to Tracy Johnson, editor and lead reporter for the weekly *Villazon*

Voice. In its wake rolled a van bearing the logo of an L.A. TV news program.

Busybodies from the press—ugh. Rachel loathed the spotlight, and she couldn't allow them to talk to Nina, who had to be interviewed and driven to the hospital for an exam.

The suspect shook his head in disgust, as if the newcomers simply compounded an already obnoxious situation. For once, she and he agreed on something.

When the child sniffled, Rachel took her hand. It felt small and moist. "You'll be fine, sweetie."

"Big cars!"

"They sure are."

"I'll escort her to the hospital," Elise said.

"Thanks." Reluctantly Rachel surrendered her charge. She had work to complete here. Booking this suspect was going to be a pleasure.

Elise helped the tot into the cruiser. They had only half a block to drive, so with luck the girl would be reunited with her parents soon.

Chief Willard Lyons stepped out of his car. An imposing, barrel-chested figure with a thin mustache and close-cropped brown hair, he'd been hired the previous year, six months after the former chief retired under a cloud. Several embarrassing incidents had hurt the department's reputation, and Lyons's job description called for cleaning things up.

He crossed to Rachel and the suspect. "Who do we have here?"

"I haven't had a chance to check ID," she responded.

"My wallet's in my jacket," said Mr. Power Suit. "Upper left..." A frown. "I can tell it's not there. I must have put it in my pants."

Rachel patted him down for a weapon from shoulders

to ankles, trying to ignore an unaccustomed awareness of the guy as a fine specimen of his gender. But fine specimens didn't kidnap little girls. They also didn't lie about having a wallet.

"No ID," she reported.

"I must have left it at the hospital. This is my car, Officer. The registration's in the—" He broke off as a camera operator hoisted a minicam. "What the hell?"

The chief signaled to a rookie. "Keep them behind that pillar, please. Tell them we'll have a statement in a few minutes."

"Yes, sir." The officer marched toward the interlopers.

"Chief—You are the chief, right?" the suspect snapped. "I'd found this child right before your officer jumped me. I heard the Villazon cops were a bunch of cowboys, but Dr. Graves assured me there was nothing to the rumor."

At the mention of the hospital administrator, the chief's expression mutated into a frown. "You work for Dr. Graves?"

"I'm on the staff," the man answered grimly. "My office is in the medical building here."

He stood taller. Funny how a guy could appear in command despite having his hands cuffed behind him.

"You're a doctor?" the chief asked.

A nod.

Okay, make that Dr. Power Suit, Rachel thought. No wonder he acted so arrogant. He wouldn't be the first doctor to confuse himself with God.

"Nevertheless, we're going to take you in," Lyons responded.

Rachel expected the suspect to bluster. Instead, he glanced past them toward the reporters. "I think my ID just arrived—along with my alibi."

She and the chief swung around. Waving at them from

behind the rookie was Marta Lawson, a good friend of Rachel's who ran the hospital gift shop.

"Dr. McKenzie!" The short, brown-haired woman hoisted a leather packet. "You left your wallet on the counter."

A couple of newly obvious facts hit Rachel. For starters, the guy had honestly misplaced his ID. He'd probably stopped to buy a snack or a magazine on the way out.

Also, if he'd been working at the hospital, he had an alibi for his whereabouts this afternoon. Which meant he might be telling the truth about having spotted Nina in the parking structure.

Even though Rachel considered her actions justified, she'd picked on a big shot who was probably going to make trouble in front of the press. And trouble was the last thing the Villazon Police Department needed.

She knew as well as anyone that when push came to shove, the cop usually ended up taking the heat. The possibility of a sodden slope collapsing on her condominium suddenly seemed minor by comparison.

Chapter Two

Russ McKenzie had nothing against cops, but he hated bullies, no matter what form they came in. Being pushed around provoked him to a fighting rage. This made him doubly incensed because it meant losing control. In most respects, he kept his emotions under tight guard. Except with kids, of course. His warm response to children was part of the reason he'd become a pediatrician.

So when he'd heard a small, quavery voice asking for help and saw a rumpled child who complained of a sore knee, he hadn't hesitated. To calm her, he'd offered a mint from his newly purchased roll, then checked her injury while asking where her parents might be. She'd explained, haltingly, that she'd followed a group of older children and lost her way.

He'd been relieved to spot an officer. But instead of receiving a thank-you for finding the child, he'd been roughed up and treated like a criminal until Marta and other hospital personnel had confirmed his whereabouts for the day. Russ didn't like to think about how he'd have been treated had he met the child while arriving for work rather than departing.

He hadn't had to go to the station, and he'd provided

his statement and received an apology from Chief Lyons right there in the garage. Yet the perpetrator of the outrage stood scowling at him as if *he* were in the wrong. The officer might be pretty if she'd lose the pugnacious air and the odd, bicolored hair. Now that his initial anger had ebbed, he found her rather intriguing.

Leaning against a pillar, he rubbed one wrist where the cuff had chafed and tried to collect his thoughts. The last hour had sped by as more cops piled in, the media clamored for interviews and the little girl's tearful parents arrived.

They'd been distressed to learn they had to wait for an all-clear from the hospital. Meanwhile, a detective had ushered them aside and plied them with additional questions. Russ was glad the police took the girl's situation seriously. Her parents should have watched her more closely.

After obtaining the story, the news van and the local reporter had finally left. They'd treated Russ as a sort of hero, which he considered almost as ridiculous as being vilified.

Under the chief's watchful eye, the truculent Officer Byers approached. "I, uh, guess I owe you an apology."

Anger prevented a reply. He wasn't ready to make peace yet.

"More," said the chief.

"More what?" she inquired.

"You said you owe him an apology. You didn't issue one."

The woman's jaw tightened until Russ feared she might require restorative dental work. In a strained voice, she uttered, "Sorry, sir. I was trying to protect the child."

"She didn't need protecting from me." Russ supposed he ought to drop the matter, but her maltreatment had brought up deep-seated resentment. "When I moved here last month from west L.A., I hoped a small town would be a friendly place to live. Guess I was wrong."

"We *are* friendly," the chief protested. "Say, I have an idea how to atone for this misunderstanding. Rachel, why don't you take the doctor on a ride-along tomorrow? It's Saturday and maybe he's off. He might enjoy a cop's-eye view of Villazon."

Any other chief would have backed off, fearful of a lawsuit. Lyons's conciliatory tone reminded Russ of Dr. Graves's assurance that the police department was bending over backward to safeguard its reputation.

As for the officer, she looked as if she were considering taking up long-distance marathon running—in the opposite direction. Ross found the prospect of discomfiting her further amusing. Besides, what better way to get acquainted with his adopted hometown?

"I accept," he announced. "What time?"

"Sorry. I'm off-duty tomorrow and the next two days after that." Rachel didn't bother to hide her relief. Ironically, her more relaxed mood revealed an intriguing warmth. Definitely a woman of many layers, Russ thought.

"You have three days off?" He wondered what kind of schedule these cops worked.

"We work five nine-hour days in a row, then three off," she responded. "Working nine hours lets us overlap patrols so the crooks can't take advantage of shift change."

The chief persisted. "Well then, how about a ride-along next week, Doctor?"

Officer Byers's mouth twisted. Her annoyance nearly spurred Russ to accept, but he had patients scheduled. Also, he was curious about this woman. He'd never met anyone quite like her. "Next Saturday will be soon enough. You are on duty then, aren't you?"

She squirmed. "I'd rather not have this hanging over my head. I'm sure the Chamber of Commerce can provide you with a tour guide."

The chief folded his arms. Rachel sighed so profoundly that Russ had to sympathize. "Okay," she said. "I'll drive the doctor around tomorrow on my free day, although I'm sure I'll bore the socks off him."

The woman's bluntness tickled him. "Whatever you'd like to show me, I'm sure I'll find it fascinating."

"Ten, fifteen minutes and you'll be either screaming to go home or fast asleep."

"I'll take my chances."

Russ supposed he must be nuts to want to view local landmarks with an Amazon who apparently wished he would drop off the face of the earth. Maybe he'd spent too many evenings alone, catching up on medical journals and staring at the sparsely furnished rooms of his house. Except for the old friend who'd encouraged him to move here, he didn't have anyone to hang out with in Villazon. For whatever reason, the prospect of spending a few hours in Rachel Byers's company appealed to him.

The chief's cell rang. He listened with evident satisfaction. "Excellent. I'm sure the parents are more than ready to take her home."

"She's okay?" Russ asked when the chief clicked off. Until now he'd been so distracted he hadn't considered that perhaps the girl really had suffered a misadventure during her lost hours.

"A sore knee where she fell on it, nothing more." Lyons shook hands with Russ. "Thanks for finding Miss Franco. I can't tell you how glad we are that she ended up in your hands rather than someone else's."

"Me, too." Russ scribbled his home address on the back of a business card and handed it to Rachel. "What time?"

"Three o'clock." The words came out clipped.

"Suits me."

She met his gaze. "You really did look suspicious."

"Officer Byers!" snapped the chief.

"I'm gone." She made tracks for her patrol car.

"Quite a character," Russ observed.

"She's conscientious. A good cop." The chief reiterated his regret at the way Russ had been treated.

"I'm glad we worked it out," he responded.

In no hurry to leave, Russ watched Lyons's vehicle and a black-and-white depart in tandem. Officer Byers lingered beside her cruiser, absentmindedly rubbing her hip as she scribbled notes on a clipboard.

Being knocked against a pillar must have left a bruise. The fact that his own body ached from the way she'd manhandled him didn't diminish Russ's regret at inflicting pain. "Sorry if I hurt you," he called.

Her face came up. Wide cheekbones, clear hazel eyes. "Oh, hey, I can always use a workout." With a wave, she slid inside.

Not the type to hold a grudge, he thought. That impressed him.

Left alone in the echoing garage, Russ felt his mood plummet. Maybe he missed the excitement. No, not really. Or was it Rachel's stubborn frankness? Well, a little.

Halfway home, he recognized the real problem. The encounter with little Nina had intensified a deep-seated longing to meet the daughter he'd given up for adoption five years ago. Consenting to give her up was the greatest regret of his life.

When his girlfriend informed him of her pregnancy,

Russ had been exhausted from the stress of his internship and stunned by the news. He'd halfheartedly offered a proposal that Janine had wisely rejected.

Disputing her decision to grant custody of Lauren to Janine's parents hadn't even occurred to him. He couldn't have raised an infant alone, especially not while facing a mountain of medical school bills. So he'd signed the relinquishment papers at a lawyer's office without requesting to see his newborn daughter.

The grandparents no doubt took good care of the child, and Russ understood why they refused to let him visit. But he missed the daughter he'd never even held.

Now that he was settling in a small town and, thanks to an inheritance, no longer owed money, he hoped for another chance at raising a family. He'd like to find the right woman—a gentle, caring person eager to have kids. He imagined them sharing an orderly, well-run home like his parents'.

In the meantime, he looked forward to tomorrow's tour with the crusty Officer Byers. It ought to prove diverting.

RACHEL COULDN'T DECIDE what to wear.

She hated the whole business of picking out clothes. One of the major appeals of being a police officer was the uniform.

Usually on free days she threw on a pair of slacks and a sweater, which was pretty much all she owned. But today she had to represent the department, in a sense. Plus, after she dropped the doctor off, she planned to swing by Hale Crandall's party.

Peering in the mirror, Rachel ruffled her two-toned hair, which she'd observed Russ regarding in horrified fascination. She'd be willing to bet his taste in dates ran to sleek and sophisticated.

Hot ladies probably sought his phone number everywhere he went. In addition to that alluring M.D. hooked to his name, the guy had broad shoulders and tight buns. Nice mouth, too. Doubtful he'd consider her romance material. Also, the only thing worse than being treated as one of the guys would be landing in some hotshot's bed as his latest conquest. Just in case he *did* go for tall women with bicolored thatch on the roof, maybe she ought to wear the uniform.

Rachel, who usually had no trouble making up her mind, couldn't choose. She didn't dare call Elise, who disdained the idea of dressing to please a guy. Marta was almost as fashion-challenged as Rachel, which left a single choice: Marta's cousin Connie.

Connie Lawson Simmons, ex-wife of traffic Sgt. Joel Simmons, was the girliest girl she knew. Heck, Connie was probably the girliest girl *anybody* knew. She decorated her house with enough crystal, china and gewgaws to open a gift store, which was exactly what she'd done. She now owned three such shops, including the concession at the hospital.

In high school, where Connie had been a cheerleader, she used to sniff whenever Rachel walked by as if picking up a bad odor. Rachel had considered Connie a case of lint between the ears.

They'd been nineteen-year-old sophomores at Cal State Fullerton on the day a speeding car plowed through a red light and caved in the passenger side of Connie's sedan, where Marta was riding. Waiting at the curb en route to a police-science class, Rachel had pulled Marta to safety moments before the engine caught fire.

Although Connie had escaped unharmed, the accident left her cousin with head injuries and multiple fractures. She'd survived to face years of rehab.

Rachel and Connie had grown close as they sat at Marta's bedside and later assisted with her exercises. Despite dissimilar personalities, the three had remained friends through eleven years of ups and downs, and all volunteered at Villa Corazon, a volunteer tutoring center Marta had helped establish. Villa Corazon. That meant City of Heart, a play on the town's name.

Feeling like an idiot, Rachel called her friend and explained the situation. "What do you suggest?"

"Is there time for us to go shopping?" She could picture Connie, blond hair caressing her shoulders and lips parted in a manner that drove men crazy. "Because I'm sure you don't have anything in your closet."

Rachel didn't take offense. Not only was this true, it scarcely counted as an insult compared to the words that used to pour from Connie's lipsticked mouth whenever she lost her temper with her ex-husband. Or her next-door neighbor, Hale Crandall, on those frequent occasions when he ran afoul of her.

"It's too late." Less than an hour remained. After finishing work at midnight and playing an on-line video game until 3 a.m., Rachel had slept till noon. "I'm not trying to date the guy. I just prefer to avoid looking like a dork."

Connie didn't hesitate. "Dig around and see if you have a skirt. Also a green blouse."

"Why green?"

A disbelieving snort. "To match your eyes!"

"My eyes are hazel." On that point, Rachel felt certain.

"They're mostly green." A beat later, Connie added, "Bad idea about a skirt. You'd probably put it on backward."

"I hate skirts anyway." Rachel had never realized she had a best color. "Green, huh?"

"I *might* own a top that would fit you." That was a

huge concession, considering how particular Connie was with her stuff.

"May not be necessary. Hold on." Cell phone in hand, Rachel poked through her closet. Brown, blue, maroon. At last, in the depths, she discovered an emerald turtleneck that she vaguely recalled receiving from her sister one Christmas. "I found a green sweater."

"How about black pants?"

"Right here." Rachel lifted a pair off the hanger. "Wait. They could be navy blue."

Connie groaned. "Carry them into the daylight!" Then, "On second thought, you'll need makeup. I can be there in ten minutes."

She'd bring mascara and green eye shadow, Rachel thought. Scary prospect. "I'll handle it. Honest. I'll duck over from Hale's party and show you."

"Hale's throwing a party?"

Uh-oh. That idiot detective should have warned his neighbor. It might at least take the edge off her temper when the party reached full swing.

Connie had never forgiven Hale for encouraging Joel's drinking and party-going behavior, which had been a major factor in their split. Now she was stuck living next door to Crandall, with the result that practically any transgression on his part sent her into a rage. It seemed to Rachel that Connie resented Hale almost as much as her ex.

"It's a barbecue," she admitted. "Starts at five."

"If those creeps are too loud, I'll call 911 on 'em. Imagine what having his own men busted would do to Chief Lyons and his image campaign!"

"How about waiting till I leave? Better yet, give us a break." Rachel would hate to land in trouble two days running, or to see her buddies in a jam. "Maybe I can keep a lid on things."

"I might drop in to see you and the good doctor. You *are* bringing him, right?"

"No way!" Rachel couldn't imagine him mixing with her pals. And his presence might give others the idea she had a boyfriend.

That wouldn't be bad if it were true. She kept wishing she'd feel sparks for some nice solid Joe, the kind who invited her to Dodgers games or classic car rallies.

As a teenager, Rachel had ruined several friendships and one budding romance by nearly smothering the other person. Maturity had enabled her to recognize the displaced child's lingering neediness and overcome it, maybe a bit too thoroughly.

Then along came a guy like Dr. Power Suit who stirred a few embers of the old longing. She might as well enjoy the glow, because given their fundamental differences, it wouldn't last.

After hanging up, Rachel carried the pants to the window as Connie had suggested. They *were* black, but she chose gray slacks instead. Less formal.

A glance outside showed a couple of workmen scrambling over the slope behind her condo, taking measurements. Probably from a geology firm the condo association had hired to assess the landslide danger.

Rachel squinted at the cloudy sky. Today's forecast didn't call for rain, thank goodness. She'd hate for one of California's frequent mudslides to wipe out this condo. Mostly because it represented a huge investment on her modest salary, but also because she might lose her cherished collection of sentimental items, including a floppy stuffed dog her adoptive parents had presented her on her first Christmas with them.

Another treasure was the psychology report her handicapped sister, Kathy, had laboriously researched and typed. Inside the cover, a professor had marked a large red A and the comment, "You show great insight." Rachel had been thrilled when Kathy gave it to her.

Despite cerebral palsy and birth parents who'd left her to the mercies of the social welfare system, Kathy had a shining spirit and a sharp mind. At twenty-two, she was close to earning a college degree. Rachel cheered her every step of the way.

She'd hate to lose any of this stuff. But in the end, what mattered were people, not things.

On the way to pick up Russ, she stopped to rent some DVDs about off-road biking and motorcycle racing—lots of noise and action, without the confusion of a plot. Or any half-naked women, either.

She tossed them into the back and headed for Russ's address. It lay on the west side of town in a development called Amber View because of the surrounding brown hills. Or at least, that was their usual color. Due to recent rains, they were verdant with lush growth.

At the end of a cul-de-sac, the house resembled a traditional cottage right down to the white picket fence and cozy front porch. Kind of homey for a bachelor pad, Rachel mused. She'd assumed from the lack of a ring and the guy's eagerness for a tour that he wasn't married, but she might be wrong.

Rachel's spirits sank at the possibility of encountering a Mrs. McKenzie. How ridiculous—as if she and that arrogant doctor had anything in common! But he wasn't exactly arrogant, she conceded. Merely strong-willed and outraged at being falsely accused of a heinous act. His wife was probably beautiful and well educated.

She'd wince at the sight of Rachel's hair. Jeez, maybe she ought to follow Connie's advice and risk another potentially disastrous color job. Or, as Marta had humorously suggested, get a buzz cut and hope the hair grew back curly.

Bracing for an awkward situation, Rachel rang the bell. From the interior she heard masculine footsteps and then the door opened.

Daylight gave depth to the guy's slate-blue eyes and highlighted the strong bones of his face. "Hey," Rachel said.

"Office Byers." He scanned her approvingly. "Nice outfit."

"You, too," she responded. A dark-blue jacket over an open-collared shirt—sexy as heck with designer jeans.

Behind him, a big-screen TV and a wall of audiovisual equipment dominated the living room. A lounge chair in the middle of the carpet and a black leather couch along one wall constituted the only other furnishings. The decor screamed bachelor. Besides, had a Mrs. McKenzie existed, she'd have stuck her nose out by now.

Surprised by how relieved she felt, Rachel confined her next comment to, "We'd better get going."

"A lot to cover before dark?" An eyebrow lifted skeptically.

"Be a shame to cut our tour short if I have to assist at an emergency."

"Does that happen often?"

Rarely in this town, but the Villazon PD had a mutual-aid pact with surrounding cities. "Once in a while."

The doctor emerged smelling of sophisticated after-shave, a welcome change from the hairy-male scents Rachel's colleagues wore. If this were a date, she might feel tingly at the prospect of snuggling beside him in her car.

Okay, she *did* feel tingly.

"Anything in particular that interests you?" she asked as they climbed into the sporty two-seater. "On the tour, I mean."

"I'd be happy with an overview and a bit of history." Russ bent stiffly, perhaps as a result of being pushed against his car yesterday. The encounter had left Rachel with a crescent-shaped contusion on one hip. She considered any duty-related bruise a badge of honor.

Wrenching her mind away from body parts, she focused on matters of historical interest. There weren't many in a town that blended into its neighbors. "Some legendary stuff used to go on at the high school, like the time the football team hoisted the principal's car on top of the gym for Homecoming. That was my junior year."

The quarterback's father owned a construction company, where the son had learned to operate a crane. Rachel took pride in the fact that no one had ratted on him.

"I was thinking more in terms of pioneers." Russ smiled. "But I like your version."

As she started the ignition, Rachel realized she hadn't carried a male passenger since she'd bought the car last year. Russ's legs were so long her hand grazed his thigh when she reached for the gearshift, and as they rounded a corner, their shoulders bumped.

"Kind of friendly in here," she muttered.

"'Friendly'?" he teased. "I like the way you talk."

"What way I talk?" She didn't have an accent. She spoke standard Californian, spiced with the occasional Spanish phrase such as "*hasta la vista*, baby."

"You talk like a cop," Russ responded.

"That's what I am." At a stop sign, Rachel waited while two skate-boarders shot from behind a parked car and skittered across the street. "There's a couple of accidents waiting to happen."

"I didn't see them coming." Her passenger frowned. "Usually I'm on the alert for kids."

"Hope we don't end up peeling them off the pavement." He chuckled.

"What?" She didn't see anything funny about her remark.

"I like that you don't make the usual small talk about jobs and, oh, whatever," Russ explained. "It bores me, maybe because I'm not good at it."

That surprised her. He struck Rachel as the glib type.

"I don't care for small talk, either," she admitted. "Girl talk is okay, though."

"Why?" he asked.

"'Cause I need my friends' advice."

"On what?" The guy actually appeared interested.

She recalled her earlier line of thought. "These days, they try to tell me how to fix my hair. You may have noticed the dye turned me into a refugee from Bozo the Clown school." After a moment she added, "I don't guess women ever offer you advice about what to do with *your* hair." More likely, they tried to run their fingers through it.

"Rarely." He glanced out the window as they exited the development. "Do you have any idea what those gnarly trees are? Or what kind of fruit they're bearing?"

"That's an avocado grove."

"Really? I didn't realize they grew around here."

"Used to be a lot of them." Rachel was pleased to discover she'd absorbed more details about her community than she'd realized. "They're Hass avocados, the kind with warty black skin. Absolutely the best-tasting. You fix guacamole with any other variety, you have to stir in salsa for flavor, but these suckers are perfect mashed with a dash of garlic salt. Every

Hass avocado in the world is descended from a single tree in La Habra Heights. That's not far from Villazon."

"Is the tree on the tour?" he asked with a hopeful air.

"It died a few years ago. There's a plaque where it used to stand," she offered.

"Only a plaque? I'll pass."

She drove past In a Pickle. As she explained its origins, he said he might return later to buy a souvenir jar of pickles but didn't want to risk having the lid come off in her car.

Rachel appreciated his consideration. "Marta and I rescued a dog once and it threw up all over my old car," she said. "I never completely cleared the smell out. There's nothing worse than beagle barf."

"Is that so?" Russ chuckled again. Rachel didn't see what was funny about an upchucking dog.

"Even vinegar didn't kill the odor. It just made the car stink worse." They were traversing Arches Avenue. "You've seen the civic center, since you work across the street. The only other historic site is Alessandro's Italian Deli."

"A deli is a historic site?" Russ inquired.

"Well, not the actual deli," she conceded. "On that site used to stand the First Bank of Villazon. There's a rumor that Richard Nixon opened an account there when he had a law office in La Habra."

"Was that anywhere near the avocado tree?"

"No. La Habra Heights is a separate community north of La Habra. His office isn't there anymore, by the way. They tore it down. Broke the preservationists' hearts." Rachel had no illusions as to how Villazon and environs stacked up against L.A. People traveled long distances to see the Hollywood Walk of Fame and the Page Museum with its skeletons of mastodons and sabertooth tigers. "I realize a deli isn't exactly the La Brea Tar Pits."

"On the other hand, I'll bet the deli sells better prosciutto," Russ hazarded.

"You're making me hungry." She glanced at the dashboard clock. Nearly five. "I'd better drive you home." Indicating the rear of the car, she explained, "I have to take those DVDs to Hale Crandall's house. He's one of our detectives."

When Russ twisted for a glimpse, his knee bumped her wrist. Rachel felt a little giddy. She'd been experiencing a pleasant buzz from the guy all afternoon.

"Are they evidence?" he inquired.

"They're motorcycle movies. For a party."

Swinging back, Russ brushed her again. More buzz than a swarm of bees. "I don't know a lot of people in this town," he said. "I'd love to go to the party. Any chance I can tag along?"

Rachel was so taken aback she could only stutter, "Uh…uh, I guess. But it's a cop gathering," she protested belatedly. Blabbing to Connie should have taught her to keep her mouth shut. "Backyard barbecue with a hefty serving of testosterone." She hoped that last bit discouraged him. Chief Lyons wouldn't like her dragging Dr. McKenzie over there to watch the guys guzzle beer.

"Great," the doc responded. "I love barbecues."

Rachel couldn't uninvite him without being rude. That would tick off the chief worse.

The other cops would needle her later about bringing a date. And if Connie got an eyeful of this guy, she'd have plenty to say. Like, *Tell me again why you aren't jumping his bones.*

Glumly, Rachel headed for Hale's house. She had a feeling the main dish grilling over the coals was going to be her goose.

Chapter Three

In actual fact, Russ didn't relish the prospect of attending a party with a bunch of sweaty macho guys. He'd rather spend the evening cruising around with Rachel, listening to her loopy presentation and trying to figure out when she was kidding and when she was in earnest, but he was enjoying her company too much to quit now. So he would put up with whatever this party involved rather than go home alone.

He'd never met anyone like her. His parents, a professional couple who claimed to be advocates of social equality, might bend over backward to raise money for the oppressed but showed a subtle snobbery toward those from a blue-collar background.

One of the reasons he'd moved to Villazon was to escape their narrow social circle, which had drawn him in while he lived and worked so close to them. His old friend, a child psychologist named Mike Federov who served on staff at Mesa View Med Center, had praised the town's friendliness and its healthy mixture of economic and ethnic groups.

Russ preferred to accept people as individuals. And Rachel Byers was unquestionably an individual. Maybe her co-workers would turn out to be interesting, as well.

Their destination proved to be a neighborhood of ranch-style homes in the southern part of town, a few blocks past a shopping center that included a discount furniture store, a gift shop and a supermarket. A row of jacaranda trees lined the street, showing only the first hint of buds that would later blossom into vivid lavender.

"The guys tend to act a little wild on their days off," Rachel warned as she found a space along the crowded curb.

"Meaning what, exactly?" Russ inquired.

"They're kind of physical." She collected the DVDs.

"In what sense?" His idea of getting physical at a barbecue involved nothing more than hefting a hamburger.

"Ever wrestle with your brother? Or your sister?" she said as she climbed out.

Russ had developed a distaste for fighting in high school, when he'd had to deck a few guys to end persistent bullying. Although he'd won, he hadn't enjoyed the experience.

"I'm an only child. While I've done weight training, I never cared for contact sports." He seized on a more interesting topic. "How many siblings do you have, anyway?"

"Depends on how you figure it." With that enigmatic comment, she veered onto a walkway, marched up the steps and entered the house without knocking. Since he assumed this must be acceptable behavior, Russ followed.

They appeared to have walked into a pool hall. Cigarette smoke, masculine chatter and the crack of a cue against a ball greeted them. At a billiards table, half a dozen men were so busy playing that they barely acknowledged the new arrivals. Their Hawaiian shirts and cargo shorts made Russ feel overdressed in his jacket and jeans.

On the walls above a mismatched array of chairs and couches, someone had tacked frayed motorcycle posters.

Beer cans and food wrappers crowded a few small tables and less-trafficked areas of the floor.

He and Rachel proceeded through a den with a big-screen TV across which aliens zapped each other. The circle of players didn't even glance up. Despite their age and size, they reminded Russ of video-addicted adolescents.

In the kitchen, doorless cabinets revealed shelves sparsely stocked with canned goods. The countertop overflowed with chips, dips, crackers, cookies and a half-empty box of doughnuts.

Russ peered around for actual food. The appetizing scent wafting through the wide-open sliding door indicated that it awaited outdoors.

A couple of guys interrupted their snacking to return Rachel's high-fives. "This is Dr. McKenzie. He's new at the hospital."

"Guess we'll be seeing you in the E.R., then." A beefy fellow with an air of authority offered his hand. "I'm Captain Ferguson. Call me Frank."

The others also greeted Russ in a friendly manner. Russ didn't bother to correct the impression that he'd been invited as a sort of comrade-by-association. Besides, pediatricians *did* consult in the E.R. on occasion.

Rachel sniffed the charcoal-scented smoke wafting through the sliding door. "Burgers ready?"

"You ought to hold off eating." Derek Reed, who'd introduced himself as the community relations officer, surveyed her lazily. "Hale's setting up a competition. Just your speed."

"You mean a game?" Russ asked. Whatever these guys had in mind, he suspected it wasn't croquet.

"I wouldn't call it a game exactly," remarked a fellow who'd given his name as Joel Simmons. "Hope you brought your swimsuit, Rache."

"Nah. I'll have to borrow." Leaving to the imagination exactly what she expected to borrow in a houseful of guys, she led the way to the patio.

A long table held plates, buns and condiments. Beyond it, a group of men and women lounged in plastic chairs watching basketball on a portable TV. To their left, a muscular aproned man—presumably the host—tended a humongous hooded grill.

Russ and Rachel retrieved soft drinks from an ice-filled cooler. "I'll save the beer for later," she explained. "Better be on my toes if there's a challenge."

An assortment of dented bicycles leaned against the cement wall that surrounded the yard. Russ was about to ask their purpose when a burst of smoke poured from the barbecue as the cook lifted the hood. "That's Hale. We better find out what's on the agenda before he gets busy serving." Rachel strode in his direction.

She made introductions. When their host heard Russ's occupation, the detective said, "Good idea, bringing a doctor."

That sounded ominous. "What's with the bikes?" Russ asked.

"They were left over from the police auction last week. I bought 'em cheap."

Russ had read about the sale, which raised money for the department by disposing of unclaimed stolen or lost goods. That didn't explain why Hale had decided to decorate his backyard with them, a point that wasn't lost on Rachel.

"Bicycles, pool. They don't exactly go together." Picking up a pair of tongs, she snagged a blackened green pepper strip, blew on it and tossed it into her mouth. Her eyes grew teary.

Hale grinned. "Hot enough for you?"

She dashed the heat with a swallow of soda. "Jalapeño?" She'd plainly assumed it to be a bell pepper.

"Worse. Thai dragon." The name said it all. "So you want to hear about the bikes?"

Although Rachel seemed to have trouble speaking clearly, she managed to nod.

Hale proceeded to outline a contest. Competitors chose a bike and pedaled around the pool. After making a hairpin turn at one end, they were to hop off the bike, dive in and swim across. The entire procedure would be timed.

Rachel chugged more soda. "What's the prize?" she wheezed, still suffering the effects of the pepper.

"Case of beer."

Of course, Russ thought.

"Cold?" said Rachel.

"My fridge isn't that large," Hale responded. "You in?"

Russ couldn't let his new friend risk her neck. "Riding bikes on wet pavement sounds dangerous. Have you played this before?"

"Nope. Just thought of it," Hale responded proudly, and laid cheese slices atop a couple of burgers.

"Did you try it yourself?" Russ challenged.

"Sure. Matter of fact, I set the baseline. Thirty seconds." Hale gestured toward the pool. "Piece of cake."

Recognizing the futility of citing the risks, Russ tried a different tactic. "Have you checked your homeowners policy for liability?"

"The department has great medical insurance," Hale returned casually. To the other guests, he bellowed, "Come and get it!"

Her mind obviously made up, Rachel requested the loan of some shorts and a T-shirt. Hale directed her to the second bedroom on the right.

As she disappeared into the interior, Russ reminded himself that he wasn't Rachel's date or her keeper, just a tag-along. She obviously had a thrill-seeking personality.

After Hale finished dishing out burgers, Russ seized the opportunity to press, "I really don't think this is a good idea."

The other man considered briefly. Then he asked, "What kind of doctor did you say you were?"

"Pediatrician."

"That explains it." Hale nodded with satisfaction, as if he'd discovered the source of what he considered excessive anxiety. "Don't worry, Doc. It isn't as if I'm letting a kid do this."

Hopeless.

Rachel wasn't the only daredevil in the crowd. During her absence, a wiry fellow grabbed a bike, issued a war cry and hit the pedals full force, zipping around the pool fully dressed except for bare feet.

The racing-style bike swerved at the end and slipped a little as he climbed off. Applause went up from the spectators as he leaped over the still-spinning wheels, hit the water and churned his way to the far side.

"Twenty-six seconds!" Hale hooted. "He's in the lead!"

The pressure of police work must accumulate until these guys were dying to let off steam, Russ mused. He only hoped nobody got hurt. Especially not Rachel.

A second contestant set off to a round of cheers, but lost his balance on the second turn. He had to plant both feet on the ground to avoid falling.

"Default!" Hale yelled.

"Ow!" A string of curses blistered the air as the man regarded his badly scraped soles. He limped off, presumably to find first aid.

More people emerged from inside for a fresh round

of burgers. Between bites, they challenged each other to participate.

"You're outta luck, you losers. The winner's here." Rachel marched out with a swagger. She'd traded her clothes for a USC Trojans T-shirt and oversize shorts with an extension cord doubling as a belt. Long legs ended in shapely bare feet. She looked rough-and-ready and incredibly sexy.

Russ contemplated a further effort to stop her, but the crowd was calling out encouragement. Clasping both hands above her head, Rachel performed an impromptu previctory prance. At this point, he guessed she'd dive into an empty pool before she'd beg off.

The question of how the chief might react crossed his mind. But the chief wasn't here, and Captain Ferguson didn't appear to object.

"Where'd you find that cord?" Hale demanded of Rachel.

"Your room." She stopped dancing around.

"Can you be more specific?"

"Don't worry. I'll reset your clock, if I live."

He glared. "You have any idea how hard it is to set that alarm? The buttons stick."

Joel hooted. "Guess you'll have to find somebody to wake you up in the morning!"

The comment brought razzes and whistles. Shrugging them off, the host told Rachel to get moving or he'd declare her in default.

Russ tensed as she picked out a bike. "She should at least wear a helmet," he told Derek.

"It's dangerous to whack your head on the water in one of those," the officer replied. "Might cause brain injury."

"She'd have to take it off before she dove in," Russ conceded.

"Then she'd lose." That appeared to be the overriding consideration.

Too late to intervene, anyway. Torn between excitement and apprehension, Russ watched as Rachel's athletic body set off, pedaling like mad around the concrete. Excellent coordination. Great balance, too, as she overcame a slight skid. The crowd fell silent.

His stomach clenched as she screeched to a halt on the lip and leaped off in the direction of the water. Then something went wrong.

Her foot must have caught a piece of the bike, because she landed at an off angle, going so fast she hardly seemed aware that she was too close to one side. Or perhaps she just wasn't willing to waste time correcting her position. The bike kept moving across the concrete until it hit a metal garbage can with an ear-splitting crash.

"Go left!" somebody shouted.

"You're too close!" called another bystander.

Russ started around the pool, hoping to run interference. Too late. Obviously disoriented, Rachel smacked against the far corner of the pool and disappeared into the depths. A brief silence ensued.

"Twenty-one seconds!" Hale slapped his leg. "I'll bet that record's gonna stand."

"Isn't she hurt?" a woman asked.

"I'll bet she's just playing possum." Joel didn't sound very certain, though.

In the pool, Rachel's inert form drifted below the surface. A whole platoon full of trained officers and not one of them made a move. There she was in the deep end, not even struggling. Eyes half-closed. If she'd hit her head… Dismissing the dire possibilities, Russ focused on his task.

After whipping off his jacket and kicking off his shoes,

he dove in. Cool heaviness closed around him, pulling at the clothes as he strained toward her.

As he'd learned in long-ago swimming classes, he gripped Rachel's head from behind, out of reach in case she started to flail. He almost wished she would, but she floated limply as he towed her to the edge.

All her spirit and energy had vanished, and he missed them keenly. Missed the unique person he'd only started to appreciate.

When they reached the pool's edge, Rachel gasped. A relieved Russ sucked in air. Then strong hands hauled them up.

"Good job, Doc." Beneath his tan, Hale had gone pale. At last the peril appeared to have penetrated his thick skull. "She okay?"

Rachel sputtered and coughed as she lay on the cement. A moment later, she wheezed, "Had the wind knocked out of me." Another few breaths and she added, "Did I win?"

"Yup," Hale said. "By a wide margin."

Rachel raised her fist a few inches in a gesture of victory. Russ wanted to hug her and scold her at the same time. "How's your head? Did you hurt your foot?"

"Ankle's bruised. Head's fine."

Someone tossed a couple of towels their way. While drying off, Russ checked his wallet. Except for dampness around the edges, it had survived intact, unlike his watch, whose digital face had gone blank. Worth the sacrifice, he decided. Next time, he'd buy a waterproof model.

A crash of wood against wood drew everyone's attention to a gate flung open in the fence between yards. A petite blonde with outrage written on her face stormed in.

"What the heck was that racket?" Her furious gaze took

in the dented bikes and overturned trash can. "Hale, you lunkhead, what do you think you're doing?"

"Oh, great. We woke the dragon lady," Joel muttered to no one in particular.

"Who's that?" Russ inquired quietly.

"My ex-wife, Connie." Joel ground his teeth. "That used to be my house. Hale and I should never have put in that gate." Ruefully he added, "Used to be fun sneaking over here to drink beer while I was supposed to be doing yard work."

The blonde advanced on their host, who found his escape route blocked by the grill. Russ caught the end of her tirade. "…can't hear myself think!"

"We're done," Hale assured her, unable to retreat any farther without barbecuing his backside.

"Done with what?"

"A little contest." He cleared his throat. "Good news! Rache won."

Connie spotted the figure sprawled on the concrete and rushed over. "Are you all right? Hale, she ought to sue you!"

"I'm fine." Rachel sat up. "Hale, are there any more burgers? I'm starved." Taking Connie's hand, she hauled herself to her feet, nearly toppling the blonde in the process.

Connie surveyed her friend with a frown. "I thought you were going to dress nice. Why are you wearing *that?*"

"I borrowed it from Hale."

The reference to clothing confused Russ. Why had the two discussed Rachel's clothing choices? Before he could draw any conclusions, the newcomer addressed him. "You must be Dr. McKenzie. I'm Connie Simmons."

The fact that she knew his name meant Rachel had informed her about the outing and, presumably, sought advice. Interesting.

"Pleased to meet you." Russ shook hands, embarrassed to be caught under such circumstances. "I assure you, I don't condone this activity."

"Neither does any sane person," Connie declared. "You look a bit the worse for wear."

"He fished me out." Lowering her head, Rachel toweled her hair. "You should have seen me sinking like a pair of old sneakers."

"Thank you, Doctor. I'm glad someone around here has a brain." Connie swung toward Hale. "I ought to tell the chief about this insanity."

"Don't be a jerk," growled her ex-husband.

Connie's eyes narrowed. Her hostility appeared to be well justified, in light of the irresponsible behavior Russ had witnessed. "Let's talk about who the real jerks at this party are, starting with—"

"Burger?" Hale proffered a plate, interrupting an incipient tirade.

The former Mrs. Simmons scowled as if she'd like to shove it down his throat. But she took the food.

Rachel was starting for the table when Connie intervened. "Go. Change. Now."

"I'm hungry."

"You should see what you look like."

Rachel glanced at where the wet T-shirt revealed curves that some of the male officers were ogling with interest. "For heaven's sake. You'd think I was Elise or somebody." Glaring at the men, she groused, "Oh, all right," and slogged away, limping a little.

Russ was glad he'd made a point of not staring. He couldn't help noticing her tempting shape, especially not when his arms retained a sensual impression. Whoever Elise was, she couldn't possibly compare with this woman.

"I wonder if I can still use that extension cord." Hale sighed. "Hey, Doc, feel free to borrow dry socks and whatever."

"Thanks." Russ reached for his jacket just as, in the pocket, the cell phone rang. Although he wasn't on call, the hospital operator might contact him in an emergency, so he excused himself and answered it on the way inside. "Dr. McKenzie."

"Mike Federov. Can you spare a minute?"

"Sure." Dropping the towel on a kitchen chair, Russ eased onto it. The somber note in his friend's voice told him this wasn't a casual call.

"Sorry to bother you on the weekend, but I figured you ought to hear this." Mike explained that while visiting his parents, who had a wide circle of friends in West L.A., he'd just learned of a tragedy several weeks earlier that concerned Russ's daughter.

Lauren's grandparents had been returning from a weekend in Lake Tahoe with friends when their small plane crashed, killing everyone on board. Lauren hadn't been with them, thank heaven.

Russ ached for the five-year-old girl, his daughter, who'd lost her family. At the same time, it occurred to him that the whole picture had changed. Concern twisted through him, followed by a tiny ray of hope. "Who has custody? Janine?"

"I hear she's the guardian appointed in their will," Mike confirmed.

"Is she…how's it working out with her and Lauren?" He couldn't imagine Janine rejecting her daughter at this stage. Still, having the girl thrust into her care unexpectedly must be difficult.

"Nobody seems to know."

"She must be terribly upset about her parents. I'd like to offer my condolences." Russ was eager to provide his ex-girlfriend with moral support. He'd always felt that he'd let her down years ago. Perhaps he could make up for that now.

Mike provided Janine's phone number, which, with his usual thoughtfulness, he'd obtained in advance. He also said that he didn't believe she'd ever married.

Russ thanked him and clicked off. He decided, however, to wait until later to call her. Better to clarify his thoughts first, and besides, this wasn't an appropriate place for such a personal conversation.

He was debating whether to accept Hale's offer of fresh clothing when Rachel emerged freshly dressed. She'd tucked wet hair behind her ears.

"Famished," she noted as she snagged a handful of crackers. "Hey, Doc, you look cute damp. Ever try out for a wet T-shirt contest?"

"Not recently." He grinned. Around Rachel, he felt surprisingly unselfconscious. He opted for declining Hale's offer of dry clothes, except for the socks.

As they returned to the patio, the conversation with Mike kept invading his thoughts. Much as Russ yearned to spend more time with Rachel, his first priority had to be his daughter, and that meant doing whatever was necessary to assist her and her mother.

Until this tragedy, Lauren had had a stable two-parent family. Since apparently Janine remained single, Russ didn't intend to let his little girl grow up without a father.

The more he reflected, the more determined he became not to shirk his responsibility a second time. And not to lose this chance to be part of his daughter's life, whatever that required.

In the midst of her colleagues, Rachel appeared fully

recovered, laughing and joking. Russ wondered if there was any way to see her again. But he couldn't even consider it until he talked to Janine.

Chapter Four

Rachel hadn't been kidding when she suggested the doc enter a wet T-shirt contest, assuming such things existed for guys. With that shirt stuck to his chest and his hair as rumpled as if he'd just tumbled out of bed, he made her blood race.

"Thanks again for pulling me out of the drink," she said as she drove him home.

"No problem." His tone was subdued.

Where were his thoughts, anyway? If fate had a trace of mercy, they'd be focused on her. Normally, Rachel loathed having some guy rescue her butt, and that included the occasions when she and her fellow trainees had taken turns during Police Academy. But even in her dazed state—or maybe because of it—she'd gotten a rush when Russ hoisted her from the pool.

Strong masculine arms encircling her. Warm contact dissolving the chill. He smelled good, too.

Under other circumstances, Rachel might have contemplated the possibility of making love to the guy, but this wasn't Joe Six-Pack. This guy did funny things to her nervous system, and his sophistication intimidated her a little. Getting involved might mean more than she was ready to handle.

All the same, no point in parting prematurely when they could be enjoying each other's company. "So, you got plans for the rest of the night?" she asked.

Russ tore his gaze from the passenger window and frowned at the clock on her dash. "Is that accurate? My watch died. I thought it was later."

In February, evenings always seemed longer due to the early darkness. "Yeah, it's nine-fifteen. Kinda early to ditch a party, but you seemed antsy."

At the party they'd viewed a DVD and part of a Lakers game, and had a go at the video console. When she'd noticed Russ's concentration lagging, Rachel had suggested they decamp.

"Do you suppose it's too late to place a phone call?" he asked. "I meant to wait till tomorrow, but I doubt I'll be able to sleep."

Aha, a clue to his preoccupation. "Depends on the time zone." Unable to contain her curiosity, she added, "May I ask who?" A girlfriend, perhaps. Might as well hear the bad news sooner than later.

"Ex-girlfriend," he responded.

The "ex" part appealed to Rachel. But if the woman was truly out of the picture, Russ wouldn't be planning to call her on a Saturday night, would he? "Sorry. I didn't mean to be nosy."

To her right, at the old pickling plant, she observed a shadow moving and was about to slow down for a better look when a dog trotted into the lamplight. A short distance off, someone whistled, and the pooch dashed away.

To some cops, off-duty meant blind, deaf and dumb except in cases of dire peril. Rachel's instincts, however, refused to hibernate on command.

"Do you know much about children?" the doc inquired.

If the question related to his ex-girlfriend, he didn't explain the connection.

"I volunteer at the local homework center. I did a lot of baby-sitting growing up, too." Rachel waited for enlightenment. This *had* to be leading somewhere.

"How do you imagine you'd react if…" Russ hesitated. "What I'm about to say is confidential, okay?"

"Absolutely."

"Suppose you'd had a baby girl and given her up for adoption, and then the adoptive parents died and there you were, raising this kid," he ventured. "Suddenly your ex-boyfriend shows up and says he intends to be part of his daughter's life. How would you react?"

Rachel didn't hesitate. "Depends on the guy. If he was an abusive jerk, I'd seek a restraining order."

"What if he was a decent guy who really cared about being a father?"

Did Russ mean…himself? "I'm not good with imaginary scenarios." Another point occurred to her. "Anyway, if adoptive parents die, the care doesn't revert to the birth mom."

Ahead, Rachel observed a van weaving in its lane and was glad when it swung into an apartment parking lot. Home for the night, she hoped.

Russ cleared his throat. "You've probably realized by now that the father is me."

Well, that certainly erased all doubt. "How did this come about?"

"Janine got pregnant while I was an intern, five years ago." Warming to the subject, he described the decision to relinquish a child named Lauren and how he'd just learned of her grandparents' deaths. "I have no idea what Janine's plans are or whether there's another guy in the picture.

Frankly, that isn't my concern. I simply want to meet my daughter and make sure she's okay."

Kind of late for that, sniped the rejected child inside Rachel. Still, in fairness, the infant hadn't been old enough to miss her parents, and she'd gone to a loving family.

"My family takes in foster kids, so I grew up around them." She saw no reason to trot out any additional personal details. "Here's my opinion—she needs stability as much as love. So if you're going to put in an appearance, you'd better be prepared to follow through."

"That's a good point."

Russ resumed his window staring as she navigated into his housing development. Reaching the cul-de-sac, Rachel again noticed the coziness of his cottage. This guy must have been acting on nesting instincts even before he learned of the grandparents' demise.

She hoped her remarks hadn't discouraged him. The girl could do far worse than to gain a father like Russ. "Go for it," she advised as the car halted.

"What? Oh. Fine." He reached for the door handle.

"I wasn't trying to boot you out!" She hurried to clarify. "I meant, don't let Janine give you the brush-off. Drop by her place. Show that you've matured." Painfully, Rachel concluded, "If you guys were in love once, maybe there's something left."

Pale moonlight traced the angles of his cheeks. "We weren't in love. I'd been exhausting myself as an intern, and Janine was a business grad student with big ambitions. We both regarded the relationship as temporary."

Rachel couldn't imagine a woman landing a guy like Russ and not hoping to keep him. "There must have been chemistry." They hadn't conceived a baby while shooting hoops. "Also, you may have misjudged her feelings."

"If so, she gave no sign of it," he responded. "Nevertheless, I agree that I should have been more supportive. In any case, I'll bet she regrets missing our daughter's early childhood as much as I do."

"You mean the grandparents banned her from Christmas and birthdays and all that stuff?"

A furrow formed between his eyebrows. "I doubt that."

"So forget the guilt trip. If you want to be close to Lauren…but maybe you don't." A twinge of old hurt prompted Rachel to challenge, "If you're easily discouraged, I guess fatherhood doesn't matter much to you."

"Who says I'm easily discouraged? Like hell!" Anger frayed his voice.

Despite the irritation directed at her, Rachel didn't take it personally. "Then go for it!"

He opened his mouth as if to argue further, but stopped. "You're quite a motivator. Ever coach Little League?"

"Naw, but I was on the wrestling team in high school." She didn't intend to get sidetracked by *that* story. "Call her now. To heck with how late it is."

A smile eased the man's intensity. "My bad temper doesn't faze you?"

"You call that bad temper?" she scoffed. "I saw what you could dish out yesterday when I tried to cuff you."

"You're one of a kind." He leaned toward her, and for one tingling instant she thought they might kiss. Instead, he said, "If you need someone to help knock off that case of beer in the trunk, remember where I live."

Buddies. As if she didn't already have enough of those. Still, Rachel liked the guy, and she'd rather be his friend than a stranger.

"Keep me current on what happens with Lauren," she requested.

"You bet." He waited while she scribbled her cell number on the back of a business card and handed it to him. "I'll do that."

"Great." She lingered to watch him stride up the walk, enjoying the view.

She wondered about Janine. Petite? Curvaceous? He'd described her as a businesswoman, which meant a sharp dresser with salon hair. That must be his type. A million miles out of Rachel's league.

On the way home, she wondered what it'd be like if she were reborn with a shape like, say, Elise's. To collect wolf whistles without trying and discover flowers on your desk from secret admirers must be nice. But not having to fend off unwanted advances from an old coot like ex-chief Vince Borrego, who'd put the moves on Elise to the point that she'd filed an official complaint two years ago.

Viewing the complaint as disloyal, many fellow officers had given Elise the cold shoulder. She might have remained frozen out except that Joel Simmons had witnessed one of the incidents. He'd admitted as much in the course of an internal investigation into a second case involving allegations that a lieutenant, Norm Kinsey, had beaten a prisoner and that Chief Borrego had covered for him.

Some members of the force had considered Joel a traitor, too. Hale, however, had stood by his friend, and Rachel had discreetly supported both Joel and Elise. Eventually, Borrego had retired under pressure and Kinsey got fired. As the department struggled to heal its wounds under Chief Lyons, old enmities had been set aside.

On reflection, Rachel supposed being cute and curvaceous had its downside. Nothing wrong with height and heft and enough guts to win the case of beer jouncing in her trunk.

Her spirits rose as she hung a left from Arches Avenue

onto the side street that led to her condo development, Archway Acres. She planned to spend an hour or so reading and enjoying a brew and then...

What was a fire truck doing in the parking lot? She glanced around for signs of a blaze or other emergency and spotted a couple of police cruisers. Beyond them, a half-dozen civilians were loading stuff into their cars.

Squinting in the light of a streetlamp, Rachel sought a reason for the apparent evacuation. She didn't have to look far. On the door of each unit was posted a yellow placard.

Yellow tags required residents to leave, at least temporarily. That status was a rung below red tagging, which indicated homes slated for destruction.

Gloomily Rachel recalled the workmen inspecting the slope earlier. Pulling forward, she halted beside a patrolman she recognized. "Yo, Bill!" she called. "What's up?"

He peered into her car. "Hey, Rache. You live here?"

"Yeah." *Or I used to.*

"How was Hale's party?"

"Awesome." Enough small talk! "Well?"

A sympathetic grimace. "Inspectors found instability in the slope. The condo association's going to hire engineers next week. We're only letting people fetch their stuff with a police escort, but you can take responsibility for yourself."

"Any chance of me sleeping here?" She ached to stretch out in her own bed. The odds of the slope collapsing tonight seemed minuscule.

"Sorry. No exceptions."

Rachel itched to argue that this was her property and she had a right to stay, but she'd behave the same way in Bill's place. A mud- or rockslide could crush people in their sleep; that had happened in several cities ringing Los

Angeles. Public-safety personnel had to protect folks from a foolish sense of invulnerability.

"Thanks." As she parked to one side, she wished she'd bought the biggest SUV on the market instead of this puny little roadster. She could only transport a bare minimum of possessions.

No way was she abandoning the beer, though. Her buddies would never forgive her.

Russ HUNG HIS JACKET in the closet and tossed his wrinkled shirt and stiff pants into a hamper. Had his co-workers witnessed the usually reserved Dr. McKenzie diving into a pool and rescuing Rachel, they'd have buzzed about it for days. Amazingly the event had scarcely fazed the police officers.

As Russ pulled on a sweater and fresh pair of jeans, he pictured Rachel swooping around the concrete on that ridiculous bicycle. Her fearlessness suited a person who could never predict what might happen during a shift.

His anger about yesterday's encounter had long since vanished. In fact, he had to admit she'd behaved reasonably under the circumstances.

And he'd enjoyed this afternoon and evening more than any experience in a long while. With her easygoing attitude, she deserved her colleagues' obvious approval. Being around Rachel meant living in the moment and accepting a refreshing level of frankness.

How different from his own experiences! Russ recognized the barriers he'd erected between himself and almost everyone else. Perhaps as a result, people from the past appeared as blurry shapes—Janine, his parents, even himself at a younger age.

His most clearly defined memory of Janine remained her face when she broke the news about her pregnancy and decision to relinquish the baby. Stressed out, she'd been all sharp edges, from the pointed chin to the narrowed eyes. Besides that, he recalled only random details about his ex-girlfriend: shoulder-length brown hair, quick movements, an eagerness to reach the next step on the career ladder.

Her private emotions and goals remained an enigma. At roughly thirty-three, Janine had surely long since ceased to be the outgoing graduate student he'd met at a party shortly before beginning his internship. By contacting her now, he risked a messy entanglement of child support and recriminations. Diving into a pool to rescue Rachel had been easy by comparison.

Buoyed by her encouragement, Russ went into the kitchen, where the almost medicinal purity of the white walls and oak-accented counters soothed his mood. Sitting at the oak table, he pulled out a pad and pen to prepare for his conversation.

At the head of the list went a request for regular visitation, including the occasional weekend. In return, he'd offer financial aid and a college fund.

Russ set down the pen, disturbed by the legalistic harshness of the black-on-white agenda. This was neither a debate nor a negotiation. Mostly, he had to persuade Janine of how much a relationship with his daughter meant to him.

Initially, he'd experienced only relief about the adoption. That he might later regret the decision hadn't crossed his mind.

He'd begun to think about her during his residency. Observing the development of babies, toddlers and preschoolers under his care had made him wonder about the well-being of his *own* child.

In a sense, Russ had watched her grow over the following months as he observed the changes in youngsters about the same age. Lauren became far more than an abstraction as he ticked off the months and the milestones, the first words that mothers reported, the humorous incidents that might parallel Lauren's, the dawning self-awareness.

After age three, when overt signs of growth yielded to more-subtle mental and emotional gains, Russ had gradually ceased to keep track. But he continued to maintain an album of photographs sent him by appreciative parents.

Now he might finally meet Lauren and, perhaps, become her father for real. Yet their future together might well depend on a single conversation with a woman he hadn't spoken to in five years.

When Russ fetched a glass of orange juice for his dry mouth, the glass felt damp in his hand. So much at stake. He wished Rachel had stuck around for moral support.

Close to 10:00 p.m. He'd better proceed.

After dialing the number, Russ listened to the rings. Two…three. Then a female voice said, "Yes?"

Although his voice threatened to stick in his throat, he plunged in resolutely. "Janine? Russ McKenzie. I just heard about your parents. I'm so sorry."

A pause. Warily: "Thanks. What can I do for you?"

"I'm told your parents left you custody of Lauren. I'd like to help…financially, I mean. And to be part of her life." He forced himself to stop rather than chatter on, and waited tensely.

"She's five years old, not an infant. We can't go back and rethink our decision." A trace of irritation laced her tone.

He marshaled his powers of persuasion. "I'm aware this is unexpected. I have no desire to intervene in *your* life. Obviously you've moved on…."

"That's putting it mildly," Janine muttered. "Whatever

you have in mind, drop it. You don't factor into this picture, not one tiny little bit."

Flat-out rejection. Russ refused to accept it. "I'm sure I'd react the same way if our roles were reversed. All I ask is a chance."

"I make the decisions regarding Lauren. She's my responsibility. You've been out of the picture for five years and that's where you're staying."

He hung on to his temper. "I accept my share of guilt, if that's the right word. And I'd have kept my nose out of this except for your parents' deaths. Now I want to be part of planning her future. Until this happened, you weren't planning on raising her, right? So it's not as if I'm intruding into an established relationship."

"I'm still not planning on raising her," Janine replied testily.

The declaration caught him by surprise. "What do you mean?" Immediately and painfully, he recognized a possibility he'd overlooked: that another relative intended to step into the picture. An aunt or great-aunt, perhaps, who'd already grown close to Lauren.

"She can't stay here. I've been like an older sister, nothing more. Even though my parents told her I was the birth mother, I've never—" Janine broke off to command, away from the phone, "Put that down! It isn't a toy. Byron will have a fit if you break it!"

In reply, a little voice said, "I'm sorry, Janine."

Lauren! Russ nearly stopped breathing. If he could, he'd rush to the other end of the line right now.

But who the hell was Byron?

"You're supposed to be in bed," his ex-girlfriend snapped.

"I got scared. Please come tell me a story." The breathy uncertainty twisted his heart.

"In a minute. Go to bed." Janine sounded angry, although he didn't understand why. Perhaps the anger was intended for him rather than Lauren.

"Don't forget." A rustling noise faded as, Russ presumed, the little girl retreated.

Her distress vibrated through him. He ached to shout, *Go comfort her! You're her mother.* Yet he was the last person with any right to criticize.

Janine spoke into the phone again. "Sorry about the interruption. You can see what it's like here."

"Who's Byron?" He tried to pose the question casually.

"My fiancé. Our wedding's in April," she said tightly. "And if you think Byron's thrilled about having a pre-schooler invade his house… He's older than I am, by twelve years, to be exact. His kids are grown, and his plans—*our* plans—don't include raising a child."

Russ was so outraged he could hardly respond civilly. What kind of man simply cast out a child because of the inconvenience? But again, he was in no position to criticize. "Is she going to stay with another relative?"

"In case you've forgotten, I'm an only child," Janine answered. "My only cousins live on the East Coast. One's a single mom with two kids, another cherishes his wild bachelorhood, and there's a couple I wouldn't trust with a goldfish."

"What are the options?"

"I've been talking with a lawyer about arranging an adoption. The world's full of people with empty arms and beautiful homes." The statement rolled off her tongue as if she'd rehearsed it. Or as if she were quoting someone. Probably, he guessed, the absent Byron.

"She's a five-year-old, not a newborn." The prospect of losing his daughter forever tore at his heart. "You may not love her, but you represent continuity. Being handed over to strangers…I can't help believing that will traumatize her."

"The lawyer's advertising for a nice couple who'd love a child. Okay, it'll mean an adjustment for her. What do you expect me to do about that?" A certain shrillness warned that she'd been pushed far enough.

"What's she like?" Russ asked.

"Why do you care?" she countered suspiciously.

"I'm trying to understand how this whole situation is affecting her. How she might feel about going to live with strangers."

Tightly she responded, "Lauren is very bright and has a mind of her own. She'll do fine."

Russ couldn't back off. No matter how resilient his daughter might appear, he'd studied child psychology during his training and seen the effects of emotional abandonment in his practice. The problems might not surface until adolescence, but when they did, the results included depression, rebelliousness and drug abuse.

"I'm sure she seems okay, but she must be hurting like crazy," he told Janine.

"You think *she's* the only one with problems?" she shot back. "Let me tell you what these past three weeks have been like. On top of burying my parents, I've had to deal with their estate, locate day care, watch Lauren in the evenings and try to dredge up some maternal instincts— I'm not totally insensitive to what she's been through. Then she caught stomach flu and I missed two days' work, in addition to the week's leave I'd already taken. If Byron weren't my boss, I'd have been fired by now."

She was right. He had no idea what she'd been through. And he couldn't wait to find out, because he intended to make her existence a whole lot easier. Starting now.

"I'll take her," Russ announced. "Permanently. Hand me the papers and I'll sign."

The ensuing silence lasted long enough for him to register that he had no child-care experience and hadn't even met Lauren yet. He'd blurted out a life-changing offer without a moment's forethought.

Russ harbored no illusions about the challenges involved in becoming a single parent. From his daily routine to long-term goals, key parts of his reality were about to hit the fan. Still, he meant what he'd said. He'd tackle the job step by step.

Finally Janine spoke. "Lauren belongs in a family. That means two parents. Russ, I appreciate your intentions, but you're as much a stranger to her as anyone the lawyer might produce."

A stranger, when he'd mentally tracked each step of her development? Perhaps so, at a superficial level. But not in his heart.

"I'm her father," Russ persisted. "Eventually she'll understand that she belongs with me. That she wasn't rejected, but welcomed. That has to make a difference."

On the far end of the line, Janine released a long breath. "I'll admit it would simplify matters, but Russ, you work all day. And you're emotionally—how shall I put this?—constricted."

She meant cold, he registered. "I'm reserved with adults but not around kids."

"Dealing with children in an office is nothing like having them underfoot day and night. You're not suited to fatherhood, not by yourself." She sounded regretful.

"I've changed." Or was about to. That small, shaky voice had touched Russ deep inside. "I've bought a three-bedroom house. And I—"

"Russ! This isn't about the number of bedrooms you own!" Janine seemed to be picking up steam. "This is about your ego, or guilt, or whatever's motivating you. If you were ready to settle down, you'd have done it by now. You know what I won't tolerate? Your playing at being a dad and then handing her back to me in a few months. So no, I won't consider it!"

The immature guy Janine had dated was gone, but how to convince her of that? If he didn't produce a bombshell, he might lose his child for keeps. Then Russ remembered what she'd said a moment earlier. *Lauren belongs in a family.* If that was Janine's bottom line, why not meet it?

"You interrupted me." He took a deep breath. "I was trying to explain that I'm engaged." He half expected the earth to open up and swallow him for such a brazen lie. It would be, Russ conceded, no more than he deserved.

But he was desperate. And he *had* set marriage as a goal when he moved to Villazon. At least his intentions were honorable.

He waited anxiously for Janine's reaction.

Chapter Five

"Really?" Relief replaced his ex-girlfriend's indignation. "Congratulations, Russ. When's the wedding?"

Unaccustomed to lying, he hadn't considered the ramifications, he realized with a jolt. Such as a name, vital statistics, and the scary possibility that Janine might insist on meeting the woman. "We haven't set a date."

"Are you certain she's ready to become a stepmom on such short notice?" his ex pressed.

"She loves kids." For some reason, Russ pictured Rachel. "In fact, she volunteers at a homework center."

"Is she a teacher?"

Although tempted to agree, since that might impress Janine, he decided to stick to a scenario that required the least invention on his part. "She's a police officer."

"You're engaged to a cop?" A choking noise, or perhaps stifled laughter, issued over the phone. "What do your hoity-toity parents think about that?"

He hadn't realized Janine considered his parents snobs. Well, they were, and they probably *would* object to his fiancée if word reached them. Russ didn't care.

"They'll learn to love her. Rachel's straightforward and honest and compassionate." Every word rang with such conviction that he almost forgot this engagement was an invention. "You'd like her, Janine."

Gone too far, he saw in a flash. Her next request was likely to be…

"When can we meet?"

He didn't have an answer, but perhaps he didn't need one. During the summers while in med school, Russ had supplemented his lab job by selling high-end cutlery, and he'd learned to spot the perfect moment to close a deal. Janine required only a nudge to seal this arrangement.

"Soon," he promised. "I'll have to consult her schedule. Cops work odd hours. In the meanwhile, I can pick up Lauren tomorrow."

"You mean for a visit?" Janine hedged.

"For good." He pushed harder. "This area's full of kids. A real old-fashioned community. Did I mention I live in Villazon?"

"Isn't that up north?" she asked dubiously.

"East of L.A.," he corrected. "Adjacent to Orange County. A great area for families. How's noon?"

"I, uh…" It seemed Janine's usually rapid brainpower had momentarily deserted her.

"Good," he continued as if she'd agreed. "What was that address?" To Russ's delight, she provided it with only a trace of hesitation.

"Thanks." Another issue struck him. "Has she got a lot of stuff? I could rent a trailer." Collecting Lauren's possessions would reinforce the permanence of the move.

"Most of it's still at my parents' home. I can hire movers but…" Janine coughed. "Russ, I'm not comfortable making this decision so hastily."

A bit more persuasion and he'd be home free. "Janine, it's absolutely the right choice. Lauren will have the security of growing up with her father, and Rachel and I already discussed adopting kids." Partly true—she *had* mentioned that her family took in foster children. In case any doubt remained, he added, "By the way, Byron sounds like a great guy. I'm sure he'll be thrilled that you resolved the situation."

"That's true." The reference to her fiancé appeared to settle the issue. "I hope you don't think I'm an unfeeling mother. Lauren's a sweetheart."

"You're doing the best you can under unexpected circumstances. And of course you'll be welcome to visit." While he wasn't crazy about the notion of Janine popping in, the familiar contact might ease the child's transition. By then he'd have to invent a broken engagement.

"That'll be up to Rachel, won't it?" To his surprise, Janine chuckled. "Russell McKenzie marrying a cop. What a kick!"

"I consider myself lucky to have found her." Doubly lucky if Rachel didn't discover what a liar he'd become and arrest him for fraud.

"I'll see you tomorrow." She stopped, and for a beat he feared she might renege. "A trial period, Russ. How about a month?"

"That's reasonable." He considered suggesting they set ground rules for deciding to make custody permanent and decided against it. The less specific, the easier to talk his way out of any minor setbacks.

"Well, I'm surprised on a lot of levels, but I suppose it's for the best," Janine conceded. "Now I've got to figure out how to break the news to Lauren."

Russ wondered how she'd planned to explain her plans to give the child to strangers. Best not to raise the issue when matters were going so well. "Please say that her father wants her. Is she even aware I exist?"

"She used to ask about you, and I told her the truth, that you weren't ready to raise a child." Sadness underscored the words. "My parents kept a family album for her that includes a few pictures of you. They got them from mutual friends, I guess. They felt it was important for Lauren to have a firm sense of identity."

"They sound like wonderful people." He owed them a great deal.

"I miss them a lot."

"Of course you do." Although normally he'd be glad to serve as a shoulder to cry on, Russ had another priority. "I'm glad we resolved this to everyone's satisfaction. I'll see you both at noon."

After a brief goodbye, he hung up. He left his phone number, but hoped Janine wouldn't suffer second thoughts.

He felt like an astronaut who'd launched himself into space without proper training. So many details he hadn't considered. How to take care of Lauren on a daily basis. Meet her emotional needs after such dramatic changes. And fake an engagement.

How on earth was he going to handle that?

As Russ paced through the house, figuring out the logistics of bedrooms and bathrooms, his thoughts returned to Rachel. He'd used her name and promised to introduce her. While he might get away with a delay of one or two weeks, eventually he'd have to…

Keep his promise. Was that possible?

Only if Rachel agreed to play along. He doubted she'd ever told a lie in her forthright life, yet a child's happiness hung in the balance.

Russ smacked a door frame with fierce resolve. He was going to make this work, no matter what. For Lauren's sake.

ON SUNDAY, Rachel awoke in a bedroom filled with colored-glass figurines and crystal flowers. A heavy rose scent pervaded the coverlet and sheets, while an oval mirror above the vanity table showed a bleary-eyed woman far from eager to face the new day homeless.

The thick scent reminded her of a foster home where she'd stayed briefly after being removed from her mother's place. Rachel had been afraid to move for fear of breaking some fragile item, and sure enough, she'd stumbled into a cocktail tray covered with teacups. At least if she broke some of Connie's stuff, she could pay for it, instead of being handed back to social workers.

In the partially open closet, she glimpsed the only clothes she'd snagged: a couple of uniforms, jeans and pullovers, their sturdy fabrics a contrast to the floral curtains at the window. On the vanity, a set of silver implements gave the cold shoulder to Rachel's worn hairbrush.

She yearned for her condo. If she weren't a police officer charged with upholding the law, she'd sneak in there this morning.

Last night she'd weighed her options. Too long a commute from her parents' home, and besides, Tom and Susan Byers's place was a madhouse. In addition to Rachel's sister Kathy, her brother Nick and a pair of long-term foster kids, a parade of screaming infants and distressed toddlers arrived at all hours.

Rachel's next idea had been Marta, but she couldn't picture the two of them sharing a studio apartment. And motels were expensive, especially when you might have to stay for weeks.

You had to hand it to Connie for being a good sport. She'd not only consented to take in a stray, she'd held her temper when a couple of the guys still partying next door trooped over to investigate Rachel's arrival, cutting a swath through her flowerbed.

"Stay as long as you like," Connie had said after the guys departed. "That's why I have a guest room."

Hard to picture what kind of guest she'd envisioned when she'd outfitted the place, though. Certainly not a five-foot, eleven-inch visitor who wouldn't be able to perform so much as a pushup without crashing into something. Still, Rachel supposed a person who owned three gift boutiques was entitled to stuff her house with gewgaws and gimcracks.

Rolling to the side, she checked the ornate bedside clock. Past 2:00 p.m. Day off, but she was wide-awake, so she might as well get up.

After gathering her stuff, she went to the hall bathroom, where she cleared china and glass doohickeys from the counter to make space for her gear. The frilly shower curtain parted to reveal a sparkling tub stocked with rosette-carved soap. Rachel made a mental note to buy real soap. Heaven help her if she showed up at the station smelling like a flower shop.

Hot water stung the abrasions on her arms and eased the residual stiffness from yesterday's bike mishap. Man, that had been fun. She wouldn't mind a rematch, especially if it included a heroic rescue by a hunky doctor.

She wondered how matters had gone with his ex-girl-friend and the little girl. Lauren was only a year older than Rachel had been when the court removed her from her family. Tragic about the grandparents. Losing a family couldn't be easy, even with a backup parent available.

Dressed except for shoes, she padded down the hall, skirting a small stand topped with a candle arrangement. In the kitchen, the dark wood table shone as if newly polished, while glass-fronted cabinets displayed porcelain dishes painted with garden scenes. Rachel poked through drawers until she found a paper plate.

Connie bustled in from the connected den, wearing an embroidered peasant blouse over a ruffled skirt. With her tiny frame, slightly almond-shaped eyes and knock-'em-dead boobs, she exuded a femininity that drove guys crazy. Didn't look a day over twenty-five, either, although she, Marta and Rachel had celebrated their thirtieth birthdays last fall.

She uttered the magic words: "How about coffee?"

"Fabulous." Rachel eyed the patterned fabric on a kitchen chair and, postponing the moment when she had to actually sit on the thing, went to peer into the fridge. She spotted a salad, sliced chicken, carrot sticks and celery, all shrink-wrapped. "Got any breakfast-type food?"

Connie measured ground beans and water into the coffeepot. "There's soy-based cereal and low-carb bread. By the way, you have a message. I answered your cell phone." She produced it from a pocket. "You left it in the living room, and I didn't want to wake you. Dr. McKenzie called."

Hearing his name gave Rachel a thrill, as if she were a teenager with a crush. Crazy. Russ was probably seeking advice about his daughter, or else he'd left something in her car. "Thanks." She pocketed the phone. "What's the message?"

"He's dropping by in half an hour. I'm glad I heard you stirring or I'd have had to wake you." One eyebrow rose inquiringly. "He mentioned a surprise. Any clues?"

"If I knew what it was, it wouldn't be a surprise." Rachel took out a loaf of bread, a tub of "light" margarine and a small pot of what appeared to be green jam. The desperate would eat anything.

Connie frowned. "You put mint jelly on your toast?"

"Oh. I thought it was kiwi preserve." Lucky it hadn't proved to be jalapeño spread. Or, worse, some of that Thai dragon stuff. "Russ is coming here?"

"Yes." Connie fixed a coffee tray with a miniature pitcher of skim milk and a small bowl of pink packets. "I think he likes you."

A blip of excitement on the internal radar screen. "What makes you say that?"

"He seemed eager to see you." As soon as the coffee finished dripping, she carried two delicate cups to the table.

Was that all? Rachel had been hoping for a revelation that only an ultrafeminine sort like Connie could provide. "Yeah, he likes me. As a friend." Rachel tore open two pink packets, spilling white powder on the table. "Sorry."

"No problem." Her friend wiped the spill with a paper towel, then curled onto a seat.

Rachel sat down tentatively, afraid of crushing the dainty chair. "Did you have this furniture when you were married to Joel?"

"Yes. Why?"

"It doesn't strike me as guy friendly." Or big-strapping-woman friendly, either, she added mentally.

"I had delusions of civilizing that oaf. Foolish me."

The toast popped up. Reaching for it, Rachel jostled the table and spilled coffee into the saucers. She apologized again.

"Don't sweat it." Despite the words, a wrinkle settled between Connie's eyebrows. Had it been summer, Rachel might have pitched a tent in the yard to spare her friend further inconvenience. Instead, she prayed for the slope repairs to proceed rapidly.

She'd nearly finished her rather rubbery toast when a

scraping noise from outside drew her attention. Russ already? But he wouldn't approach from the rear.

Across the den, through the French-style panes of the back door, appeared the unshaven visage of Hale Crandall. He made a sorry picture in an untied terry robe, striped pajama bottoms and flip-flops.

"I have *got* to buy a new lock for that gate," Connie muttered. "Usually he at least throws on some clothes."

"Probably wants to borrow some of that beer I won. I'll check." Carefully shifting the chair, Rachel rose.

Outside, with the air of a man offering temptation, Hale hefted a sack of doughnuts. Rachel was thankful she was already standing, or she'd have upended the table in her haste.

She sped down two steps and through the den, past a flowered sofa and a coffee table laden with china shepherd-esses. "Fantastic! Where'd you get those?" Judging by his attire, Hale hadn't ventured out today and the Doughnut Emporium didn't deliver, despite frequent suggestions by her co-workers.

"They're a thank-you for yesterday's party. Jorge dropped them off." That would be Jorge Alvarez, a fellow detective. "I considered eating the entire dozen myself until I remembered your refugee status. There's a couple of chocolate ones left."

"Great!" After admitting him, Rachel carted the bag up the dividing step to the kitchen. "What kind do you like, Connie?"

Their hostess scowled at Hale's unkempt form. The scents of cinnamon and chocolate won out, however. "Peanut sprinkles."

At the table, Hale reversed a dainty chair and plopped his striped bottom onto it. "I saved two of them for you. How about showing some gratitude?"

Connie yanked a doughnut from the sack. "I'm only tolerating you because Rachel's here."

"But you gotta miss an elemental male presence in the morning." He grinned, taking pleasure in provoking her.

"It isn't morning. And you might have the decency to put some clothes on." Connie fetched a fork and knife and, to Rachel's astonishment, proceeded to cut the doughnut into bite-size pieces.

Hale tilted the chair forward for a better view. "Wow, what manners! The Queen of England could take lessons."

Connie waved a hand in front of her nose. "Hale Crandall, you stink! Do you ever take a bath?"

He feigned innocence. "Don't I smell like I took a bath?"

"No," Connie and Rachel responded simultaneously.

"That's what swimming pools are for. Guess I'll go for a dip." As he got to his feet, Hale reached for the sack. Rachel barely managed to snatch a second doughnut. "Enjoy your breakfast, ladies." With an insolent air, he slap-slapped down the steps and out through the den.

"Can you believe that slob!" Connie narrowed her eyes toward the patio before snapping her attention to her empty plate. "Wait a minute. He said there were *two* with peanut sprinkles."

"You should have grabbed it," Rachel advised.

"That jerk took the bag!" Recovering her poise, she shrugged. "Who cares? He made me lose my appetite, anyway."

Rachel didn't attempt to excuse Hale's slovenly behavior. But she thanked him silently for preventing starvation. She'd have to lay in supplies to make it through the week.

"I can still smell him!" Snatching a can of air freshener from the counter, Connie filled the air with cloying sweetness. Rachel nearly gagged. Make it through the week? She'd be lucky to survive a couple of days.

The two women cleaned up and carried fresh coffee into the den, where a bit of channel switching revealed a basketball game. They were getting comfortable when the doorbell rang.

Russ! The prospect of seeing him sent sparkles through Rachel's bloodstream. She followed Connie through the dining and living rooms on a twisty path between delicate furnishings.

As the door opened, Rachel, trying to peer past Connie, noted a tweed jacket and sky-blue shirt. She saw a hint of uncertainty followed by a smile when he spotted Rachel.

A rush of warmth. He *was* glad to see her.

"What a sweetie!" Connie cooed, and then Rachel saw the child on the porch beside Russ. Around the moppet's face curled a mass of long, light-brown hair, as stylish as if she'd emerged from a salon. From beneath a white pea jacket peeked a pink blouse above a ruffled rose skirt and knee-high white boots. Certainly not a bedraggled-orphan type like the foster kids who landed on the Byerses' doorstep.

"Rachel, I'd like you to meet my daughter, Lauren," said Russ, who'd apparently already introduced himself to Connie.

"Hi." Impossible to insert another word, with their hostess sweeping the arrivals inside and fussing over the darling pink-and-white outfit. Rachel retreated into the living room.

Nice of the ex-girlfriend to let Russ take their daughter for the day. But had he run out of activities already? Hard to imagine any other reason for him to drop by.

Ignoring Connie's compliments, Lauren marched over to Rachel. "Dad says you're a cop. Where's your gun?"

"In the bedroom." She'd have to make sure Lauren didn't go exploring, Rachel thought.

"Show me how to shoot," the little girl commanded.

Taken aback, Rachel shook her head. "A gun isn't a toy."

"She can't do that, honey. Guns are dangerous," Connie added.

"Not to me! Show me how to shoot *now!*" Her tone warned of an incipient tantrum.

Rachel wondered exactly what was going on inside that little head. Her best guess: this must be a power play, although why Lauren was directing it at her, she couldn't say.

Russ touched his daughter's shoulder. "Let's find another topic to talk about, sweetheart."

Lauren lifted her chin stubbornly. "Rachel, teach me!"

"Sorry, kid. No can do."

Russ watched them cautiously, perhaps weighing whether to intervene further. Apparently he trusted Rachel, though, because he stayed silent. That he didn't simply drag his daughter away seemed to indicate this interaction mattered, but she had no idea why.

"I don't like you!" Lauren raged. "You're mean!"

Rachel crouched in front of the little girl. Those big brown eyes sure were appealing, in spite of the rudeness. Besides, her emotions must be swinging wildly in response to losing her grandparents. She was trying to figure out where she fit into this new universe and, to her credit, didn't intend to sink without a fight.

"My job is to do what's right, even if I tick people off," Rachel informed her. "Would you like me to tell you lies?"

"No." A note of defiance.

"Or make promises I can't keep?"

A shake of the head.

"Good. You can count on me to be honest and fair, even if people don't like me," Rachel continued gravely. "And I won't let you do stuff that might hurt you, any more than your father or your mother would. Now, why do you want to shoot a gun?"

The little chin quivered. "'Cause I wanna be powerful."

Rachel took a stab at mind reading. "A cop is the most powerful person you can think of, huh?"

"Yeah." The girl folded her arms defiantly.

"The thing about power is, you have to use it wisely," Rachel told her. "Besides, you already have power."

"No, I don't." She sounded uncertain.

"Sure, you do. Somebody spent their hard-earned money buying you beautiful clothes," Rachel pointed out. "Your daddy drove you all the way here to introduce you to his friends. You have power over people who love you. You should be careful not to misuse that power."

"I don't." Lauren frowned. "Do I?"

"You called me mean. That hurt my feelings," Rachel responded.

"You're not mean," the child conceded.

"How about me?" Russ asked. "That's what you claimed when I wouldn't buy you two desserts after lunch."

"You wouldn't? Now, that *is* mean," Rachel cracked.

Lauren giggled. "Grandma let me have two desserts sometimes."

Russ hugged his daughter. "Well, I have to use my Daddy-power carefully. I'm a doctor, which means I'm especially careful about your health. But as we get better acquainted, we'll figure out which rules can be broken now and then."

Connie had been observing this interchange with growing confusion. "Better acquainted? I gather I've missed part of this story."

Rachel seconded that motion. She'd sensed since Russ arrived that his visit was more than casual.

"My daughter's coming to live with me," he told the two women. "Which is tricky, since we'd never met before today."

"Permanently?" Concerned that her disbelief might upset Lauren, Rachel threw in a joke. "I see swimming pools aren't the only things you dive into headfirst."

"That's actually more true than you realize. Which brings me to my point." Russ glanced at Connie. "If it isn't too much of an imposition, I'd be grateful if you could occupy Lauren for a few minutes while I talk to Rachel."

Connie rose to the occasion, despite what must be intense curiosity. "Lauren, let me show you my doll collection. You can undress and dress them if you're gentle." When the child hesitated, she added, "There's a policeman action figure. Want to play with him?"

The notion of putting clothes on and off toys sounded incredibly dull to Rachel. Lauren, however, rose to the bait. "Okay." A short pause. "Can I, Russ?"

"Yes, it's fine, angel." He didn't push her to call him Daddy. Rachel was glad, because attachments couldn't be rushed.

Taking the child's hand, Connie led her out of the room. She kept the dolls in a glass breakfront in the master bedroom, well out of hearing range if they spoke softly. Good, because apparently Russ had a private conversation in mind.

She'd be glad to help the little girl adjust to a new town. If that was all he sought, why did he seem so tense?

Self-consciously, Russ sank into a brocade chair. Rachel sat on the sofa, a stiff affair that fit the elegant decor, which included a golden filigree fire screen and, above the mantel, a gilt-framed oil painting of carnations.

The silence lengthened. Whatever the man had to say,

she wished he'd spit it out. "This must be quite a tale," Rachel remarked to break the ice. "The last I heard, you'd set your sights on occasional visits."

His hands clasped his knees, a further sign of nervousness. "Janine had decided to search for an adoptive family. She's engaged and hubby-to-be doesn't want some kindergartner complicating his privileged existence."

"So Janine just gave her to you?" A cavalier attitude, in Rachel's opinion, but perhaps in the child's best interest.

"I pushed hard," he admitted. "She's granted me a one-month trial period to prove this can work."

"And you believe it can?" She didn't mean to challenge his sincerity, only to point out what an enormous task he'd assumed. This was a bachelor with a living room full of video gear.

"It has to. I'm her father." He released a long breath. "You should have heard her in the background last night, begging for attention. Lost and scared and…well, you get the picture."

Rachel's heart went out to the child. "She must have been her grandparents' darling. And she's a bright kid. She'd understand she was being given away."

"Exactly." He cast her an appreciative look. "The problem is…" He stopped.

She waited for his thoughts to unblock. No hurry. Besides, she was enjoying the electricity in the air and the guy's low-key, yet unmistakable masculinity, a refreshing change from macho specimens like Hale.

"Janine insisted that Lauren belongs in a family," Russ explained. "She remembers me the way I was five years ago, not remotely ready for parenting."

"How did you change her mind?" This ought to be interesting.

He cleared his throat. "I had to say I'm engaged."

That was weird. "To who?"

"Well, you."

"You're putting me on!" Rachel had heard plenty of whoppers in her day, but this topped them all.

"I'm sorry. Janine was on the point of refusing, and I doubt I have any legal right to challenge her decision." He leaned forward into a ray of sunshine that highlighted the pleading in his expression.

Rachel was still trying to figure out how this scenario worked. "So, like, you claimed you met me two days ago and I knocked you for a loop, or what?"

"I didn't go into detail." He uttered an uneasy cough. "She asked to meet you, maybe later in the week. That is, assuming you're willing to pose as my fiancée."

Rachel had never been much of an actress. "I'm guessing you didn't think this whole business through."

He ran his palms along his jeans. Must be sweaty. "I'd appreciate your help. This means a lot to me."

The handsome, sophisticated doctor, who probably had to chase women away with a scalpel, had chosen Rachel as his intended. His *imaginary* intended. His trust was flattering, if misplaced.

She doubted she could pull off such a deception if her life depended on it. She was definitely not cut out for undercover work. But if she failed, what would happen to Lauren?

Rachel had no quarrel with the idea of adoptive parents, given that the Byerses had saved her bacon. Even so, it had taken years for her to come to terms with the fact that her mother cared more about booze than about her own child. Rejection can play havoc with a person's self-esteem.

"She understands that you're her father and not some nice fellow who treated her to lunch?" she probed.

"Obviously, I'm not the man who's been raising her,"

Russ conceded. "But her grandparents gave her my photo and made me part of the family history. She recognized me the moment we laid eyes on each other."

A promising first step, Rachel supposed. Still, they had a long way to go to establish a real parent-child relationship. "Foster kids tend to have a honeymoon period and then start acting up like crazy. Sure you can handle it?"

"One way or the other, I'll muddle through, because I refuse to give up," he insisted. "I've deeply regretted losing my daughter, and I won't blow this second chance. Which brings us back to my request. Will you pretend to be my fiancée? Meet with Janine and play the part for as long as necessary?"

"I can't pose as something I'm not," Rachel said. "Also, I keep thinking of complications. Like, word's sure to leak out, which means I'll have to pretend to a whole lot of other people. Besides, I promised Lauren I'd never lie to her."

Russ swallowed hard. "You're entitled to say no."

"What'll you do?"

He rose and paced across the carpet. "Admit to Janine that I made up the engagement. I'll have to convince her to trust me, anyway, which will be extrahard after I tried to fool her, but that isn't your fault."

He nearly collided with a large china dog that had been obscured by the sofa. He halted, then stood staring at the thing, mind undoubtedly working in so many directions he couldn't focus.

Rachel's heart squeezed for him and Lauren. Then a solution smacked her in the face. A totally outrageous, insane solution, almost as crazy as his announcing a pretend engagement. "Maybe you won't have to."

"Won't have to what?"

"Won't have to tell her you made it up." Rachel resisted, barely, the instinct to bite her lip for courage.

"Why not?" He regarded her with fists clenched and jaw tight, as if afraid to hope for too much.

"Because," Rachel said, "we can get engaged for real."

Chapter Six

The first day of Russ's internship, when he'd finally been assigned patients of his own, he'd experienced a disconnect. Despite years of training, he'd been tempted to glance around in search of the *real* doctor. The same sense of unreality came over him now.

His vision sharpened, lending hyperclarity to the room's tones of ivory, turquoise and coral. Engaged? For real? Although he'd shared vivid experiences with the woman sitting across from him, they weren't really even well enough acquainted to be considered *friends*.

Russ strained to unclog his throat. "Engaged means we're planning to get married," he protested hoarsely. "Diamonds, lace, wedding cake and so on."

"Lots of people plan lots of things," Rachel remarked as casually as if they were discussing what to order at a restaurant. "Our traffic sergeant was engaged for two weeks before the woman ran off with her ex-boyfriend. One of our dispatchers got married for two days in Las Vegas and had the whole thing annulled. She claimed she was too drunk to know what she was doing."

Russ blinked. What bizarre stories. Fascinating, though. "Surely you don't consider those two examples normal."

She responded with a shrug. "Being a cop is hard on relationships, so for us, that stuff *is* normal."

He wanted to be absolutely clear on the terms. "Are you saying it's no big deal if we break it off later?"

She considered, wearing a solemn expression that went oddly with the two-toned hair and bare feet. "Let's put it this way. There are worse reasons to tie the knot than to protect a child, but I'll accept a trial period, kind of like Janine offered you and Lauren."

Relief drained the tension from Russ's muscles. "I can go for that." Her statement rendered the pact little more than a formal approach to dating.

Then she added, "Maybe you can help me look at wedding dresses, just for kicks."

How bizzare. His ability to keep Lauren might depend on how well he got along with a woman who, two days ago, had flung him against a car and infuriated him to the point of violence. A woman who rode bicycles around swimming pools and scarcely seemed to notice that she'd almost drowned. And who claimed engagements meant next to nothing, then discussed wedding gowns in the next breath.

The funny part was that he found her so invigorating, he might enjoy playing her fiancé. He only hoped that in the end she didn't honestly expect them to walk down the aisle. The idea of being herded into marriage, whether by Janine's demand or by Rachel's rather peculiar principles, stirred the same anger he felt whenever someone tried to push him around.

Oh, for heaven's sake, this arrangement was temporary. A person couldn't be forced into marriage, and she'd made it clear that wasn't what she intended.

"Well?" Rachel probed. "What do you say?"

"The part about a wedding gown is giving me pause," he admitted.

"We can check out tuxedoes, too. You'd look cute in a penguin suit." Her smile lit up the room. "Or a swimsuit. Or nothing—forget I mentioned that."

The memory of the T-shirt plastered against her breasts sent a pleasant warmth through him. "I'll be happy to overlook it, if that's what you want."

"I guess we'll find out." She didn't so much as blush.

He might as well quit fighting the inevitable, Russ reflected. In the end, for Lauren's sake, he had little choice but to go along. And the prospect of spending a few days or weeks in Rachel's company wasn't the least bit unpleasant.

That left a few important details to work out. "What are we going to tell people when they ask the reason for this hasty decision?"

She had a ready answer. "You're the shiny knight who rescued me. We fell head over heels as I swooned in your arms. They'll buy it. I do dumb things all the time."

The last of Russ's qualms dissolved in laughter. "Right now, Lauren and I are the ones who need rescuing."

"Fine by me," she responded. "I love kids."

"She wasn't acting very lovable when we arrived," Russ noted. "You brought her around." He'd appreciated the way she'd seen through Lauren's bratty behavior to the vulnerability beneath.

"With everything that's happened, I'm sure she feels out of control," Rachel answered. "She's going to test us until we earn her trust."

"I'm aware that pushing the limits is typical of children." Russ had advised a number of parents regarding such behavior. "Unfortunately, recognizing the dynamics doesn't teach us how to change them."

"The only kind of dynamics I'm good at usually end with somebody flat on the pavement," Rachel replied ruefully.

"You were good with Lauren."

"In my family, we had hot and cold running foster kids in the house," she said. "If you didn't figure out how to handle 'em fast, you were sunk."

She'd certainly had an unusual upbringing. He was about to request more details when Connie fluttered into the room. "Lauren's absorbed in the dolls, especially the cop. She seems to have developed a soft spot for him. What've you two been doing?"

Russ wasn't sure where to start. "We have some news."

"Yes?"

They exchanged glances, and now Rachel *did* blush. As for Russ, the right words eluded him.

"Well, what?" Connie demanded.

"We're engaged." Rachel plopped her feet on the coffee table, nearly dislodging a china St. Bernard dog.

The blonde's expression wavered between amazement and doubt. "You're not serious!"

If they were going to convince the world, Russ had to embrace the situation. "Rachel's agreed to marry me. I understand your surprise, but we're in earnest."

"Oh, yeah?" challenged her friend.

"Double yeah with fried onions on it," Rachel replied with mock childishness.

"Yesterday, you said you had to show a total stranger around town, so this obviously isn't a longstanding affair," Connie retorted. "We can eliminate love at first sight, since I heard about your rumpus in the parking garage. And it's too soon for you to be pregnant. So what's going on?"

Russ wavered. He still wasn't certain exactly how honest they ought to be.

"Lauren's birth mom was going to give her away until Russ invented a bride-to-be," Rachel blurted with typical candor. "That's the only way he can win custody."

Well, what the heck? Russ doubted anything less than the truth would have satisfied their hostess.

Connie drummed her fingers on the door frame. "Are you certain this engagement is absolutely necessary? Because it's a harebrained idea."

Taking over the lead, Russ detailed the circumstances with Janine, including the unexpected death of her parents. He kept his voice low, reassured by the faint sound of his daughter chattering to the dolls in the bedroom.

Connie tilted her head pensively. "Well, at least it's a pretend engagement. You'll break it off as soon as the custody issue's settled, right?"

Rachel glanced at Russ before answering. "Not exactly. It's real."

"How real?" This woman had the tenacity of a pit bull.

"There's a chance we might get married."

"Would that be a ten percent chance? Twenty percent?" her friend asked. "Or about the same odds as, say, a blizzard hitting L.A. in August?"

Russ jumped in. "Fifty percent." Rachel nodded enthusiastically.

The blonde perched on a chair. "So you might actually walk down the aisle or you might not. Depending on what?"

"How hot the sex is," his bride-to-be quipped.

Russ tried not to dwell on an image of Rachel's lightly tanned skin pressing against his and their legs tangling beneath the sheets. With Lauren in the house, he hoped he'd be in no danger of yielding to temptation.

"We're doing this for Lauren's sake, and I appreciate Rachel's help," he said more gruffly than he'd intended.

"And I'd love to be Lauren's stepmom," Rachel said.

Connie studied her speculatively, then swung her gaze to Russ. "Is she moving in with you?"

"Oh, hey, can I?" Rachel regarded him with an unmistakable flash of hope.

On the verge of refusing, Russ reconsidered. Although he'd decorated the third bedroom as an office, he'd included a foldout couch for visitors. Given her knack for reading his daughter's moods, Rachel's presence might help Lauren adjust. Besides, as Connie had explained on the phone, she'd be returning to her condo before long. "Sure, if you'd like."

Both women heaved sighs of relief. These two must be grating on each other's nerves, Russ thought. Considering their dissimilar personalities, he was amazed they'd become friends in the first place.

Connie chuckled. "Guess I was kind of obvious about that, huh? Don't take this the wrong way, Rache."

"You don't have to tell me I'm a bull in a china shop." Rachel chortled. "A person can't stretch her legs around here without kicking over two candle arrangements, three little pigs and the seven dwarves."

Connie made a face. "You exaggerate!"

"Not much."

A reluctant nod of recognition. "Guess I'm overdue to rotate some of them into the stores. That was the original plan." To Russ she explained, "I own Connie's Curios at the intersection of Villa and Arches avenues, about half a mile from here. We have a branch at In a Pickle."

"She also owns the gift concession at Mesa View Medical Center," Rachel noted. "Marta runs it for her. They're cousins."

If he'd considered Rachel and Connie an odd couple, the blood relationship between this dewy blonde and boyish Marta struck him as stranger still. The discovery served as another reminder that in a small town, he should never assume people weren't connected.

"The gift shop's excellent. One of the best I've seen." In addition to flowers, personal-care items, snacks and stuffed animals, the hospital boutique carried books, games, rental DVD players and the latest DVDs, well displayed and stocked.

"Well, speaking as the expert on small decorative items, if you two expect to convince the world you're engaged, you'll need a ring," Connie informed them.

"A ring, huh?" Visions of thousand-dollar price tags danced in Russ's brain. He also hadn't begun to tally the impact of day care and other new expenses on his tight budget. "We'll have to keep it simple."

Rachel averted her gaze. "Yeah." Beneath the word, he read disappointment. For heaven's sake, how seriously was she taking this engagement?

"I have an idea!" Connie sprang to her feet. "You can borrow mine. One of these days I plan to reset the diamond, but in the meantime, you might as well use it."

"Wow!" Rachel's colorful hair bounced. "That's so generous!" Dubiously she added, "You don't think Joel will recognize it?"

Connie didn't hesitate. "Are you kidding? He'll be clueless."

Rachel wearing a ring to work—that made this arrangement public. And no doubt Marta would spread the word at the hospital, as well. The spiraling nature of the situation disturbed Russ.

"I'm not entirely comfortable with this," he admitted. "Everybody in the world's going to hear the news." The immediate world, anyway.

Rachel tapped her fingers on her thigh. "That's the idea, isn't it? To make it seem real?"

"I don't want to raise false expectations, including yours," Russ said. If they were going to break it off, he'd rather do it now. "Frankly, you're sending mixed messages. Moving in. Wearing a ring. How much of this is real to you?"

"The part about wishing I were Lauren's stepmom is true," she said wistfully. "And I *have* to believe we're actually tying the knot or I'll never manage to convince Janine."

That cleared up nothing. "I'm still not sure what you mean by 'believe.'"

With a rueful smile, she answered, "I stopped believing in Santa Claus eons ago, but every year I decorate a tree and set out cookies by the fireplace."

How delightful. "Who eats them?"

"Me." After a moment, she murmured, "But not until after midnight. Just in case he *does* show."

Before Russ could sort out this confusing statement, Connie returned with a jewelry box. Lauren followed, clutching a blue-clad male doll about a foot high. "Look, Russ, I can keep Officer Bud!"

"Are you sure that's all right, Connie?" He feared his daughter might be taking advantage of their hostess.

"You bet. The darn thing reminds me of my ex." She extended the velvet box. "So does this. Hope it brings you more luck than it brought me."

Rachel's attention riveted on the case as she opened it. Moving closer, Russ caught a twinkle of blue-white light from a large stone set amid an emerald swirl. A stunning piece, he thought as his new fiancée slid it onto her finger.

"Thanks, Connie." Holding her hand aloft, she regarded the ring with shining eyes.

Lauren stared at it. "Connie said you and Russ are getting married."

Rachel took a deep breath. "I sure hope so."

Russ recalled that she'd sworn not to lie to his daughter. And that she hadn't entirely given up on Santa Claus. *How much of this is real to you?* Maybe a whole lot more than he'd anticipated.

He prayed that he hadn't made a very big, very awkward mistake.

ONCE RUSS AND LAUREN LEFT, Rachel went to pack her stuff. A simple matter, since she hadn't brought much.

On her finger, the ring twinkled like a faerie gift. Rachel hadn't expected to care about anything as froufrou as a diamond ring, especially a borrowed one. Yet its exquisite beauty made her feel pretty and desirable, like the popular girls in high school who'd never acknowledged she existed.

Connie used to be among those girls. Funny how people changed.

Speaking of Connie, her friend barged into the room and stood with arms folded. "Okay, I held my peace and played along, but now I'm going to pose the burning question of the day… Are you nuts?"

"People walk down the aisle every day." Rachel continued folding clothes into a bag. "As for Russ, he's cool with it."

"In case you've forgotten, you *aren't* walking down anything except a primrose path. You're posing as fiancés because the man's desperate."

Rachel wasn't ready to let go of this magical sense of belonging. "He can't be that desperate. Of all the women in the world, he chose me."

"Did you see his reaction when I mentioned buying a

ring? The guy was practically backing out the door," Connie pressed.

"The doc's reserved. But he's not the type to run away." She could count on him in a crisis, as Rachel had discovered yesterday. "Also, he invited me to move in with him. That has to mean something."

"You invited yourself." Agitated, her friend sank onto the bed. "Seems to me you're a lot more into this engagement business than he is."

Happiness began slipping away. Rachel made one more grab for it. "I like the guy. What's wrong with that?"

"You're going to get your heart broken, that's what!" Connie replied. "He's gorgeous and he's a doctor, which means he's used to having women fall in love with him. I'll bet he doesn't even realize how much pain he causes."

Probably true. But if Rachel listened, her common sense might make her return the ring and go on sleeping in a china-doll guest room. Besides, she'd made a promise to help Lauren. "You may be right, but I don't care. I'm thirty years old, for Pete's sake, and there's not a big market for women who can outshoot and outwrestle guys. I'm going to take a chance that the prince might actually fall for a supersize Cinderella."

Connie radiated disapproval. "Playing house with a guy you're falling in love with could have all sorts of unpleasant consequences, especially if you're falling in love alone."

Rachel thrust wadded socks and underwear into the corners of a suitcase. "If I'm kidding myself, that's my problem. When I'm old, I want more to reminisce about than how many crooks I took down! For once, I can be an insider, the girl with the sexy boyfriend, and I'm determined to enjoy every minute. Who can say? He might discover I'm the one he's been searching for all along."

A rueful air replaced the frown. "Oh, Rache! Take it from a woman who's been there. If the guy isn't a perfect match, don't try to change him. I wasted three years on Joel, and I don't even have a kid to show for it. Not that I wanted one, at the time."

A kid. Lauren. Rachel's spirits leaped at the prospect of playing with her. And with Russ. "Men always flocked around you. This may be my only chance."

"You deserve better," Connie replied loyally. "One of these days you're going to find a fellow who'll buy you a ring of your own."

Rachel lifted her hand, enjoying the flash of blue light. "I prefer this one."

To her shock, Connie jumped up and gave her a hug. "Don't underestimate your appeal. Lots of the guys find you attractive. Hale told me a couple of them were disappointed you had to work and missed the Super Bowl party."

"Well, that's encouraging, although I can't imagine who." Another bit of curiosity nagged at her. "Since when do you and Hale have heart-to-heart talks about me or anything else?"

"He helps me with yard work once in a while. Since we don't have much else in common, we discuss mutual acquaintances." She returned to her earlier topic. "So don't let the doctor break your heart."

"Thanks for the advice. And for the hospitality."

"Honestly, it's been my pleasure."

Rachel lugged her stuff out to the car. She left most of the beer, which she'd stashed in Connie's garage refrigerator. No doubt it would migrate back to Hale's house sooner or later.

Unseasonable sunshine turned the afternoon to California gold, and a faint floral scent drifted through Rachel's open window as she drove to Russ's development. Seeing the bungalow again, she registered appealing details: two-toned honey-and-tan trim setting off the beige paint, a large front porch flanked by clumps of calla lilies, and an abstract design etched into the glass of the front door.

It was such a beautiful place compared to the run-down apartment complex where Rachel and her mother used to live. Vague images lingered of dirt and weeds in the yard and the sour scent of an unclean kitchen. She'd longed for an enchanted cottage like this one, and what a glorious opportunity to help a girl who must be aching inside just as Rachel had been, so long ago.

She was proceeding along the walk when Russ opened the front door and stepped out. He made a distinguished figure, with his graying temples and confident carriage.

Then she saw his taut stance, the wariness in his eyes, and her spirits plunged. After a short while to reflect, he apparently had regretted inviting her.

Connie was right. He'd been honest about his discomfort and his intention to break off their engagement once they'd convinced Janine. Why had she nursed delusions about princes and enchanted cottages? A princess didn't wear boots and strap a gun to her hip.

A twist of sorrow was all the emotion she tolerated before striking a cheerful note. "Don't worry," she announced as she approached the porch. "I wasn't serious about getting married. Let's just enjoy this while it lasts."

Relief showed on Russ's face. That might have hurt, had she allowed it to. But dwelling on disappointments didn't suit Rachel's nature.

Giving him a friendly, impersonal nod, she hauled her luggage inside.

Chapter Seven

On Tuesday, Rachel arrived a few minutes early for her new shift, which began at 6 a.m. Although she was happy to be working days following six months on swing, a lot of guys hated rising before noon, so she found herself in an empty briefing room with twenty minutes to spare.

She tried to focus on the posted flyers and announcements, but her mind kept flicking over Monday's events. Since the department operated on a "five nines" schedule, which meant five nine-hour days followed by three days off, she'd had an extra day to settle in at Russ's.

Yesterday morning he'd enrolled his daughter in kindergarten. He'd also taken Lauren to a licensed day care at the home of a young mother in the neighborhood. Apparently the meeting had gone well, because he'd agreed to let Mrs. Sommers collect the little girl when school ended at noon, beginning today.

While father and daughter were out, Rachel had found a locked cabinet to store her gun, inspected the smoke alarms and bolt locks, and purchased a carbon monoxide monitor at the hardware store. Having been raised by parents who met foster-care standards, she considered those basic precautions.

Rachel had eaten an early lunch with Marta, then spent the rest of the day with Lauren while Russ worked. The kid had definite tastes—yes to tuna, no to peanut butter—and an understandable tendency to cling. At the park, Lauren had insisted they swing side by side, and when they stopped at the supermarket, she'd required no reminders to stick close.

Later that evening Rachel had struggled to maintain her distance from Russ. She hadn't entirely succeeded.

As they fixed dinner, she'd bumped into him twice. After Lauren went to bed, a tussle for the remote control had involved further bodily contact and laughter. He hadn't seemed to mind.

She'd avoided any mention of shopping for a wedding dress or introducing him to her folks. The only reference to their engagement had occurred when he said that Janine wanted to meet his fiancée.

What a peculiar push-pull Rachel experienced about the whole business! Until next weekend, she had to carry on with the pretend engagement in front of the world. And perhaps for a while longer, until custody became final.

As for her condo, the homeowners' board had hired experts to fix the slope. However, the management company had warned in an e-mail that residents should anticipate at least another few weeks of banishment.

More officers wandered into the briefing room. Determined to wrest some information from her inattentive study of the wanted posters, Rachel reread one about a prison escapee. A robber named Noel Flanders, who'd been arrested in Villazon eight years ago, might have ties to the area. A large tattoo of a skull and crossbones on his neck ought to make him easy to ID even if he dyed his bushy red-brown hair. But, she mused, he'd probably fled across the border to Mexico by now.

Rachel turned as Joel, today's watch commander, strolled in with Hale. As a detective, Hale didn't have to put in an appearance this early, but the guy worked harder than you'd assume for a party boy.

They drifted toward Rachel. "How're you and the dragon lady getting along?" Joel sniped.

"Oh, I'm not living with Connie anymore."

Hale blinked in surprise. "They fixed your slope?"

"Hardly." Rachel extended her left hand and braced for a flood of questions. "I moved in with my fiancé."

Dead silence fell over the room. Her voice had obviously carried. Oh, man, she hated being the center of attention. Every doubt she'd entertained and a plethora of new ones swarmed over her. *But I'm doing this for a good cause.*

Elise Masterson shot her a dubious glance. Bill Norton, the patrolman who'd been working the yellow-tag scene Saturday night, said, "Don't tell me it's that doctor I heard about, the one who pulled you out of the pool."

"That's him," Rachel confirmed.

"He sure works fast!" Bill grumbled.

He was complaining? If her co-worker took a personal interest in her, that was news to Rachel. Maybe Connie had been right. Well, the guy should have spoken out sooner.

Hale gripped her hand, raised it into full view and regarded the sparkler with a pained expression. "Oh, come on, Rache, people don't just… Hey, that sure looks like Connie's old ring."

Uh-oh. Who'd have figured *Hale* would notice?

"No way," Joel scoffed. "Her diamond was a lot bigger. I oughtta know. I paid for it."

Rachel smothered a laugh. If she'd had to fork over the bucks, she'd probably overestimate the size of the rock, too.

"Guess you're the expert." With a shrug, Hale released

her hand and ambled out. Briefing was for patrol. As a detective, he attended to his own cases.

The fuss died down as Joel signaled the start. For the next half hour, the officers took notes on restraining orders, stolen cars and suspects at large, particularly a husky, bald man—not very creatively nicknamed Baldy for publicity purposes—who'd robbed several area pharmacies at gunpoint. The watch commander also assigned some officers to patrol Archway Acres and escort condo owners who needed to pick up stuff to go to their unit. Mercifully, he spared Rachel that duty.

When he was done, a couple of officers came over to congratulate her on the engagement. "When's the wedding?" was the most frequent question, to which she admitted they hadn't set a date.

"Be sure to invite the chief. I hear he played matchmaker." Elise's teasing tone indicated she'd recovered her aplomb.

Rachel hadn't considered in what light Lyons might regard this affair, especially once she and Russ staged their breakup. The chief was hypersensitive about any activities that reflected negatively on the department's image.

"I just hope the newspaper doesn't make a fuss," she responded.

The *Villazon Voice*'s article about Nina's rescue hadn't come out yet, but given the paucity of news in town, Rachel expected Tracy to make much of it. Russ's engagement to the cop who'd nearly arrested him ought to be a big deal, too.

As if matters weren't ticklish enough, Captain Frank Ferguson, the chief's right-hand man, materialized next to Rachel. "What's all the fuss?"

Most of the cops were heading off to their cruisers, as she devoutly wished to do, but she gritted her teeth and filled him in. Frank, an easygoing department veteran in his late forties, accepted the information calmly.

"I'll inform Chief Lyons," he said. "I'm sure he'll view it as a positive development in community relations."

"Thanks," Rachel said gratefully.

"They should have made *you* the chief," Joel told the captain in a low voice. "We wouldn't need someone to run interference if you were in charge."

Frank waved away the compliment. "We're lucky to have such a top-notch leader."

Despite a year on the job, Lyons remained basically a stranger to the department. Still, Rachel considered Joel's remark indiscreet. She chose to avoid office politics whenever possible.

The day's only excitement occurred that afternoon when, at the request of hospital security, she broke up a heated argument between a husband and wife in the lobby. The sight of her uniform inspired them to start blaming each other for creating a problem, but her threat to arrest them both for creating a disturbance silenced them. The saddest part, to her, was that they'd been arguing about how to spend an expected inheritance from an ailing relative.

"Pack of hyenas," muttered Sgt. Derek Reed, who'd been meeting with hospital staff in his role as community liaison. Although providing backup wasn't among his duties, he'd leaped at the chance as if itching for action.

Rachel watched the couple stalk past the gift shop and out of the building. Surely they'd begun their marriage starry-eyed and deeply in love, and now look at them. "These situations bring out people's worst side, I guess."

"I'd rather leave everything I own to charity than to grasping relatives like that." Derek broke off complaining to add, "By the way, congrats. I hear there's cause for celebration."

"Darn right." Rachel would have preferred to leave the subject at that, but Marta made a beeline toward them from the boutique. These days, a slight limp and a jagged scar half-hidden by makeup were the only reminders of her near-fatal accident eleven years ago. Other than Connie, Marta was the only one who knew the truth about the engagement.

She gave no sign of her inside knowledge. Instead, she chatted cheerily to Derek about the quarreling couple, who'd stopped by the gift shop earlier and nearly fought World War III over which bouquet to purchase. Glancing between the two of them, Rachel realized with a start that Marta found Sgt. Hit-and-Run attractive.

That was too bad. Marta's boyish figure and short, light-brown hair didn't fit the playboy's preferred blond-and-buxom type. He at least appeared to listen attentively to her, but then, Marta was so outgoing almost everyone warmed to her.

Rachel excused herself to return to duty. Perhaps as a friend, she ought to stick around and encourage the conversation, but she didn't work for Cupid; she worked for the Villazon PD. Besides, she was hardly an expert at swaying men's hearts.

At shift's end, Rachel completed her paperwork promptly. On the way out, she passed Chief Lyons in the hall.

"Frank tells me best wishes are in order." Lyons might have been distant, but he possessed the no-nonsense air of a man who'd spent years on patrol. Some of those who'd applied for his job were reputed to have spent so much time and effort smoothing their rise to power that they barely remembered they were cops. "Kind of sudden, if you don't mind my saying so."

"Who'd have guessed playing tour guide could be so rewarding?" she responded. The lighthearted remark spared her the necessity of lying outright.

"I'd better add 'matchmaker' to my résumé." He paused. "On second thought, better not. Romance isn't my strong suit." A widower for the past dozen years, Lyons had struggled to raise a rebellious teenage son. Whether for personal reasons or to prevent any breath of scandal, he reputedly avoided dating even outside the department.

Rachel dredged up an innocuous reply and escaped. She would rather storm a building full of armed suspects than make nice with the brass.

It was close to four o'clock when she parked at Russ's house and walked around the corner to the day care address. Despite its two-story height, the house had a cozy air with a roofed porch and potted pansies lining the walkway. Through a side fence, Rachel glimpsed colorful play equipment. So far she approved.

She rang the bell, glad that she'd changed out of her uniform at the station. You never knew how people might react.

Inside, childish footsteps pelted toward the front. "Whoa, Ken!" called a woman's voice. "Remember the rule. Only grown-ups answer the bell."

"Okay, Mommy." Clearly one of the caretaker's children.

The door swung open. The woman standing there looked familiar, yet Rachel couldn't place her. Medium height, delicate features, shoulder-length straight brown hair. Cataloging her features produced no additional insights.

"I'm here to collect Lauren," Rachel said.

"You must be…" The brown eyes widened in recognition. "Rachel!"

A memory surfaced. "Keri?"

"Wow! So you're engaged to that handsome doctor. Good for you!" The door swung wide.

Keri Borrego, daughter of then-chief Vince Borrego, had been in college when Rachel joined the force, and they'd met at her parents' annual barbecue for the department. Both single, they'd enjoyed chatting there and at various other police functions. Then Keri had married a real estate attorney and moved away.

Her father's forced retirement and her parents' divorce must have been tough. But marriage and motherhood obviously agreed with her.

"I wasn't aware you'd moved back to the area." As she spoke, Rachel surveyed the living room's child-friendly furniture. A couple of couches, a TV on a sturdy low table and a large shelf of picture books left plenty of space for three boys racing toy trains around a track.

One youngster shouted, "Vroom, vroom!" as he whizzed a locomotive through the air. Keri merely smiled. A tolerance for noise must be a requirement for anyone supervising kids.

"About six months ago, Ed took a job with a law firm in Whittier. I'm happy to be back in the area." Keri indicated the children. "That's my son Ken over there with his two friends, Tommy and Cade, and my twins, Kim and Mary, are in the den with Lauren. I'm licensed to watch six children."

"How did things go today?" A new school and a new after-school center might have thrown Lauren off balance. Rachel didn't underestimate the potential for tantrums.

"She became a bit stressed this afternoon," Keri confided. "My teenage helper herded the boys outside while I read quietly to the girls. That soothed her."

A bit apologetically, Keri added, "I suppose it's indulgent of me to pay an assistant, but by three-thirty I'm tired and my patience wears thin."

"I doubt I'd last more than a couple of hours with six kids." Rachel had supervised foster siblings occasional evenings and weekends. The experience had been fun but exhausting.

"I can see why you impressed Russ," Rachel remarked.

"He's quite a guy, stepping in to raise his daughter on short notice. She's lucky to have you both."

Keri provided a quick tour of the downstairs. The gated stairs and childproof outlets reassured Rachel. She also appreciated the streamlined kitchen, not a china knick-knack in view.

They paused at the entrance to a large den. On the far side, Lauren and two younger girls were sprawled on a rug, playing a board game. A chubby teenager helped them count play money.

Catching sight of her, Lauren leaped to her feet so fast she scattered game pieces. "You're here!" She ran forward, then stopped. Apparently her relief at seeing a familiar face extended only so far.

"Hi, sweetie. I promised to pick you up unless all heck broke loose in town, so here I am. Have fun today?" Rachel asked.

"Yeah." The little girl hovered close by, not quite touching.

Over the child's head, Rachel acknowledged an introduction to Keri's after-school helper, Lisa Chin. The girl looked about fifteen.

"Lisa lives next door." Keri tucked Lauren's possessions into her backpack.

"You moved in with that cute pediatrician, right?" Lisa finger-combed long dark hair streaked with strawberry highlights.

"They're getting married!" Lauren proclaimed proudly. Rachel merely smiled.

"A couple of divorcées are going to be severely disappointed," Keri teased. "When he showed up at the homeowners meeting last month, they figured they'd hit the jackpot."

Rachel laughed. "I'll see you both tomorrow, unless I'm hung up at work."

"Busting bad guys, huh?" Lisa said.

"You bet!" Lauren confirmed.

Taking Lauren's hand, Rachel slung the backpack over her shoulder and strolled out. On the walk around the block, she listened to an account of the day's events. Lauren liked her new teacher, but the kids weren't nearly as nice as the friends from her old school.

"Give them a chance. And what about—" Rachel searched for the names of the twins "—Kim and Mary? They seem friendly."

"They're babies," Lauren scoffed. "They're in *preschool*."

"Totally uncool."

A giggle. "Yeah!"

As they mounted the porch steps, Rachel felt a rush of tenderness for this small, intense person. As long as the engagement lasted, she vowed to be the best substitute mommy in the entire world.

ON TUESDAY RUSS worked a schedule reminiscent of his pressure-cooker internship. He slated patients during his lunch hour to compensate for the time he'd spent yesterday making arrangements for Lauren. Then from 3:00 to 6:00 p.m. he worked his regular volunteer stint at the outreach clinic housed on the hospital's lower level.

One of the factors that had attracted him to Villazon was this low-cost clinic sponsored by the medical center. While California provided insurance for poor kids, many still fell through the cracks.

To him, volunteering fulfilled a longstanding goal. For the first few years after completing his residency, Russ had served a high-paying clientele, logging as many hours as possible to pay off student loans. An unexpectedly large inheritance from his grandfather had enabled him to retire the debts and afford a down payment on a home, as well as pursue his desire to care for kids in need. So he donated part of each Tuesday to treat problems that ranged from asthma and ear infections to more serious afflictions.

Since Russ refused to leave any child unexamined, he didn't finish until nearly six-thirty. The intense focus required to diagnose and prescribe for so many patients left him pretty stressed out, despite the sense of satisfaction.

In West L.A., he'd listened to classical music on the short commute home and released his tensions by antici-pating a quiet, stress-free evening. During the past few days, however, Rachel and Lauren had turned his once-pre-dictable world upside down. And the drive took only ten minutes, not nearly long enough for the tightness to seep from his muscles.

Nor did Russ's disposition improve when the whirring rise of the garage door revealed an interior too crammed for him to pull inside. Someone had stacked a bed frame, mattress and bureau inside, along with boxes of books that he'd stored in the second bedroom.

Russ tried to subdue his irritation. Obviously, his daughter's possessions must have arrived. Janine had e-mailed yesterday that she'd hired a truck to bring them, but the driver was supposed to call Russ's cell number to schedule the drop-off.

Why couldn't people follow simple directions? he re-flected dourly. And why had Rachel stuck everything in the middle of the garage instead of somewhere more convenient?

He forced himself to recognize the effects of hunger and fatigue on his mood. A man's home might be his castle when he lived alone, but since he'd chosen to lower the drawbridge, he'd better cut his new housemates some slack.

Russ drew in several deep breaths while locking the car. Scents of bare earth, flowers and cooking reached him, a welcome change from the exhaust fumes of Los Angeles. Relative equanimity restored, he opened a side door into the kitchen.

Disorder reigned. Pots, pans, utensils, spices and food packages cluttered the counters, which he'd left in pristine shape, and the air hung heavy with the aromas of maple syrup, broiling meat and burnt bread. White powder smeared a corner of the floor.

Lauren, a streak of yellow mustard on one cheek, was setting ketchup and margarine on the table. "Russ!" she shrieked. "Rachel, Russ is home!" And ran to throw flour-dusted arms around him.

I will not snap at my innocent child, Russ resolved. Hanging on to his temper, he ignored the white fingerprints festooning his suit jacket.

But until now, he realized, he hadn't considered the nerve-shredding impact of his new lifestyle. He'd seen in his practice that not everyone was cut out for the daily pressures of raising a family. And interacting with a perpetually irritable parent chipped away bit by bit at a child's self-esteem.

He had to master this flaw. Otherwise, his hasty leap into fatherhood had done his daughter a great disservice.

Janine had warned him. Russ hoped he wasn't going to have to admit she'd been right.

He closed his eyes and prayed for self-control.

Chapter Eight

One look at Russ's face told Rachel she should have anticipated how he'd react to her culinary chaos. She'd scarcely noticed the mess because she'd been so engrossed.

His strained air spoke louder than words. Apparently he *liked* a kitchen sterile enough to double as an operating room. She'd figured he simply hadn't finished decorating yet.

"I'll clean up when we're done." She added an apologetic shrug. "Guess I got carried away."

Above a flour-smeared suit that had been pristine moments ago, he wore a deer-in-the-headlights expression. "No problem." The phrase choked out of his throat.

"I burned the buns." Lauren held on to her father. "In the toaster. They're for the hamburgers."

"I love burned buns." A good sport. Or perhaps merely shell-shocked.

"I'm broiling the meat." Rachel squashed an impulse to suggest Russ install a grill on the patio. He didn't appear to be a barbecue-in-the-backyard type. "Also, by special request, pancakes."

"For dinner?" he asked dazedly.

Lauren hopped in place. "They're my favorite!"

Moving to the stove, Rachel flipped the second batch.

"I decided to indulge in comfort food this evening. We're also having fruit salad. We can do the green healthy routine tomorrow."

Russ's jaw worked. She wondered what bothered him most—the poor nutrition or the chaos. Then she considered that being forced to park in the driveway probably hadn't thrilled him, either.

"Sorry about the garage. Lauren's furniture arrived right before five, and I didn't want to leave the old stuff outside in case of rain," she explained. "We can reorganize later."

"Sure." Gently untangling his daughter, he brushed his suit over a wastebasket. "There's no point in my changing before dinner. How can I help?"

Rachel was about to suggest he pour the drinks when Lauren burst out, "My books came! I'll read you my favorite."

"Great." When she dashed off, he hovered uncertainly. "Am I supposed to follow her or what?"

Better to postpone the shock of observing the makeover she'd done on Lauren's bedroom. "Stick around. You can pour her milk while you're waiting." Rachel switched off the gas under the frying pan, grabbed pot holders and opened the broiler to remove the burgers.

"Fine." He fetched three glasses. "Water okay for you?"

"My favorite." As Rachel transferred meat to a serving plate, she said, "I appreciate your patience. I didn't mean to take over your house, but things happened fast."

He aligned the glasses on the table. "I'm not complaining. You're here at my request. Well, sort of."

"Another night at Connie's and they'd have had to lock me in a padded cell," she joked. "As for Lauren, parents have to go with the flow."

"That's never been my forte." He sounded grim.

"Entertaining second thoughts?"

When he didn't reply, she knew she'd hit close to the truth. Although Rachel was tempted to grab him and insist that absolutely no way could he change his mind, she had to go easy on the doc. He'd stumbled into uncharted territory. A few doubts didn't spell retreat.

"It'll pass," she said mildly, and scooped the flapjacks onto a plate.

"I hope so."

Lauren pelted in holding a picture book, *The Velveteen Rabbit*. Russ's gaze traveled between her and the table piled with food. "One page has to be enough for now. Otherwise dinner will get cold."

"Okay." She opened to the front. "Once upon a time, a little girl named Lauren met a fairy. The fairy gave her three wishes." Lauren shut the book. "Let's eat!"

Gently, Russ lifted the book and regarded the print. "Where does it say that?"

"Right there!" she replied indignantly.

His forehead creased. "The story's about a stuffed rabbit."

"She's at the prereading stage." Rachel had held enough foster kids on her lap and listened to their wild tales to recognize the process. "She understands the magic of the printed word, even if she can't decipher it yet, so she invents her own tale."

Russ shot her a grateful look before addressing his daughter. "Very creative, sweetie." He handed her the book. "Put that away so food can't land on it, okay?"

Satisfied, Lauren dashed out.

"My pediatric experience doesn't appear to translate very well," he admitted to Rachel. "I understand kids in theory."

"You catch on fast." She removed the apron from her

jeans and knit top, then sank onto a chair that rocked beneath the impact. "This thing's out of kilter."

"I've noticed."

Such a flaw cried out for remedy. "You never thought to sand down the legs?"

"I use the other chairs." Russ shifted the platters so the plate of burned buns didn't jut out over the table's edge. "A classic case of avoidance, don't you think?"

"I can fix it if you like," Rachel responded.

"I'll do it eventually."

She interpreted that as a warning that this remained his house and these were his possessions. Heck, she knew that. On the other hand, he'd better figure out quick that sharing required easing off the controls.

Once Lauren returned, they dug in. Eating mellowed Russ, and Lauren held center stage in the conversation. She liked the playground at school, she told them, but the snack had been yucky. "Crackers and carrots! Ugh!"

"Who provided the food?" Russ asked, ladling a second helping of fruit salad into his daughter's bowl.

"The room mom." A brief reflection. "Today's letter was *C*."

"That's why the crackers and carrots." At Rachel's impatient signal, he added a few more pieces of pineapple. "That's a fun way of teaching the alphabet."

"They could have served cupcakes," Rachel remarked. "Or cookies. Those both start with *C*."

"Cantaloupe would be healthier." Russ frowned into the fruit salad. "Although I'd say we have a bit too much of that. I'd prefer cherries."

Lauren joined the game. "Candy! That's a *C* word!"

"In fruit salad?" teased her father.

"No! For snacks!"

"While we're using the letter *C,* at least they didn't turn you into cannibals," Rachel said.

Russ nearly choked on a bite of pancake. Lauren dropped her fork. "That's gross!"

"Sorry." Rachel decided to move on, fast. "If tomorrow's letter is *D,* they'd better serve doughnuts."

"And Danish!" Lauren cried gleefully.

"Dental floss," said Russ. "Afterward, I mean."

His daughter wrinkled her nose.

Following dinner, they all pitched in to restore order in the kitchen. Lauren carried plates and condiments, Russ loaded the dishwasher, and Rachel tackled the counters and floor.

Then, unable to delay the moment of truth any further, she trailed father and daughter down the hall to what had been, only a few hours ago, a starkly utilitarian chamber done in beiges and browns. She stopped behind Russ at the entrance to the darkened room.

He waited in the doorway while Lauren switched on her newly installed lamp. Through a rose-colored shade, light flooded a scene of floral excess that, in Rachel's estimation, lacked only a dose of perfume to render it totally cloying.

She wouldn't have bought this kind of stuff on a dare. But then, she wasn't a frills-and-flounces kind of girl. Lauren obviously loved the decor.

A pink comforter and bolster matched the canopy atop a four-poster bed, which was flanked by an ornate white dresser and table. In the corner, an overstuffed armchair squeezed against a curlicued bookcase. Since Lauren had insisted on unpacking everything, Rachel had piled the horizontal surfaces with dolls and stuffed animals. Connie would certainly have approved.

Russ folded his arms. "I assume your previous bedroom was larger than this one."

A big nod.

"I'm sorry if you feel cramped." He eyed the bedside table. "You don't need every single piece, do you?"

"Yes!"

"But you'll be tripping over them!"

"That's all right," Lauren said. "I'll take them home with me."

Russ froze. Rachel ached for the child, who, despite the events of the weeks since her grandparents' deaths, still didn't understand the permanence of the situation.

Russ moved into the room and knelt beside his daughter. "Honey, this *is* your home now."

Her dark brown eyes filled with tears. "I want Grandma and Grandpa!"

"I know you miss them, but you'll be happy here." When he reached for her, she backed off.

"They'll come fetch me!" she protested, grabbing her new policeman doll.

At this age, death didn't seem real to kids. Rachel's aunt, the only member of the family who'd visited, had died of heart failure eight months after Rachel's placement. She'd been angry for months, certain Aunt Theresa could return if she chose to.

Russ continued in a low, earnest tone. "I'm sure Janine explained about the plane crash. Honey, even though your grandparents loved you more than anything, they're gone."

"No!" Lauren squeezed Officer Bud so hard Rachel feared it might break. "Take me home."

"Your grandparents don't own that house anymore." He seemed to be casting about for an explanation she could grasp. "Janine does."

"I'll stay with her. I hate it here!" She stamped her foot.

"You don't mean that."

"I hate you!"

Rachel held her breath. If Russ was already regretting his decision, the child had handed him an excuse to throw in the towel. She recognized, and at some level he must also, that the tantrum sprang from fear and pain. Still, if he shrank from making a commitment, he might con himself into believing he was only obeying her wishes by returning her to her mother.

Instead of replying, Russ moved to the easy chair. "Did your grandparents used to sit here and read to you?"

Stiffly, Lauren nodded.

He glanced thoughtfully around the overstuffed chamber. "Did your dolls and bears gather to listen?"

"Sometimes." She buried her face in the doll. At least the foot stomping had ended.

"I'll bet they miss Grandma and Grandpa, too, don't they?" Plucking a fuzzy bear from the shelf, he marched its little legs along the chair's arm and lowered it beside him.

Rachel's throat clenched. His action seemed utterly natural, yet she suspected this man hadn't played with stuffed animals since infancy.

"My toys cry at night." A tear marked Lauren's cheek. "I tell them stories. The ones Grandma used to tell me."

"Does that help them feel better?" Russ selected a panda, which stumped down to join the bear.

"Yes." She dangled Officer Bud at her side.

Taking the doll gently, Russ tucked it into the crook of his arm. "Where's *The Velveteen Rabbit*?"

She ran to the shelves. Bringing it to him, she climbed into her father's lap as he began to read the story of a toy that was loved so much it became real.

Rachel slipped out. She couldn't face anyone until she hid unwelcome tears and got a grip on the emotions boiling to the surface.

Her chest hurt. Inside, an abyss opened, threatening a gut-wrenching crying spell such as she hadn't endured since adolescence. *Breathe slowly. Don't give in.*

Most adults failed to understand how much toys meant. Kids invested them with such strong personalities that, as in the book, their playthings seemed like real friends. Amazing that Russ, who hadn't struck her as particularly playful, had grasped that truth intuitively.

If only she'd known a father like that during her early years. Later, Tom Byers had tried to fill the void with his bluff, jovial manner, but due to her earlier experiences, Rachel had had difficulty trusting him. Mostly she'd tagged along with the other children in the home, satisfied to remain under his protection but a little apart.

How lucky Lauren was. If only every child could have a father like that.

Rachel retreated to the sunroom, where louvered glass overlooked the rear lawn. Darkness had fallen, rendering the yard a mass of shadows. Beyond the fence, safety lights dotted the parking lot of the warehouse complex that abutted Amber View.

Rachel stared out, fighting for composure. She focused on the austere lines of lights marching into the distance and the unsentimental square shapes of the buildings.

When Russ entered, she remained motionless. He flicked on a lamp, which hurt her eyes. "What's wrong?"

She tried to dredge up an offhand comment to keep from answering directly. Her mind went blank.

The divan dipped beside her. Russ had changed into casual clothes that smelled of fresh detergent, she noticed.

"Are you having trouble digesting the pancakes and hamburgers? That was an odd combination."

He thought she had gas? To Rachel's embarrassment, laughter and misery combined into a loud hiccup. "Darn."

"At least you're speaking. Try again but leave off the sound effects."

She sniffled. Giving away too much.

Russ peered closer and said in wonder, "You're crying. Why?"

She managed an unconvincing shrug. "Old tapes. Childhood crap. Don't worry about it."

"Now that we're engaged, you can confide in me." His arm brushed hers. The closeness felt so comforting that if Rachel hadn't been so tall, she might have crawled onto his lap like Lauren.

Yeah, right. Officer Byers sobbing her heart out on the doc's clean clothes. "Nothing to confide."

"You're one of the strongest people I've ever met, and something's obviously bothering you." He slid an arm around her. "Hey, I'm in father mode. Spill it. Don't tell me you're afraid to."

Continuing to argue was pointless. Might as well tell her story. "I mentioned that I grew up with foster kids, right? The part I left out was that I was one of them."

"You lost your family?" Sympathy tinged his voice.

"Lost?" She thought of Nina in the parking garage, with the doctor stopping to help and anxious parents rushing to claim her. A scary situation but neatly resolved. "What happened was a lot messier than that."

Russ pressed his cheek to her hair. "Tell me."

How could compassion cause such anguish in her? Rachel stiffened, and he moved his arm onto the back of the sofa.

"I've said enough." Even now, more than a quarter century later, the pain not only lingered but, given half a chance, festered. "I got adopted by the right family, and that's all that counts."

"What happened to your birth parents?" Russ persisted.

In view of their living arrangement, she supposed she ought to tell him. "My real dad split while Mom was pregnant. He'd also abandoned a couple of kids by other women, so I don't fool myself that he'd be thrilled if his cop daughter tracked him down."

"Go on."

"Mom and I lived with her boyfriend, Ernie." She recalled little except small, dark rooms and the stink of moldering onions from the overflowing trash. Unable to describe the couple except through sarcasm, she explained, "They only quarreled when they drank, and they never drank except when they could scrape together enough money to buy booze."

"Which is saying you lived in constant turmoil," he summarized.

Exactly. "After a while you take the screaming for granted, like having a TV on in the background." Analyzing the ugly memories helped more than she would have expected. "You recognize the different levels of quarreling, like whether they're crabby because they ran out of ice or whether somebody's in danger."

"Are you aware that you stopped talking in the first person?" Russ said.

"What?"

"You quit saying 'I' and began using 'you.' Distancing yourself."

"You'd have kept your distance from Ernie, too." She'd reached the tricky part. Better to dive in fast. "He spanked me for any infringement. If he was hung over, loud breathing counted as an offense."

"Are we talking a swat on the rump or worse?"

The knot in Rachel's chest had grown large enough to anchor a sailing vessel. But she'd traveled this far, so she might as well finish. "He wasn't sadistic, but he lashed out with anything he could grab. A rolled-up newspaper. A beer bottle. His belt."

"You were how old?" The question bristled with anger.

"Four when a neighbor spotted my bruises and refused to buy the 'she fell in the bathtub' excuse. The D.A. brought charges, and I guess Ernie went to prison for a while. A few months later a social worker found Mom in an alcoholic haze. I was standing on a stool, heating soup in a pot, unsupervised." The Byerses had related that story to Rachel.

"That's when you moved to the foster home?" He stroked her hair. This time, the gentle touch soothed her.

"Right. Mom tried to win me back for a while. She couldn't stick with rehab, though. After a drunk-driving arrest, she relinquished her claim. Too much trouble to quit boozing, I guess. If she'd died, at least I could have pretended she cared."

Her eyes were burning again. Rats.

"Did you try to contact her as an adult?" Russ asked.

"She died when I was thirteen. An aneurysm, I heard." Rachel had received the news stoically. At that age, she'd retained only vague memories from early childhood and hadn't yet matured enough to see her mother as a person.

"No other relatives?"

"My aunt Theresa visited a few times, but her health was poor and she didn't live long. Nobody else." She refused to seek out uncaring relatives. "I figure if they were worth a damn, they'd have taken me in when I needed them."

"That's probably how Lauren would feel someday," he observed. "Thank you for helping me keep her."

"Glad to." She rested her head on Russ's shoulder.

Thank goodness none of her buddies could see her acting so pathetic. Leaning on others wasn't what she did. Tonight, though, the physical contact felt good, possibly because she'd relieved the pain of old losses, or because she simply liked this guy.

"Now I understand why you tried to clean my clock when you thought I'd kidnapped that little girl," he murmured.

"Any cop would feel the same. My personal background has no bearing on my work." She'd resolved from the start not to yield to emotions. "If I overreact, I pose a danger to the public and to my fellow officers."

"I didn't mean to imply that."

"Just clarifying." She rested there, buoyed by his nearness. "You'd have made a good shrink, Doc. You show a talent for getting inside people's heads. You did a great job of handling Lauren, too, with that business about reading to her toys."

He didn't immediately answer. Rachel simply waited. That was the trick to listening.

"Don't give me more credit than I deserve," he said contritely. "As you may have guessed earlier, when I came home tonight, I started questioning whether I'd made the right decision about taking in Lauren."

She nodded, and he explained, "At the end of a trying day, I'm accustomed to peace and quiet. Instead, the two of you flew in my face. Not your fault, but it made me irritable and a little resentful."

"But you wouldn't reject a child over that," she said.

"Of course not. But I believe it's unfair to raise a child with negative emotions." He was breathing fast, considering he hadn't moved.

"Only saints don't have negative emotions," Rachel returned. "I wasn't sure how you'd take it, though, when she yelled about hating this place and you and wanting to go home."

His chest rose and fell. "I realized she must be testing me. Making sure I'd stick around even though she misbehaved. Ironically, when I saw how vulnerable she was, I felt this great wave of love for her. It's scary, that I had considered backing out even for just a moment."

"You were tired," Rachel pointed out.

He shook his head. "That's no excuse. As a doctor, I've lectured parents about setting aside their mental state to focus on the child. Arrogant, huh?"

Rachel had exhausted her supply of sympathetic remarks. "Yeah, you're a real pain in the butt."

A tickle in the ribs caught her off guard. Checking her instinct to wrestle the man to the floor, she settled for a light punch on the arm.

Russ leaned over and cupped her face with one hand. She blinked, startled, and then curved instinctively toward him. Their lips touched, then his teased hers and probed deeper. Rachel had thought of kisses as mere preface, but this was intoxicating.

Melting against him, she relished the scent of Russ's skin and the edge of his teeth. His fingers tugged through her hair, and heat built inside her. Stroking his arms and chest raised tantalizing images of what lay beneath the sweater. She drew the knit fabric high, revealing a flat stomach. Bent and traced a line with her tongue.

"Whoa." He stopped her with a light touch.

Oh, right—open door and kid not necessarily a sound sleeper. She sat up. "You want to adjourn to another room?"

Russ averted his face. "That might be pushing this engagement business a bit far."

Did he have to take everything so seriously? "I was just fooling around. Hey, don't you ever follow your instincts?"

"Animals have instincts. People have common sense." His offhand tone took the sting from the words. "Sex complicates things."

"What's complicated about sex?" Sleeping together and friendship weren't mutually exclusive. The problem, Rachel admitted reluctantly, was that Russ stirred her in ways she didn't fully understand. Maybe she did the same to him, or maybe he was being self-protective. "Okay, okay. Point taken." Moving on, she inquired, "What kind of video games do you have?"

He regarded her dubiously. "That's it? You say 'Point taken' and then we duke it out on a virtual battlefield?"

"Yep," Rachel said. "Bet I can mop up the floor with you."

"Bet you can't."

They adjourned to the living room. While she was deciding which of several dozen games to choose, she told him about the attention Connie's ring had inspired at the station.

Russ glanced at her warily. "You told everyone you're engaged?"

"Hard to avoid, with me wearing this rock." She flipped through an online menu. "Didn't you mention it to the other docs?"

"We don't talk about our personal lives."

"If you showed up wearing a ring, every female within ten yards would notice."

He didn't comment. The fellow obviously wasn't used to the office banter that Rachel took for granted.

"I made my choice." She held up a disc. "Prepare to be pounded into the ground."

"By you and which hockey team?"

Those were fighting words. They plunged into the game, battling across continents and solar systems, better matched than Rachel had expected.

She won, all the same.

Chapter Nine

Perhaps because he retired earlier than usual, Russ had trouble falling asleep. Usually he lost consciousness instantly, a habit he'd developed during his internship, but tonight his body hummed with an awareness of Rachel's fire and her lack of inhibitions.

Her nearness threatened to drive him past his usual caution. Imaginings haunted him, fantasies about wild passion. But that wasn't his style. In the long run, his nature demanded a more-temperate pairing and an orderly life. An intense involvement could only end in recriminations that might hurt them both. And possibly Lauren, as well.

Unable to relax, Russ arose and pulled a robe over his pajamas. He decided to check on Lauren.

In the glow of a night-light, her petite shape huddled beneath the pink coverlet. Brown hair spread on the pillow and one arm encircled Officer Bud. He watched the light motion of her breathing, swept by the realization that she was really here. Not a visitor or an abstract notion, but a distinct individual. His daughter.

In the two and a half days since they'd met, Russ had been too busy to reflect on the larger picture. Tonight, in his heart, he'd made a commitment to stick with his daughter, and that meant a future shaped by her personality, needs and growth. He prayed he wouldn't let her down.

The sight of her sleeping so peacefully contrasted sharply with Rachel's painful tale. She'd been younger than Lauren and equally defenseless when she'd suffered abuse. Russ's anger flared, not only for her but also for himself.

What he'd endured paled beside her experience. Still, cruelty took a long-term toll on a child's psyche.

During junior high, several larger and tougher students had bullied him and his best friend, Mike Federov, ridiculing his slight stature and Mike's mild-mannered nature. In high school, after a growth spurt left Russ gawky and rail thin, the same thugs and their pals had dealt out humiliation both physical and emotional.

Ashamed to show weakness, he'd hidden the bruises from his family. The few occasions when Russ had shared school-related concerns with his parents, he'd regretting doing so. They paid far too much attention to the latest child-rearing theories popular among their friends, and very little to his feelings.

In fourth grade, when he'd groused about receiving a C he believed was unfair, they'd complained to his teacher over his objections, which had embarrassed him and created tension in the classroom. A few years later, when he'd mentioned that several boys were singling him out for insults, they'd switched gears and demanded he stop complaining and solve his own problems. Despite their education and social consciences, Max and Lois McKenzie lacked the right instincts for providing emotional support.

So, in high school, he'd taken up bodybuilding. The added bulk and confidence he'd gained, along with a couple of off-campus fistfights, had discouraged the bullies. He'd also defended Mike, who'd more than repaid the favor by helping him conquer calculus. They'd remained friends ever since.

In the front room, Russ paused outside the office where he'd unfolded a bed for Rachel. She'd left the door ajar, and he glanced inside to make sure she was settled.

Through a window, light from a streetlamp revealed a splash of dark hair and an arm curved around what appeared to be a lump of fabric. Curiosity compelled him to move a few steps closer, until he discerned a doll so raggedy that only two button eyes remained of its face.

The doll obviously gave her comfort. Smiling, he withdrew, touched at discovering that the tough lady cop still had a little girl inside.

He returned to a master bedroom neatly appointed with an oak bedstead and bureau. Nothing old, nothing sentimental. Russ preferred not to grow attached to objects.

But he'd lost his heart to a little girl who was infinitely more precious than any object. That made him vulnerable in a way he hadn't felt since adolescence.

Much as he liked Rachel, becoming physically involved would be a mistake. Russ wasn't ready for that kind of closeness with a woman.

Fatherhood had too powerful a claim on him right now.

A PERSISTENT RINGING yanked Rachel out of a dream. She'd been searching through a maze for… Another jangle, and the rest vanished.

Lamplight at an unfamiliar angle reflected off a computer screen almost close enough to touch. She was, she recalled, in Russ's office. Setting her doll aside, Rachel swung out of bed.

It was 10:17 p.m. She'd hit the hay half an hour ago,

worn-out by a long day and seething emotions. Seemed a lot later, she mused as she stumbled into the living room.

Russ strode past her from the hallway. "I'll handle it." Was she imagining things or did the man wear crisply pressed pajamas?

He switched on the porch light. Rachel nearly withdrew until a shaky female voice requested her by name.

Russ turned with a puzzled expression. "You have a visitor."

As Rachel peered out, cold air raised gooseflesh around the T-shirt and exercise shorts she'd worn to bed. "Hello?"

On the porch, Lisa Chin huddled inside a sweater. "I'm sorry to bother you. This guy peeked in my window and scared me. I was hoping you might check around."

"You live in the neighborhood, don't you?" Russ asked. "Come in."

She moved into the room. "I'm Keri's neighbor. I help at the day care." The girl shivered.

"Tell me about this Peeping Tom," Rachel urged.

"It was just a few minutes ago." She'd been about to change for bed when she'd noticed a silhouette outside. "He was sneaking through the side yard when he glanced in my window. Sometimes I forget to shut the blinds completely."

"You're sure it was a male?"

"The shape and the way he walked, yeah." Lisa kept her hands in her pockets. "I mean, you're tall, but you don't resemble a guy."

Russ's mouth twitched in a hint of a smile. He didn't comment, however.

A Peeping Tom could be a nosy adolescent, a burglar casing the property or a potential rapist. "You should call in a report. The police will check it out," Rachel advised. "Any chance you could identify him?"

"No, but…" Lisa's nose wrinkled. "I was seeing this guy from school that I didn't tell my parents about 'cause I'm not supposed to date. We broke up a few weeks ago. In case it's him, I'd rather not create a big fuss and upset my folks." That clarified why she hadn't come with a parent.

Rachel requested the boy's name. "Gary Landau" didn't ring a bell. If he'd been in trouble before, the matter hadn't reached her ears. "Who did the breaking up?"

"Me."

"Did he threaten you?"

"Nothing like that," she insisted. "Gary's parents are in the middle of a divorce. He's been upset. I'd hate for the cops to treat him like a criminal when he might just be…confused."

"If you were my daughter, I'd want to know what was going on," Russ pointed out.

Lisa sighed. "My parents are first generation. They have these superconservative ideas, like all I should do is study." Returning to the subject of the prowler, she added, "I've heard that homeless people cut through here to sleep in the avocado grove. It was probably one of them."

"Homeless people may be harmless or they may not. Hold on." Hurrying into the office, Rachel pulled on heavier clothes and pocketed her badge and cell phone. She also retrieved the gun from the locked cabinet and brought a flashlight.

"I'll see if anyone's lurking in the bushes," she told Lisa. "But you shouldn't have left the house. If his goal was to draw you out, you fell right into the trap."

Lisa gave a small gasp. "That didn't occur to me."

Fortunately, the girl hadn't suffered any harm. "Tomorrow at school, talk to the guy. See if he'll confess. And if this happens again, call the police for sure."

"Don't keep your parents in the dark," Russ advised. "If there's really a threat, I'm sure they'll help."

"Okay. Thanks so much!" Brushing bangs out of her eyes, Lisa headed for the door.

"Don't leave yet, Lisa. I'll escort you home," Rachel said.

Russ placed a hand on Rachel's arm and pulled her into the kitchen. "I don't like you going out there alone," he said quietly. "Why not let me handle this? It's my neighborhood."

She appreciated the protective instinct and hated to bruise a male ego, but they'd better square matters from the start. "Thanks, Doc, but you're not trained. Stay here and keep an eye on Lauren."

He appeared to be struggling against a desire to argue. Finally he said, "You're the expert. If you need help, call me."

If she required backup, she'd summon a uniform. Politely she responded, "I appreciate the concern."

They returned to the front hallway where Lisa waited. The girl looked up and smiled. "I meant to tell you, Dr. McKenzie. Lauren's a real cutie."

"Thanks. The kid has more friends than I do," Russ joked. Then he said, "Be careful out there, both of you."

"You bet," Rachel replied.

Outside, she assessed her surroundings as they walked toward Lisa's street. The sky was partially overcast and the lighting was spotty, but thanks to the neatly trimmed landscaping, there were few hiding places.

The normally chatty Lisa fell silent, as if the shadowed night oppressed her. Darkness didn't bother Rachel. She enjoyed night patrol, being alert and in charge while others slept.

On their way around the corner, she noticed that many of the houses had gone dark, while TV screens lit others. From a fenced yard, a dog yapped. Good. Noisy dogs discouraged burglars.

After Lisa slipped into her house, Rachel strolled to the end of the block, her rubber soles nearly silent on the sidewalk. Her gaze swept the scene for a furtive figure or anything out of place. Still, in a low-crime neighborhood like this, she bore in mind that an over-eager cop could prove a greater menace to the residents than an intruder.

Also, Rachel wouldn't have been surprised to glimpse wildlife from the adjacent open area. Possums and raccoons frequently searched her condo development for leftover cat food, while coyotes hunted small mammals. She presumed they frequented Amber View as well.

Rachel circled onto a street parallel to Lisa's, observing while listening in case an engine started. Tracing a license plate to this fellow Gary Landau would confirm Lisa's suspicion.

All remained still. A few minutes later, about to retrace her path, Rachel hesitated at the edge of a footpath that ran between two unfenced yards. Her flashlight beam showed that it ended far to the rear, at a rise that led to the houses on Lisa's block. It probably existed for the convenience of the development's gardeners, but what an invitation to a trespasser, she mused.

Abruptly, atop the rise, a man's shape loomed. Rachel reached into her pocket for the cell phone, but found only her iPod. She couldn't believe she'd brought the wrong device. Damn!

Impossible to make out any features, but judging by the man's confident stance, he was no teenager. Of course, he might be a resident—except that instead of retreating to the nearest house, he descended the slope, marking his way with a thin ray of light.

She switched hers off and eased close to a house,

breathing low. The man's movements remained cautious as he approached, but she didn't believe he'd spotted her.

When a branch snapped under his foot, the silhouette halted and peered around. Watching for a movement, or afraid of detection? Although Rachel considered identifying herself, she decided to wait and watch.

The subject didn't veer toward the rear door of either adjacent house. Instead, he continued down the path. In another minute he'd pass right by her.

Abruptly his presence activated a safety light on one roof, angled in such a way that it had missed Rachel. It gleamed off a gun gripped in his hand.

Damn. He was almost on top of her.

As the man dodged the glare, illumination shone across his face. Squinting, he caught sight of her shape. "Hey!"

Rachel was reaching for her weapon when she recognized the man as Keri's father. That must be her house directly behind them. Better talk fast, because he was shifting his gun into position. "Chief Borrego! It's Rachel Byers."

He paused and peered closer. "Rache? What're you doing here?"

"Checking on an informal prowler report." She stepped forward. After a glance of acknowledgment, he tucked away his automatic.

The former Villazon chief surveyed her attire. "Very informal, I'd say."

They repaired to the sidewalk. With the intruder apparently gone, Rachel saw no point in further stealth, so as they walked, she outlined Lisa's visit. "What brings you out here?"

"I was spending the night at my daughter and son-in-law's when Ken hopped out of bed and claimed he'd seen a thief. That's how he put it, though as far as I can tell, nothing was stolen." The chief nodded toward his weapon and, although Rachel hadn't asked, explained, "I have a permit. In case you hadn't heard, I've become a private investigator. Just opened an office in town."

"Wasn't going to bust you." Gossip had placed him at an investigative agency in Santa Ana. He must have moved recently, probably to be close to Keri.

When she'd served under him, Rachel had been aware of Borrego's reputation for hard drinking, and his raunchy sense of humor had stemmed from the days before sensitivity training. But he'd always treated her fairly.

She didn't excuse the man's wrongful behavior. He'd hurt the department and Elise with his harassment, and he'd tolerated misconduct from one of his top lieutenants. However, he'd lost both his job and his marriage. Must have had an impact, because even in the patchy darkness, she could see he'd replaced his beer gut with muscle and gained a briskness in his gait.

They agreed that the prowler was most likely either a homeless person, a confused ex-boyfriend as Lisa had suggested, or a kid who lived close by. By now, apparently he'd either gone indoors or left the area.

When the conversation became more general, she learned that Vince was renting an apartment in Villazon. He'd lost his house to his ex-wife.

"My grandkids are growing up," he told Rachel. "I missed most of Keri's childhood, working long hours and partying afterward. No more of that. I'm a regular attendee at Alcoholics Anonymous and I quit smoking, too."

"Good for you." To her surprise, he continued alongside her past Keri's house. "Aren't you going in?"

"My daughter says you're engaged." Lamplight brought out the deep wrinkles around Vince's eyes, a testament to

Get FREE BOOKS and FREE GIFTS when you play the...

LAS VEGAS GAME

Just scratch off the gold box with a coin. Then check below to see the gifts you get!

YES! I have scratched off the gold box. Please send me my **2 FREE BOOKS** and **2 FREE GIFTS** for which I qualify. I understand that I am under no obligation to purchase any books as explained on the back of this card.

◄ DETACH AND MAIL CARD TODAY! ▼

354 HDL EF49	154 HDL EF59

FIRST NAME   LAST NAME

ADDRESS

APT.#   CITY

STATE/PROV.   ZIP/POSTAL CODE   (H-AR-02/07)

7	7	7	Worth TWO FREE BOOKS plus TWO BONUS Mystery Gifts!
🍒	🍒	🍒	Worth TWO FREE BOOKS!
🔔	🔔	♣	TRY AGAIN!

www.eHarlequin.com

Offer limited to one per household and not valid to current Harlequin American Romance® subscribers. All orders subject to approval.

former bad habits. "She speaks highly of your fiancé. Okay if I meet him?"

"Sure, if you don't mind that he's in his pajamas." She didn't see why he was so eager, though. "Why not wait? You'll probably run into him at the day care center."

The old chief answered earnestly. "I'm trying to get involved in the community. Feel like I owe this town and my family a big debt. According to my daughter, the doc volunteers at a health clinic. Figured there might be a role for me."

Rachel couldn't picture Vince slapping on bandages or answering phones. "What about the homework center? Villa Corazon."

"You mean tutoring?" He straightened. "I could handle that. In fact, it might be fun. My landlady's involved, isn't she? Yolanda Rios."

"You're renting in her fourplex?" Yolanda, a retired teacher, had founded the center with Marta's aid five years ago in a garage. Two years into it, shortly before Vince left town, she'd received permission to take over a former community center near the high school.

"Yes. Nice lady. Maybe I'll check it out."

They reached Russ's cottage. "Still want to come in?"

"As long as I'm here."

Rachel's hesitation vanished when she considered that if they weren't acquainted, Vince might run into Russ some night in the dark and mistake him for a prowler. She didn't like to picture that gun pointed at the doc's chest.

They found her fiancé in the living room, reading a medical journal. He seemed slightly ill at ease about socializing in his bathrobe, but shook hands with Vince and exchanged greetings.

As they discussed volunteer opportunities, Rachel remembered rather belatedly that Elise volunteered at the homework center. Darn. What an awkward situation if Vince appeared! But most likely he'd find an activity better suited to his crime-fighting background than sitting at a table reviewing multiplication tables.

"Any sign of the prowler?" Russ inquired.

"Long gone." Vince regarded the entertainment center and spare furnishings. "I like your decorating style. Most wives would start redoing the place, but you're marrying the right woman. Rachel's practically one of the guys."

Russ seemed at a loss for words. Before he could recover, a small person in a nightgown peered at them from the hall. "What's a prowler?" Lauren had obviously been listening for a while.

"Someone who pokes around where he doesn't belong." Vince crouched at her level. "Hi. I'm Ken and Kim's—"

"Grandpa!" Her eyes widened. "I saw you!"

"At Keri's house?" he asked.

Her forehead puckered. "No. I mean…" She glanced around in confusion. "I was in my old house. With my grandpa."

"You must have been dreaming," Rachel suggested. "Maybe Mr. Borrego resembles your grandpa, huh?"

A slight nod. "Maybe."

"Hope it was a good dream." Vince patted the child's arm. "Sorry I have to leave. Keri must be wondering what happened to me. Maybe I'll see you at her house someday."

"Okay."

"Speaking of dreams, let's get you back to bed." Taking his daughter's hand, Russ led her down the hall.

"So you're planning to put down roots," Vince said to Rachel. "Good idea. I wish more cops gave their families a priority."

A strange sentiment, considering the source, but obviously he'd changed in the past two years. "Does it seem weird, being back in Villazon?" she asked.

A rueful nod. "I'm sure Lyons wishes I'd disappear permanently. Here's irony for you—his son rents an apartment in my building. Ben's a nice kid, although he admits he used to have a drug problem. Well, I'm certainly in no position to criticize, am I?"

Much as Rachel liked Vince, she hoped his return wasn't going to stir up trouble for the department. Impulsively she inquired, "So you don't hold any grudges?"

"The only person I blame in this mess is myself."

"You sure?" In the old days, she'd never have dreamed of expressing doubt about Vince's veracity. But he wasn't her boss anymore.

He took no offense. "Norm Kinsey's bitterness is eating him alive. He was a loose cannon, roughing up prisoners, and he deserved the boot, but the last time I saw him he refused to acknowledge that. It's a rotten way to live."

"I imagine so." Former Lieutenant Kinsey had moved out of town. Gone to Montana to be near relatives, she'd heard.

Vince let himself out onto the porch. "Frank Ferguson and I both try to pound sense into his head, but he has a long list of grievances, even against me. After all, I got to keep my pension. Well, congrats. Your guy seems like a winner."

Vince moved down the steps with a lot more agility than he used to show. Rachel was glad to see that he'd gotten his act together.

She was heading for bed when Russ returned. A quick study confirmed that his pajamas *were* neatly creased, although a bit rumpled from the evening's exertions. "Do you iron those?"

"What?" He followed her downward gaze. "No. They're new."

"Well, that's a relief," she cracked. "As your future wife, I'd hate to think you expect me to iron your pj's."

Russ laughed. "I'm not *that* compulsive. Although some of my friends might think otherwise."

Rachel wasn't the least bit sleepy. "We went to bed awfully early," she observed. "We could stay up and play a round of whatever you choose."

She realized the suggestiveness of her offer as a series of expressions touched his expressive face. Amusement, hunger, temptation. Resistance won. "I'll pass, but thanks. By the way, Lauren meeting Keri's dad right after her dream seems to have had an impact on her."

"What kind of impact?" They gravitated to the kitchen, where Rachel poured them each a glass of orange juice.

"She seems convinced her grandpa really is searching for her."

"She's grieving." Rachel hadn't forgotten her own difficult adjustment. "Denial is one of the stages. I had fantasies about my mother moving in with me at the Byers house. Completely unrealistic."

Out of the blue, he asked, "Who gave you the doll? The one you sleep with."

Startled, Rachel answered, "My adoptive parents."

"And you still treasure it."

"Dinah isn't an it, she's a her!" she responded with mock severity. "That doll became my best friend."

His eyes twinkled. "My daughter's sleeping with a toy policeman. What do you suppose that means?"

Although Rachel doubted he meant the question seriously, she replied, "Maybe he's her protector."

"*I'm* her protector!" More softly: "And so are you."

"Give her time." Rachel stifled a yawn. "Guess I'm more pooped than I realized."

"My regards to Dinah."

"I'll tell her."

Sliding beneath the covers, she listened to the sounds of Russ moving away through the house. Instinctively, she reached for the doll. But, she conceded, she'd much rather throw her arms around Russ and wreak havoc on those new pajamas.

Even if she had to iron them later.

Chapter Ten

Lauren's fantasies about grandparents gained rather than lost intensity over the next few days. Aware that the child could control neither her dreams nor her emotions, Russ did his best to provide a sympathetic ear, but he began to worry that she might never feel at home with him.

"Do you think I was wrong, bringing her to live with me? Maybe she'd be better off with experienced parents," he remarked on Friday to his friend Mike Federov as they returned to their respective offices. They were crossing the enclosed pedestrian bridge that connected the fourth floor of the medical building to that of the hospital, where they'd eaten a late lunch in the cafeteria.

"You believe adoptive parents are necessarily old pros?" The psychologist's blue eyes reflected skepticism. "I'm more concerned with this pretend-fiancée business than with your lack of experience. When Rachel leaves, that means yet another loss for your daughter."

"She promised to stay involved, although I grant you, it won't be the same as living with us." Russ had told his friend the truth, both because he opposed lying in general and because Mike deserved honesty. "She's been a blessing. Collects Lauren early from day care, keeps us both in good spirits and understands emotions a lot better than I do."

The comment failed to distract his friend. "What happens when her condo becomes habitable again?" he persisted.

Russ hated to think about that. Despite Rachel's slapdash housekeeping style and the danger of giving in to their physical desires, her presence brightened Lauren's spirits as well as his. On Wednesday, the tedious task of clearing the garage had turned into a lark, thanks to her jokes and funny stories, and afterward she'd introduced Lauren and him to pineapple-ham pizza.

Through the glass surround, he observed several cruisers pulling into the police station across the street. Must be nearing the end of their shift. He'd never noticed such things until he met Rachel.

"The engineers intend to terrace the slope, plant vegetation with deep roots, and cover the hill with mesh until the stuff matures," he explained. "That has to take at least a few weeks, right?"

Mike cast him a shrewd look. "Sounds as if this engagement might not be so phony after all. You're pretty eager for her to stick around."

"Friendship isn't love." The comment emerged more forcefully than intended.

"I see."

Russ nearly added that he hoped what he felt for Rachel *wasn't* love. Delightful as the initial stages of romance could be, long-term complications seemed inevitable between two such dissimilar individuals. And with Lauren undergoing such a difficult transition, she deserved all his attention.

"Any suggestions?" he queried. "About the grandparent fixation, I mean."

Mike stroked his chin between thumb and forefinger, an

unconscious gesture he'd adopted in college. Russ was amused by how much, at that moment, his friend resembled a stereotypical shrink. "I realize matters haven't always gone smoothly with your folks, but Lauren *does* have another set of grandparents. Have you talked to them?"

"Not yet." Russ had been too busy to think about his parents. When he'd informed them of Janine's pregnancy years ago, they'd approved the decision to relinquish the infant, but surely they were curious about their grand-daughter. "Do you suppose Lauren will be upset that they aren't like the grandparents she lost?"

"You can't control how people react to each other, but you can give them a chance to form bonds. Your daughter must miss having an extended family." They reached the elevator, where they had to part, since their offices were on different floors.

"Thanks for the insight." They shook hands.

"Keep me in the loop," Mike urged.

"Absolutely." As the elevator descended, Russ reflected on what lay ahead. His parents would almost certainly welcome Lauren, but what should he tell them about his temporary engagement?

He decided to contact Janine first. Once she'd seen his home and met Rachel, perhaps she'd transfer custody right away. After that, the engagement would be history and his parents wouldn't have to know.

The notion should have reassured him. Strangely, it did not.

THE SCENT OF POPCORN greeted Russ as he entered the kitchen through the side door later that evening. Although sandwich makings strewed the counters, there was no one in the room. The rat-a-tat noise of popping kernels issued from the front.

Every day an adventure, he mused as he went into the living room.

Amid the sleek furnishings bloomed a carnival-style cart, bright red with the word Popcorn stenciled in yellow on the side. Lauren shrieked with delight as another salvo shook the square glass top. "Can I eat now?"

"We'll have it with supper." Rachel, her back turned to Russ, scooped fluffy kernels into red-and-white-striped snack boxes. "We'll consider this our vegetable."

"But not a terribly healthy vegetable," he broke in. Swiveling, Rachel hoisted one of the cartons in a salute.

Lauren ran for a hug. Russ swooped up the little girl. "Where did this gadget come from?"

"Remember I mentioned the traffic sergeant who was engaged for two weeks?" Rachel filled a third container. "This was a wedding gift from his fiancée's cousin."

"And he presented it to you on the occasion of your engagement?" Russ released his wiggly daughter, who bounded over to sample the popcorn. "How generous."

"Yeah. Nice, huh?" Dusting off her jeans, she stood back. "Lucky for us he got sick of popcorn."

Russ wouldn't have chosen this particular contrast to his black-and-white color scheme, but the cheery monstrosity pleased Lauren. And he was learning that too much perfection might not be a good thing.

"It's striking," he hedged. "Let me change clothes and I'll help fix the meal."

"Not necessary. It's almost ready."

He remembered his plan to contact Janine. "Are you free tomorrow? I'd like to get my ex to visit."

"I'll be working my regular shift." Rachel handed one of the cartons to Lauren with a warning to hold it straight. "But she's welcome for dinner. The boyfriend, too."

Ah, yes, the older man who shuddered at the prospect of stepparenting. Russ owed the man his gratitude. "I'll make sure to include him."

In the bedroom, he tossed off his jacket and dialed Janine's cell. She sounded distracted when she answered, and reported that she and Byron were leaving in the morning on a business trip to New York. After inquiring about Lauren, she assured him she'd get in touch when they returned.

"Thanks for sending the furniture," he put in.

"It's a relief to get rid of it. I've decided to rent out my parents' house." She muttered a curse before noting, "I'm on the freeway. Some idiot just cut me off. I'm so busy between now and tomorrow morning, I can't think straight."

"Have a safe trip." The wait chafed, but Russ *had* agreed to a one-month trial.

"You can reach me on my cell if there's a problem." In the background, a traffic report came on the radio.

"We'll be fine." Russ rang off with a lingering sadness at his ex-girlfriend's lack of maternal feeling for their daughter. At least she didn't seem to have any regrets about surrendering Lauren.

Choosing to leave the conversation with his parents until after dinner, he changed clothes and went to eat.

To RACHEL, calling one's family was a casual matter. Just, "Hey, guys, it's me," and you caught up on the week's events. They always had interesting stuff to discuss, such as the latest foster kids' antics and how her sister Kathy was on track to graduate from Cal State in June.

Russ, however, appeared on edge after dinner. He'd informed her that he hoped to drive his daughter to meet his parents tomorrow, but kept postponing the call, first to wash the dishes and then to play Chutes and Ladders with Lauren. He hadn't discussed his plans with his daughter, either.

Rachel would be happy to miss that gathering. Russ had described Maxwell McKenzie as a prominent internist and Lois McKenzie as a charity volunteer. They sounded a bit stuffy, and besides, she wasn't keen on deceiving his parents. As for what she intended to tell her own, she hadn't puzzled that out yet.

She expected him to place the call while she gave Lauren a bath, but when they emerged, Russ was on the computer, paying bills. Procrastinating, more accurately.

Lauren, her freshly washed hair falling in natural curls, climbed onto her father's lap. Obligingly, he finished posting a payment and moved the cursor to the toolbar. "Do you have a favorite Web site?"

"Let's e-mail Grandpa and Grandma!" Lauren cried.

Russ's shoulders twitched, a movement Rachel interpreted as dismay. "Honey, we can't e-mail dead people."

"Try!" she demanded.

He exchanged glances with Rachel. They'd gone over this territory repeatedly since his daughter had met Vince, without effect. "Sweetheart, when people die, we can't reach them." He released a long breath and took the plunge. "Your grandpa and grandma were Janine's mom and dad. I have a mom and dad, too. I'd like you to meet them."

"Are they my grandparents?" the little girl asked.

"Yes. But not the *same* grandparents." His arms tightened around her. "I'd hate for you to be disappointed."

Rachel sat on the edge of her foldout bed and waited for Lauren to reply. Hard to assess how much a five-year-old grasped. "Remember that man you met, Ken and Kim's grandpa? He's different from yours, too."

"He was nice." Lauren nodded. "Okay."

Her father lowered her to the floor. "While I arrange with them, why don't you eat your night-night snack?"

Determination pinched her face. "Let me talk to them!"

"In a minute," he responded.

"Me first!"

"No. You'll have to be patient," he said with a hint of strain.

"Me!" She stomped on the carpet.

Weariness and eagerness formed an explosive combination, Rachel reflected, and clapped her hands for attention. "How about more popcorn?"

"After!" The kid didn't lack willpower.

"It's now or never," Rachel said, folding her arms, prepared to enforce that statement and carry the kid off to the bedroom if she threw a full-fledged tantrum.

"You're mean!"

"Too mean to fix popcorn?"

Lauren must have realized she was pushing her luck. "I'm sorry. Okay. Let's go."

The gratitude in Russ's gaze sent a quiver down Rachel's spine. Sharing little challenges like these brought a precious sense of intimacy. She only wished she were the type of woman guys fell in love with, instead of the kind they clapped on the shoulder.

In the living room, she put fresh kernels in the machine and activated the air popper. While Lauren danced around waving her hands as if the tiny explosions were music, Rachel kept an ear tuned to the one-sided conversation from the adjacent room, from which Russ's voice carried in snippets.

He exchanged pleasantries and launched into an explanation about taking custody of his daughter, but broke off to ask in surprise, "Really? Who told you?"

So they'd already heard about the custody. Small world, Rachel thought.

"This only happened a few days ago...last Sunday... getting her settled has been hectic...I'm sorry if you felt embarrassed."

They were laying a guilt trip on him about the delay. Rachel presumed they hadn't heard of the engagement as well, since she caught no reference to it. No doubt that would have infuriated them even more.

The conversation continued in that vein for a while, with Russ becoming increasingly irritable. Lauren was halfway through her snack by the time he steered the subject to proposing he introduce their granddaughter.

He emerged from the bedroom with his jaw clenched. "Honey, they'd like to talk to you."

"Yay!" Setting aside her popcorn, Lauren raced for the office. Rachel trailed behind.

The little girl snatched the phone to her ear. "Hi!" Since shyness wasn't her nature, she conversed freely, informing the McKenzies about her new friends and kindergarten. "I'm having a snack," she told them. "Rachel made popcorn."

Russ reached for the phone, but with a mischievous grin, his daughter ducked into the desk's kneehole with it. "Rachel? She's marrying Russ," the child announced from hiding.

Their best-laid plans had just gone awry. Rachel didn't mind so much for her own sake, but Russ was clearly bracing for trouble. "I'll tuck Lauren in bed," she whispered. "You tell them the truth about our engagement." That ought to ease matters.

A headshake. In a low tone: "They heard about Lauren from friends of Janine's. Word could reach her." Louder: "Lauren! Daddy needs to talk."

Reluctantly the girl emerged. Despite the occasional rebellion, she truly was a well-behaved child, Rachel observed. As for blurting the news about the engagement, the grown-ups had only themselves to blame for keeping secrets.

"Let's brush the kernels out of your teeth!" She hustled Lauren down the hall to the bathroom. "Was that fun, talking to your new grandparents?"

The child babbled happily about the conversation, claiming far more promises than could possibly have been made. Finally Rachel left her alone to use the potty and seized the chance to eavesdrop from the hall.

Overhearing Russ's words didn't require much effort, since he was fast losing patience and his voice was raised. "That's right, I met her in the month since I moved to Villazon. Sudden? Well, in thirty-four years, she's the first woman I—" Rachel would have loved to hear the rest of that sentence, but apparently a question interrupted the flow. "She's a police officer."

A pause. The prospect of a daughter-in-law in uniform had apparently stunned the socialite and the noted physician into silence. Not for long, though.

"What do you mean, what kind of…?" Russ uttered a snort. "Not a policy official, Mom. A police officer."

Lauren emerged and requested a story, forcing Rachel to abandon her post. When Russ joined them a few minutes later, he took over reading while his daughter snuggled against him on the bed. Rachel slipped out her cell phone for a picture.

Two startled faces fixed on her. "I want to update Lauren's scrapbook," she said.

"She has a scrapbook?" Russ asked.

"It arrived with the furniture." Rachel had tucked the beribboned volume into a bureau drawer. "Her grandparents did a beautiful job."

"We'll have to leaf through. But not tonight." He planted a kiss atop his daughter's head. "By the way, I agreed to take you both to my parents' house Sunday afternoon if that suits your schedule, Rache."

"No problem." Although less than thrilled, she saw no graceful escape.

"You'll love their house," he informed Lauren. "It overlooks a canyon."

"What's a canyon?"

"A big ditch," Rachel teased. "With trees."

"You're dissing some of the most expensive real estate in Southern California," Russ retorted lightly. To Lauren: "Please don't repeat that remark to your grandparents. They wouldn't find it amusing."

The little girl regarded him with interest. "Is that where you grew up, Daddy?"

"Yes. I'll tell you my whole life story another night." As he kissed his daughter again, Rachel withdrew.

She had to remember that her role here was only temporary. Much as she longed to remain part of the scene, she had to separate herself, for Lauren's sake. And for her own.

Russ joined her in the rear-facing den, where he stood by the window staring out at the stars. "Did I hear correctly? Did she actually call me Daddy?"

"She did," Rachel confirmed.

He threw back his head. "Amazing. I needed a lift after my parents put me through the meat grinder."

Rachel stretched out her legs from the divan. "The engagement came as quite a shock, huh?"

"About a nine-point-five on the Richter scale." Silhouetted against the moonlight, his body went rigid. "Starting with the fact that I waited this long to tell them about Lauren. Apparently they've been stewing all week."

"They should have called *you*," she said.

"I hadn't considered that. My perspective suffers in matters concerning my relatives." He relaxed slightly. "Then there's the matter of my abrupt venture into matrimonial waters, with a woman they'd never heard of."

"And a gun-toting one." Might as well mention her employment. "I'll bet that threw them."

"My parents would gladly stage a benefit dinner for the family of a fallen officer, and I'm sure my mom could deliver a brilliant speech about how much we owe the men and women in blue." He didn't continue, because he didn't need to.

People raised money to save whales, but they wouldn't marry one. Rachel deduced that the McKenzies felt the same way about cops. Still, even if they *were* snobs, their feelings mattered to Russ.

"Can't you trust them with the truth about our engagement?" That seemed the simplest course. "Surely they'd keep quiet."

"I'm never sure how they'll react. To anything." He swung toward her, his face partly in shadow. "They've always been extremely concerned about what their peers think, so their opinions change with the tide. Maybe someday they'll respect me enough to accept *my* opinions as important, but so far that hasn't happened. My friend Mike calls it crazy-making behavior."

Rachel approved of this friend already. She'd definitely go crazy around people like that. "How'm I supposed to pull this off on Sunday? I haven't a clue how a proper fiancée should act."

"Act like you love me." He gave her a wry smile.

That wouldn't be hard, she thought. Except that she doubted he meant draping herself over him or kissing him in public. "Can you be more specific?"

He paced along the louvered windows. "If we *were* engaged, how would you behave?"

"I'd make love to you until we both wandered around with silly grins on our faces," Rachel responded.

Laughter rumbled through the room. "Touché."

Feeling a cramp in one leg, she stood and stretched. "Maybe I'd better polish the old image. They'll love the split-level hair, right?"

Appreciation filled his gaze. "You'll be the freshest thing that ever happened to them."

The way his eyes shone gave Rachel a wisp of hope. "So my best bet is to bowl them over with my personality?"

"The way you bowled me over." He sounded so genuine she almost believed him. But he was teasing, of course.

"Keep going and you might get to first base. I'm a sucker for smooth talk," she joked.

He stopped laughing. Moved closer, eyes trained on her, seeking…what? They paused a few feet apart, heads tilting. Any second he'd retreat, Rachel expected, but instead he stepped forward and reached for her.

Their mouths met, and his powerful hands gripped her waist. Remembering the speed with which he'd withdrawn the last time they embraced, Rachel merely traced her palms along his silken shirtsleeves. An awareness of him as a complete person, both physically and emotionally, infused her at every level. If only she aroused even half this much longing in him!

When at last Russ lifted his head, he wore a glazed expression. Breathing rapidly, he drew her hard against him, his chest crushing her breasts. Inside Rachel, heat flared.

But then he dropped a kiss between her brows and eased back. He was unmistakably logging off.

"Oh, fudge," she blurted.

"Sorry," he murmured. "That business about making love… Definitely appealing."

"But that's as far as it goes?" she finished for him. "Well, shoot. Maybe if I'm a good little girl, in my next incarnation I'll come back as Connie."

He ceased retreating and gripped her shoulders. Forcing a confrontation. Possibly about to shake sense into her, except that any guy who tried to shake Rachel would find himself launched into space. "You believe my taste runs to buxom blondes?"

"Whose doesn't?" She'd lived in the real world long enough to nail down that fact. "Alternate choice is an exotic brunette with hair down to her butt."

He released his grip. "Here's a news flash—you're my type. I may not have been aware of what my type was when we met, but… Anyway, that isn't the issue."

She folded her arms. "Please enlighten me."

"Let me tell you a story about my parents. Since you'll meet them, this might provide insight." He perched on the arm of the divan.

A story involving his parents? Talk about Freudian! "I thought we were discussing sex."

"Sex leads to involvement." Russ spread his hands. "Which is sort of the topic."

Rachel plopped into an armchair. Might as well get comfortable. This had to be a first. Instead of hustling her into the bedroom, the guy preferred to talk. But he was so darn cute, she didn't mind.

"Years ago, when I was nine, my parents helped sponsor a camp for underprivileged kids." His gaze grew distant.

"They decided I ought to attend, not because I might enjoy camping but as an egalitarian gesture."

"You're sure that was their motive?"

"When I protested, they told me to stop acting elitist. They were still lecturing when they dropped me off, a naive, studious boy who was small for his age among a bunch of streetwise youngsters." He quickly added, "They were no tougher on me than the kids at my regular school. That isn't my complaint."

"What, then?" She hoped he wasn't about to reveal a snooty attitude toward the lower classes, among whom she belonged. Still, she related to the pain of being torn away from familiar surroundings.

"One of the counselors called my parents to report that I'd brought a set of hand-painted wooden soldiers, which were my favorite toys. None of my bunkmates had anything half as nice. I let them play with them, and as far as I know none of the kids objected, but the counselor obviously did."

"Major crisis," Rachel summarized. "After all, they sent you there to prove how egalitarian they were."

"Exactly." Strong emotions roughened his voice. "My parents told him to distribute the soldiers among the other campers."

"You mean permanently?" Rachel would have fought like a tiger had anyone tried to confiscate Dinah. "It might make sense to send the toys home, but that was just mean!"

He stared past her. "I'm sure they figured that would teach me a lesson. Well, it did. I learned that people in authority can jerk others around. Also that it doesn't pay to get attached to stuff. That year, I gave all my Christmas presents to charity."

"Didn't your parents find that odd?"

"I donated them to the poor. They probably ground their teeth about how expensive the stuff was, but they could hardly object."

"Revenge, of a sort," she noted. "Hey, here's a fun fact. I was one of those poor kids they presumably felt sorry for." If not for donated toys, Rachel wasn't sure what she'd have received most years, considering how tightly the Byerses stretched their budget. "Guess they ought to love me, huh?"

"In theory." He didn't appear to consider that likely, however.

Well, they didn't have to love her. Rachel had joined this venture for Lauren's sake.

No, you didn't. You volunteered because you really like this guy. And was growing fonder of him by the day. Which explained why the forthcoming encounter with his judgmental parents made her uneasy.

"Did they replace the soldiers after you got home from camp?" Rachel asked.

"Impossible. My grandfather gave me those soldiers. He'd had them since childhood." Russ cleared his throat. "When he found out, he was furious. My parents weren't thrilled to discover they'd disposed of an heirloom, but they refused to admit they'd been wrong…. Something just occurred to me."

"What?"

Ironic amusement colored his voice. "My grandfather died about a year and a half ago. Although I was the only grandchild, everyone was surprised that his will named me sole heir."

"Who else should have inherited?" These matters seemed foreign to Rachel, since she never expected to collect a bequest from anyone.

"My dad expected a sizable sum. He and mom had been talking about investing in a vacation home." Russ grew contemplative. "Grandpa had Alzheimer's and, while I visited his nursing home, we hadn't really connected for years, so I was as puzzled as anyone."

"Surely he didn't harbor a grudge about some toy soldiers!"

"Who can tell? Whatever the reason, he did me a tremendous favor. I paid off my med school debts and bought this house."

"Your parents didn't pay for med school?" If they could cosponsor a camp, they weren't short on bucks.

"I prefer to be independent, because where they're concerned, there are usually strings attached." Hastily he added, "I'm afraid I haven't painted a very flattering picture of my family. They're good people, basically."

Rachel didn't doubt that, since they'd raised such a wonderful son. "Just one question. How does this relate to having sex?"

A blank look. Then: "Oh. Right. Sex and involvement. As you might have noticed, I'm very cautious about letting anyone close."

This from the man who'd insisted on claiming his daughter hours after learning about her grandparents' deaths? "That doesn't appear to apply to Lauren."

He smiled ruefully. "She sneaked right past my defenses. I'm more than attached. I'm head over heels. We *have* to persuade my parents we're engaged."

After hearing the account, Rachel understood why he considered them unpredictable. A couple that insensitive to their son couldn't be trusted to honor his confidence.

"I'll do my best," she promised. "Hey, here's a major concession. I'll swing by the mall tomorrow afternoon and buy an outfit." Russ deserved no less.

"Don't go overboard," he cautioned. "Be yourself."

"And I might throw some dye on the hair." She envisioned the society matron peering down her nose at this messy thatch.

"Uh, Rache?" he ventured.

"Yeah?"

"You might ask Connie to pick the color." He braced as if for fireworks.

Sounded like a good idea to her. "She'll be thrilled." As an afterthought she said, "And she can help me choose the new outfit, too."

"Simple and classic will be fine." Reaching out, Russ squeezed her hand. "You're the best."

The best what? Rachel decided not to push her luck by asking.

They repaired to the living room to catch an action movie on TV. As the hero and his buddies mowed down their enemies with rapid fire, she found herself identifying with the bad guys for a change. Because, come Sunday, she suspected she, too, would face a firing squad.

Chapter Eleven

Russ's snapshots, from Sunday:

Lauren. Sitting on her bed, pouting and hugging as many stuffed animals as she can squeeze into her arms. Suffering last-minute remorse about this visit-the-new-grandparents idea. Still in pajamas, twenty minutes before departure time.

Rachel. Crouching by the bed, sternly addressing the toys and, indirectly, Lauren. She wears brown slacks and a tan knit tunic with a matching beret atop hair that is now a warm shade of brown.

Lauren and Rachel. Hand in hand on the front porch, Lauren dressed, finally, in a red crushed-velvet party dress left over from the holidays. Not exactly casual wear, but it beats pj's. She's holding Officer Bud and one bear, the negotiated minimum.

Lauren's snapshots—she insisted on trying the camera:

Various scenes through the car window, blurred by raindrops hitting the glass. Passing cars. Distant mist-shrouded mountains with a hint of snowcaps. Freeway signs. Upward-curving road edged by bushes.

Rachel's:

The McKenzie house. Set down from the street, view of a shake-shingle roof amid a screen of trees. Wraparound wooden deck fronting split-level modern structure that blends into the wooded canyon.

Lois and Max McKenzie, wearing tentative smiles of welcome, stood on the covered porch. Lois's short blond hair was sprayed to perfection and her slender figure sported a green, Chinese-style pantsuit. Max stood with a slight stoop, his once-dark hair turned nearly all silver. Russ didn't consider his parents old in their midsixties.

"Guess you should put this away." Rachel handed him the camera as he killed the motor.

"Thanks," he said. "I figured we should put these in a scrapbook for Lauren." Photo albums helped children integrate their experiences. Adults, too.

Lauren stared across the gravel driveway at her grandparents. "Why does she get to wear her pajamas?"

"Those aren't pajamas." Rachel peered through the light rain. "At least, I don't think so."

Russ recalled a conversation with his mother on Christmas. "Some of her friends are supporting a village somewhere in Asia. They operate shops that sell clothing and toys the villagers make, plus a bakery that hires immigrants from that region."

"Nice of them." Rachel lifted her purse. "Ready?"

Not entirely. But he nodded.

In a flurry of umbrellas, they unloaded Lauren from the

car and managed to reach the porch without getting soaked. Quick introductions accompanied them into the house.

In case Lauren failed to notice, Russ pointed out the small steps between rooms that might trip her. Despite its open layout, the house comprised a maze of odd angles and sunken rooms to fit the hillside and, he suspected, the designer's notion of aesthetics.

Trying to see the interior through Rachel's eyes, he wondered why he'd never noticed the somber effect of the decor, including the light-gray walls and dark wood furnishings. In fairness, the Southern California sunshine normally contributed plenty of cheer that was lacking today.

Rachel indicated an abstract glass sculpture atop the coffee table. "Might be wise to put that in a safe place," she told Lois. "While we're here, I mean."

"I don't believe my granddaughter will find that a problem." His mother bristled as if defending Lauren against slander.

This being the first and possibly only grandchild in the family, Russ found it unsurprising that his Mom felt possessive. But Rachel's remark had been practical, not an attack.

Fortunately his mother's sharpness didn't faze her. "Hey, Lauren's really graceful. It's me—massively clumsy. My friend Connie owns a gift shop and she won't even let me through the front door."

Max chuckled. "I doubt that."

Lois ignored her husband's comment. "You'll just have to give the coffee table a wide berth, then, won't you?" The snippy tone made the words sting, at least to Russ. Rachel let it pass.

"Great house." She studied the high ceiling with its two-story glass wall. "Do birds ever fly into this thing? I mean, splat! Little broken necks and beaks. Not a pretty sight."

"Ick!" Lauren cried.

Lois appeared to be puffing up for a rebuke until Max quieted her with a gesture. "We used to have problems. You might not be able to spot them from here, but up high we've attached a couple of hawk decals. That scares them off."

Russ stepped in to further distract his mother. "The canyon's an informal bird sanctuary. My parents keep a hummingbird feeder outside the kitchen window. You should see the birds hovering in midair. They're beautiful."

"Can we?" Lauren pleaded.

"Absolutely." Pacified, Lois led them into the kitchen, where tomato-red paint offset the steely fixtures and black granite countertops. Past the breakfast table, they gazed into a trellised alcove where the scarlet feeding cylinder hung from a hook.

"Hold on," Lois told her granddaughter. "I'm sure there'll be one soon."

As if on command, a tiny, bejeweled hummer darted to the tube and hovered as it sipped. "Oh! Pretty!" Lauren watched for several minutes before losing interest.

When Max offered a tour of the house, they readily accepted. Russ trailed the others, examining his childhood home with a new perspective. From an architectural standpoint, its use of space and unexpected angles commanded admiration, while subtly arranged works of art enhanced the serenity. Yet to him the place seemed empty. No picture books or toys dropped helter-skelter. No snack wrappers forgotten on a side table; not a castoff shoe or hairbrush out of place.

As Russ paced the upstairs hallway, old emotions dogged him. Anger, anxiety, a determination to carve his own course. Also an awareness of his good fortune in living amid the austere beauty of the canyon, with parents who loved him despite their inability to achieve closeness. They'd surely done their best with whatever skills they'd inherited from their own parents.

Amazingly, despite her dysfunctional early life, Rachel strolled through the passageway with her usual confidence. She didn't seem bothered by his mother's attempts to commandeer Lauren's affections, nor feel compelled to try to impress anyone. Her self-possession anchored him.

They reached the corner room that used to belong to Russ and had later served as a guest chamber. Since the last time he'd glanced inside, blue fabric stitched with Asian motifs had replaced the Scandinavian bedcovers and draperies. He assumed the rather garish effect had been inspired by one of her friends.

"This room is for our little girl!" Lois proclaimed. "You can visit on the weekends and stay for a week or two next summer. Would you like that?"

Solemnly, Lauren addressed her toy. "What do you say, Officer Bud?" To the grown-ups, she said, "He says okay if Rachel and Russ come."

That obviously hadn't been the plan, Russ registered. To his mother, he clarified, "She's just starting to get used to me. It's too soon for her to consider paying extended visits."

His mom's jaw jutted with determination. She yearned so strongly to forge a connection, he could tell, that she had difficulty accepting limits. "I'm sure she'd love it here. My friend Marsha has a granddaughter, and the four of us would have lots of fun!"

Before his wife could continue, Max indicated an elaborately dressed doll atop the covers. "I believe your grandma has something else to show you, Lauren."

"I almost forgot. This is for you!" The new grandmother bestowed the delicate toy upon Lauren. As the two fussed happily over the clothing, his mom's face brightened. Tuning out everyone else, they debated until they chose a suitable name for the Asian character: Jasmine.

Russ's father finally managed to steer everyone out the door. Taking her granddaughter's hand, Lois cast a triumphant look over her shoulder at Rachel. Fortunately, Rachel was too busy checking out the location of the fire alarms to notice.

Russ hoped he'd misread his mother. The two women weren't in a contest for Lauren's affection.

In the dining room, his parents brought out a tea set, along with a plate of almond cookies and dumplinglike pastries studded with sesame seeds. Lois placed Jasmine at one end of the polished teak table and produced a shopping bag. "Let's put your old toys in here," she told Lauren, and in went the bear and Officer Bud. "We'll set them by the front door so you don't forget to take them home."

Lauren stared in dismay as the bag disappeared into the living room. "Bring them back!"

Her grandmother returned. "They'll be fine. Now have a seat and I'll serve you tea. These sweets are the kind Asian children eat."

Confused by the rapid-fire remarks, Lauren obeyed, but her eyes narrowed. Russ hoped the snack would restore her high spirits. Under the table, he patted his daughter's arm until she relaxed.

"Tell us about your work, Rachel," Max said as his wife poured the tea. "I understand you met Russ on the job."

"Yeah. Nearly busted him." She regarded her cup dubiously. "I'm more of a coffee person myself."

His father, who had mellowed considerably in recent years, scooted back his chair. "I'll fix some, if you don't mind instant."

"My favorite," Rachel said.

Russ bit into his pastry and nearly choked. He hadn't been expecting a thick, gooey paste with an odd flavor. Not bad, he supposed. He might learn to like it, but he feared Lauren's reaction.

Too late—she was taking a bite. Leaning close, Russ whispered, "If you don't like it, slip it quietly into your napkin. No spitting."

Her face turning purple with disgust, the five-year-old ducked low and obeyed his request. Fortunately, Lois failed to notice. Coldly, she demanded of Rachel, "What on earth motivated you to join the police force?"

"Gives me a chance to meet such interesting people," said his fiancée, straight-faced.

When Max returned, he handed her the sugar bowl and smoothly picked up the thread of the discussion. "Did I hear correctly that you nearly arrested Russ?"

"I mistook him for a perv." Rachel appeared on the brink of adding that the term was the shorthand for pervert when she registered Lauren's rapt attention and skipped ahead. "'Course, he turned out to be a rescuer. The chief was afraid he'd sue the department, so he assigned me to babysit the new doc and show him around town."

"How unusual." Lois had grown up in L.A., with its large, impersonal force. Russ suspected her only encounters with officers had been the occasional traffic violation.

"Was it love at first sight?" Max asked with a humorous note.

"Not quite. We got together after he fished me out of a swimming pool." Rachel stirred three spoonfuls of sugar into her coffee.

While Russ's parents were absorbing this remark, Lauren piped up, "Can't you swim? I can dog-paddle." She seemed happier now that she'd helped herself to a couple of almond cookies.

"That's a good start. We'll arrange for lessons next summer, so you can be water safe." Russ considered swimming skills a necessity in Southern California. "And, yes, Rachel swims. I'm just better at it."

His fiancée reached for a pastry. "Especially when I've had the wind knocked out of me. A bunch of us cops were horsing around." She sank her teeth into the pastry and, halfway into a bite, began to sputter. After coughing into her napkin, she burst out, "What the Sam Hill is this? It tastes like sludge!"

Max, who'd avoided the pastries, laughed so hard he snorted tea out his nose. Grabbing his napkin, he wiped his face.

"Perhaps if your culinary tastes ran to something more sophisticated than doughnuts, you'd appreciate bean curd pastry!" Lois replied furiously.

Rachel set down the remainder of the dumpling. "I'm sorry. I have a tendency to blurt whatever comes to mind. I'm sure these are real popular somewhere."

"I spit mine out." Lauren's pronouncement only deepened her grandmother's obvious annoyance.

"The cookies are great." Max passed the serving plate. "Trying food from different cultures is a valuable learning experience, don't you agree?"

Rachel took two. "Absolutely. Like Dos Equis beer. That's the Mexican brand. *Dos equis* means *two Xs*. Interesting, huh?"

"Can I try some?" Lauren asked.

"Only when you master the entire alphabet." Catching Russ's frown, Rachel added, "And turn twenty-one."

Tactfully Max steered the conversation to the value of reading, which seemed a safe topic. They all declared themselves in favor of various children's books, and meanwhile, Lauren slid under the table. She sat there at Russ's feet undressing her new doll.

"Grandma!" she proclaimed from out of sight. "Jasmine isn't wearing underpants!"

"We'll buy her some next time you visit," Lois promised. "Why don't you sit in your chair? That's what big girls do."

Lauren clambered into view, bumping the table so Max's fresh cup of tea sloshed onto the cloth. Then the doll appeared, upside down and totally nude.

Russ's mother grimaced. She'd never had much patience with children, and the strain of dealing with a strong-willed granddaughter and a rough-edged future daughter-in-law had apparently sapped what little remained. "Isn't it time for your nap?"

"Jasmine needs underwear now!" the little girl wailed.

"She can borrow from your other dolls when we get home." Rachel cast a meaningful look at Russ.

He didn't require an interpreter. "You're right on target, Mom. Lauren's tired. But we'll be leaving soon. I suspect she'll sleep all the way home." He collected cups while his father gathered plates.

In the kitchen Max confided, "Your mother may take a while to recognize a diamond in the rough, but Rachel's a great find."

After setting down the cups, Russ hugged his father. Only for an instant, because they'd never been a demonstrative family. But when he stepped back, he saw tears in Max's eyes. "Thanks, Dad."

"You're also right about Lauren." The older man got busy rinsing dishes. "She's not ready for weekends with the new grandparents. As she gets older, it might be a different story. When's her birthday?"

"Next month." Russ had noticed the date while completing the forms for kindergarten.

"Your mother might insist on throwing a party. Hope that's all right." Max began loading the dishwasher. "We're both excited to have a grandchild. We've tried to avoid thinking about her all these years because of the circumstances, but I'm glad you stepped up to the plate."

"So am I." Russ wasn't sure how his daughter would feel about a party that might not involve her new friends. But then, he and Rachel could throw a separate bash in Villazon.

Except that Rachel may be gone by then. The prospect left Russ with a hollow sensation.

They rejoined the women, only to discover that Lauren's mood had further deteriorated. She was clinging to Rachel and avoiding Lois's gaze. "She's not my grandmother! I miss Grandma!"

Rachel's soothing words had no effect. "I'm not sure what set her off," she told Russ and Max.

"I merely suggested she spend next weekend with us." Lois folded her arms. "There are so many fun things we could do."

"I won't!" Lauren screamed.

"It's too soon," her husband advised.

Russ knelt near his daughter, who transferred to him willingly. "No one will force you to do anything," he assured her. "We're going home now. Why don't you give your grandparents a hug?"

"No!" the little girl protested.

"Why not?" He wished he had Mike's insight into child psychology, because he suspected something besides being tired was troubling her.

"Their…their faces." His daughter struggled to explain. "I miss my grandma and grandpa!"

Rachel crouched beside the two of them. "After I lost my mother, I got upset when my mental image of her began to fade. Mom and Dad Byers found a photograph for me to keep by my bed, so I didn't lose what little I had left."

More grateful for the insight than he could express, he thanked her. Lauren's inner picture of the Holts might well be weakening, and the introduction of two new grandparents must be adding to the confusion.

"Sweetheart, this evening we'll go through your scrapbook. Right now, let's take a photo of you with your new grandparents to add to the collection." He was glad for the reminder, since he'd meant to take a picture anyway. "Then you can see all four grandparents and you won't get them confused."

"Okay." Her grip on him eased.

"I'll fetch my camera, too." His mother hurried out.

Soon they there were all positioned on the couch, with Rachel operating each camera in turn. Her tantrum forgotten, Lauren sat on Lois's lap between Russ and his father through flash after flash.

"Now I'll take a few." Max claimed the cameras. "I want shots of my future daughter-in-law, so no arguments."

Russ tried to avoid thinking about the deception he was practicing. Although, he suspected his dad would understand if he told him.

At last they said their goodbyes, and Russ shepherded Lauren and Rachel to the car. The rain had stopped but darkness was falling. In the rear, his daughter drooped in her booster seat, cushioned by a pillow and comforted by a blanket Rachel had brought.

Once they'd cleared the canyon roads and were sailing along the freeway, he said, "Your bravery was above and beyond the call of duty, Rache."

She adjusted her beret. "How so?"

"My mom can be tough." He slowed the car to make the transition onto another freeway. "Dealing with her wasn't part of our bargain."

"She feels threatened. I can relate to that. Son falling for a woman way outside her social circle, and this same hussy making inroads with her grandchild." Rachel sighed. "Hey, our breakup ought to thrill her, right?"

Russ didn't answer, because he was starting to realize how much he dreaded Rachel's departure. He didn't know what he was going to do about that.

Perhaps for once he should stop trying to nail down the future and simply let life carry him.

DESPITE RUSS'S supportive behavior, the visit had made Rachel painfully aware of how out of place she was in his family. For heaven's sake, she'd misspoken repeatedly, even insulting his mother's refreshments with a crudeness that had no place outside one of Hale's parties.

Although not given to introspection, she kept mentally kicking herself. Fortunately, nobody else seemed concerned. Lauren awoke hungry, and they stopped at a fast-food place for a bite, where the little girl insisted on taking her teddy bear and Officer Bud inside as if afraid someone would snatch them again. She left Jasmine in the car.

Rachel was grateful for her ability to grasp the child's feelings. Lois had tried hard to get close, yet at every turn, the instinct to take control had driven a wedge between her and her granddaughter. Luckily, they had years to sort matters out.

By then Rachel would be little more than a memory. Despite her deep affection for Lauren, she harbored no illusions about a lasting bond. Lauren, as Russ's daughter, belonged in the McKenzies' upper-crust milieu, and Rachel did not.

On the rest of the drive home, her heart ached as she thought about father and daughter. She longed to stick around, no matter how unsuited she and Russ might be. After all, they *were* engaged. They hadn't entirely ruled out the possibility of—

Stop right there.

Nothing would scare a guy away faster than clinging, as she'd learned during her teen years. Besides, beyond this temporary situation in which they shared a common goal, she and Russ were largely incompatible. Hadn't today demonstrated that?

Rachel knew she should enjoy this phase of her life and then move on. So why did their pending breakup loom like an old masonry wall, poised to topple onto her head?

At home, Rachel and Lauren found undergarments for her new doll while Russ downloaded the photos into his computer, printed out the best shots and added them to the album the Holt grandparents had maintained. In the living room, the three of them sat on the front sofa in a circle of light, flipping back through the scrapbook.

"There you are as a baby. Wow, where'd you get so much hair?" he teased his daughter. "Here's Janine at your first birthday party. And both your grandparents."

The little girl paged through, eagerly drinking in the scenes. Rachel wished someone had kept a book like this for her, at least of the period after her adoption. Mom and Dad Byers had assembled a few photos in a binder, but the influx of short- and long-term foster children had made anything more elaborate impractical. As for her earliest years, those images would stir nothing but regret.

Lauren fingered a shot of Russ and Janine in a casual

pose, looking very young and not particularly affection-
ate. "Why aren't there pictures of you and me, Daddy?"

He studied the image as if he'd never seen it before.
Perhaps he hadn't. "Because I missed your first five years."

"Why?"

"Your grandparents…" He paused, then restarted.
Being careful not to lay blame, Rachel assessed. "Since I
didn't have enough money to raise you, we all agreed you
were better off with Grandma and Grandpa Holt. They felt
it was best for me to stay away."

"Didn't you want to see me?" She hugged Officer Bud.

"Yes. You were on my mind a lot." Russ shut the album.
"In fact, I'd like to show you a special scrapbook, okay?"

She agreed. Rachel presumed he meant a record of his
own past, but when he returned, he bore a photo album of
children she'd never seen before.

"These aren't pictures of you, sweetheart." He'd
resumed his place on the couch with Lauren in the middle.
"They're babies and children who were my patients. But
I took special notice of the ones about your age to help me
understand what you might be like."

He opened to a shot of himself holding a boy about a
year old. The inscription read: "Brad Akers. Birthday is
two days after Lauren's." Following the photo was a brief
description of Brad's milestones: standing at ten months,
taking his first step at eleven.

"I tried to follow your growth. Your first words, your
funny questions and comments. Of course, they weren't
really yours, but I pretended they were." He leafed through
image after image of babies, toddlers and preschoolers,
some standing or sitting alone, some with parents and a
few posing with him.

"Did you tell them about me?" Lauren asked.

"Doctors don't talk much about their own families. It wouldn't seem professional. But I *thought* about you."

That Russ had loved his child at a distance touched Rachel with unexpected force. Despite his obvious instincts to guard his emotions, he'd allowed himself to care deeply about a child he might never be able to meet.

Her own birth father hadn't left so much as a photo. She figured she must resemble him, since her mom had been petite with blond hair, but she wouldn't recognize the man if their paths ever crossed. For all she knew, she might have busted him.

Russ finished reviewing the album and reopened Lauren's. "Here's the new picture of you with my parents. I found room in the back."

Lauren frowned. "Do I have to call them Grandma and Grandpa?"

Recalling her earlier anxiety, Rachel suggested, "Why not Grandma and Grandpa McKenzie? Or Grandma Lois and Grandpa Max?"

Lauren's gaze rested on the photo. "Okay." She brightened. "I'm not confused about their faces anymore."

Russ gave her a squeeze. "That's why scrapbooks are so important."

The little girl studied the group shot Max had snapped. "I like having parents, too."

Above her head, Russ's gaze met Rachel's with surprising tenderness, almost as if they really did share— *Don't go there.*

Lauren began to yawn, so they put her to bed. Despite her nap in the car, the day's events proved exhausting, and she fell asleep in the middle of a story.

Russ and Rachel slipped out quietly. "You're amazing," she said in the hallway.

"How so?"

"That photo album. Those notes. The way you followed her growth." Impulsively, she faced him and rested her forearms on his shoulders. "Impressive, Doc."

"How impressive?" He leaned forward and brushed a kiss across her mouth.

For an instant she couldn't speak, and then she said, "Just about overwhelming." That described her reaction, all right: an utterly irresistible blend of desire and affection.

She expected him to draw back, the way he had in the past. Instead he tugged her through the doorway into the master bedroom.

Rachel wondered if she'd somehow fantasized this. If so, she intended to enjoy the heck out of it.

Chapter Twelve

The room was larger than Rachel had expected, or perhaps the expanse of carpet and subdued teak furnishings gave it that appearance. "You could hold a karate class in here and never break anything but a sweat," she observed.

Russ kept hold of her. "You've studied karate?"

"A bit. Mostly I work out in the gym at the station." A bad-smelling room not remotely as seductive and sensual as this place, she had to admit.

"Think you could take me down?" he teased.

She chuckled. "How far down?"

"As far as you like." He found her strength a turn-on, she realized with a start.

Usually at this point—on the rare occasions that she reached this point with a man—she went for the main event. Tangling, thrusting, climaxing. But from Russ she wanted more. She wanted something she couldn't quite name.

Love. Well, that was a crazy idea.

"What's running through your mind?" He plucked off the beret, which she'd forgotten was still atop her head, and tossed it onto the bureau.

"Unprintable stuff," she responded.

"That sounds promising." What had gotten into this

man? He was kissing her again. Hands exploring her rib cage and the underside of her breasts, raising a burst of sensations. "When do we start the wrestling match?"

"Karate isn't wrestling." Oh, the heck with discussing this to death. Rachel grabbed the guy and lobbed him onto the bed, landing astraddle. He made no attempt to resist. "How's this, Doc?"

"Temperature rising," he responded. "How's yours?"

She laughed. "You're monitoring our vital signs?"

"Call it training. Or instinct. Speaking of which…" His hands smoothed beneath her knit tunic and cupped her breasts through the brassiere. Her nipples strained against his fingers as Rachel braced above him, near melting point.

He arced up for another kiss and continued loosening her clothing. Rachel returned the favor by undoing his shirt and belt and stroking downward far enough to discover how hard he'd grown. Breath coming fast, too, just like hers.

No stopping now. As if anyone but an idiot would choose to.

Catching her off guard, he flipped them. Before she could react, his tongue traced a hot wet line along her throat and down to her swelling breasts.

The contact drew fire across her skin. Rachel could barely keep up with the man's fervor as the last scraps of clothing became an intolerable restriction. She tossed them away.

"You're amazing," he murmured.

"Better yet, I'm on the pill," she responded.

"Then you won't mind if I do this." He proceeded to pull off the rest of his clothes.

He looked fabulous, sculpted and eager, simultaneously demanding and gentle. The scent of his skin tantalized her beyond endurance.

When Russ parted her with a thrust, joy swept Rachel

into a previously unsuspected realm. They seemed to be swirling through a fragrant heated pool that intensified her awareness.

She could no longer distinguish external sensations from the knife-edge of pleasure. A new freedom bloomed, the freedom to be vulnerable and to merge into another person. For the first time in her life, Rachel felt…beautiful.

Waves of exquisite agony seized her, too soon. She wanted so much more. Then there *was* more—soaring higher and higher, hearing Russ's groans mingle with her gasps, until she settled into the comfort of his arms.

They remained, amazingly, in his bedroom. To Rachel, however, the place bore a striking resemblance to paradise.

She lay dozing as Russ adjusted the covers. When he kissed her hair, the gesture brought a sweet sigh.

She curled up beneath the sheet, and although she half expected him to retreat, he gathered her close.

When he switched off the light, a glow lingered briefly around his face. Perhaps Rachel was seeing the heat that emanated from him as luminescence. Or maybe she was seeing him with her heart.

Rachel had hoped someday to find the right man, but she'd never considered what being in love really meant. Suddenly here it was, overpowering every bit of common sense. She and Russ had fused at a level beyond ordinary emotions, as if some of their DNA had swapped strands.

She longed to hear him confirm that he too had fallen in love. But she didn't dare press. As when pursuing a criminal into a building you hadn't cleared, where an enemy or a booby trap might lurk around any corner, you had to hold your position until you determined the extent of danger.

In this case, no backup existed. Only risk. But wonderful possibilities if the risk paid off.

Content to take the future moment by moment, Rachel kissed Russ's shoulder and let her eyes drift shut.

HE HADN'T KNOWN he could lose his inhibitions so utterly, or belong so completely to another person. Russ wasn't sure how this relationship could work, given the vast differences between him and Rachel, but right now he didn't care.

There remained a lot to learn about each other, a lot of potential potholes in the road. A week wasn't long enough for two people to determine whether to spend their lives together. But if other people trumped obstacles, why couldn't he and Rachel?

A fantasy engagement turned real. A home for Lauren complete with a mom who seemed born to the role. Maybe it was possible, after all.

Too perfect, warned the voice of experience. *Too easy.* Russ ignored it.

He must have dozed, because the ringing of a phone woke him. Russ was still trying to pinpoint the source of the noise when Rachel sprang up and grabbed the cell from her pants pocket on the floor.

She wasn't scheduled to work tonight, but perhaps officers remained on call for emergencies. He certainly hoped nothing had happened to her family.

Then he heard the name "Lisa," followed by series of monosyllabic responses that failed to clarify why his teenage neighbor was disturbing them again. Cops had a lot in common with doctors, Russ reflected grumpily. People tended to think of you as always available.

"I'll go find him. Next time, get *his* cell number, okay?" Lisa must have apologized, because Rachel added, "Don't worry about it," before clicking off.

"What's up?" Russ watched as she began throwing on

clothing. He'd have preferred to leave Rachel dozing and take care of the problem himself, but she'd never allow it. Besides, why should either of them go out?

"Lisa's babysitting for Keri and her husband." Rachel located a sock beneath a chair. "Vince dropped by unexpectedly, and while he was there they both heard noises in the backyard."

"I thought this prowler was supposed to be stalking Lisa. Why's he poking around Keri's yard?" The first incident hadn't troubled Russ much, as it might have been simply a mistake, but this second occurrence signaled a real problem. That bothered him for a lot of reasons, not the least of which was that his daughter spent weekday afternoons at the Sommers house.

"That's the thing." The tunic muffled Rachel's words as she yanked it over her head. "Her ex-boyfriend, Gary, couldn't be the prowler. She discovered that his family moved out of state. And she was so flustered tonight that she forgot to tell Vince when he went outside to investigate. He's still out there."

"Why does she expect you to act as her messenger service?" Russ growled.

"She's afraid Vince might cut the perp too much slack, assuming he's a kid. Someone has to warn him."

Russ still didn't like the arrangement. "They should have called 911."

"I agree." She donned her pants backward and had to take them off. "But since they didn't, Vince went out there armed. Has a permit, no problem. Tricky, though, if the cops mistake *him* for the perp or he gets trigger-happy and fires on them. I'd hate to see somebody get shot."

Anxiety gripped Russ's stomach. "I'd hate to see *you* get shot."

"Yeah. Me, too." With a grin that squeezed his heart, she zipped the pants and headed out. "I won't be long."

He followed her progress aurally as she fetched her weapon and latched the front door. The whole business seemed wrong to Russ—Rachel acting as neighborhood security when he longed to shelter her. Maybe that made him an old-fashioned, domineering male. But what was wrong with wanting to protected the woman he loved?

Not *loved*. Their bond was too raw and untested. The woman he cherished, then.

Too restless to stay in bed, he threw on his robe and peeked into Lauren's room. She was sleeping soundly with what appeared to be a death grip on Officer Bud. The new doll sat on her dresser in isolated splendor.

His mother had meant well. The abrupt appearance of a granddaughter must have thrown her for a loop. As he poured a glass of wine in the kitchen, Russ conceded that he never gave much thought to how his parents felt about much of anything. Such as his relinquishing Lauren in the first place.

He'd never told them how much he'd disliked their interference in his life these past few years. Stopping by his apartment unannounced, nagging him to attend their parties, discussing his activities with mutual acquaintances in the medical community. Perhaps he should have confronted them, but he'd preferred to move thirty miles away.

The rejection by their only child must have hurt. Until he'd taken in Lauren, Russ hadn't considered how much his parents had invested in him emotionally.

In truth, he'd never worried about anyone. Right now, though, he carried his glass into the living room and peered into the darkness, wishing he could see around the corner and down the next block to Keri's house.

Rachel should have reached the place by now. He hoped she didn't feel obligated to patrol the entire area. Just deliver a caution to Vince and get her tail home again.

From a few blocks off came the sound of a car on Arches Avenue. Closer, a cat yowled. A few drops of wine sloshed onto his hand.

Minutes ticked by. Where the hell was she? He supposed Rachel took this kind of situation in stride. Probably handled prowlers on a regular basis, along with armed robbers and… Well, not often, surely. Not in a place like Villazon.

Still, her actions in the parking garage made more sense to him in this context. Not only had she believed he'd kidnapped a child, but there'd been no way of determining whether he was armed. He was glad she hadn't cut him any slack. If she went soft on people, one of these days she might get—

A sharp crack from outside jolted him. Gunfire? Heart thundering, Russ braced for more, but none came.

Hurrying to the phone, he dialed 911. But the fear pooling in his gut warned that he might have waited too long.

THE BOOM OF A GUNSHOT halted Rachel in the Sommerses' front yard. She judged that it originated behind the house.

On her cell phone, she rapid-dialed 911 and informed dispatch of what she knew. Then, weapon in hand, she edged toward the corner of the house, but hard as she peered into the darkness, she couldn't see worth a darn. The nearest streetlamp cast more shadows than usable light.

About to call Vince's name, she stopped on hearing a rustling noise by the fence. A dark form struggled with the gate latch, uttered a low curse and scrambled over the top.

This much-slimmer figure clearly didn't belong to

Chief Borrego. Rachel couldn't make out any facial details, either, owing to the suspect's ski mask.

She had to assume the guy was packing, since she'd heard gunfire. Vince could be lying dead in the yard, and this individual might be a rapist or robber sought in seven counties. Or he could be a high school prankster who'd nearly gotten his fanny tanned by the former chief's bullet.

If she confronted him, she risked a shot to her unprotected gut. If she stood down, she might be letting a murderer escape.

Rachel had only a split second to make the choice.

Chapter Thirteen

With regret Rachel let the man go. The law didn't allow her to shoot without a warning, since he posed no immediate threat and might not have committed a crime, despite the suspicious mask.

And if he *was* armed and trigger-happy, to leap out shouting "Police!" at nearly point-blank range constituted suicide. While she never shrank from danger, neither did she possess a death wish.

The figure vanished between two houses, heading toward the edge of the development. As he darted by, she caught a glimpse of brown hair with a reddish cast. Estimated height, five-ten.

Rachel updated the dispatcher and was about to check on Vince's whereabouts when the ex-chief emerged through the side gate. He held his gun pointed toward the ground as a precaution.

Rachel identified herself and explained that she'd alerted patrol. "What happened?"

Disgust creased the older man's face. "I spotted him across the yard. The creep was trying to break in my granddaughter's window."

"Who fired?" She wasn't on duty and technically

shouldn't be quizzing him, but darn it, this was her neighborhood, and the jerk might target *Lauren's* bedroom next.

"I did." Vince holstered his weapon. "After he swung around and drew on me."

"You're sure?" Distinguishing a gun from a cell phone or other innocuous device could be tricky at night.

"Absolutely. There's a lamp just inside the window." Vince scowled. "I didn't dare hit the house, so my aim was off."

"The perp never fired?" Rachel asked.

"The shot must have scared him."

By the curb, a cruiser halted, its dome flashing. No siren, presumably to avoid tipping off the suspect if he lingered in the area. A second patrol car stopped across the street. And, a few houses down, the station wagon that belonged to newswoman Tracy Johnson sidled into place. She must have been monitoring the police frequencies.

"Glad you're here," Vince muttered. "You can verify that there really was a prowler."

"You probably observed as much about the guy as I did." Rachel sure wished she'd been able to stop the man.

"Lyons won't be thrilled about my acting gun happy in a residential neighborhood. I can use all the corroboration I can get."

Until now Rachel hadn't given any thought to how this incident might look. In view of Villazon's low crime rate, the disgraced ex-chief discharging a weapon near an occupied dwelling might make the front page. Although she considered his conduct justified, it would serve as an embarrassing reminder of the department's former problems.

She resigned herself to detailing her observations to one of the arriving officers when what she longed to do was to climb back into bed with Russ. It was going to be a long evening, by the look of things.

POLICE CRUISERS, FLASHING BEACONS—Russ watched anxiously out the window for an ambulance that would indicate someone had been injured. The absence of one failed to reassure him, however.

At last he ventured into the front yard, the farthest he dared go with Lauren sleeping inside. Half a dozen other neighbors emerged also, but none had any information.

How infuriating to be unable to intervene! To stand here envisioning Rachel crumpled on the ground, a dark stain spreading across the sweater she'd thrown on so casually. *"I won't be long."* How could she make a promise like that? How could she tell whether she'd be returning at all?

Treating sick children on a daily basis, Russ occasionally had to deal with diseases that defied modern medicine's power to heal. And accidents could claim a life without warning, in the most ordinary setting. But those occurrences remained mercifully rare.

Rachel was different. Her *job* was different. It required her to face situations most people avoided. To march into dark corners and dimly lit alleys, to pursue armed felons, to stop cars that might contain fleeing killers. Every time she reported for work, she put herself into the line of fire.

He admired the hell out of her, but he didn't see how he could bear to wait around for a woman who played Russian roulette whenever she stepped out the door. Thinking about the chances she took made him angry, although he wasn't sure at whom.

Finally an officer came by, asking neighbors what they'd witnessed. "Was anyone hurt?" Russ demanded.

"No, sir, it doesn't appear that way," came the reply.

"Is Officer Byers all right?"

"Oh, you know Rache?" The young man's formal

manner eased. "Hey, you're the doc who hauled her out of the drink last weekend. Heard you two got engaged." His gaze swept the bathrobe, which Russ had forgotten he was wearing. "Looks like someone interrupted a pleasant evening."

Russ gritted his teeth. While worry was tearing him apart, this clown had his head stuck in the bedroom. "I gather she's all right."

The man smirked. "I'll tell her to hurry home to the love nest, Doc." Before Russ could march inside with what little dignity remained, the cop added, "You see or hear anything?"

Stiffly, he said, "A gunshot. I'm the one who reported it."

"Half the neighborhood called us," the officer responded cheerfully. "Thanks, Doc." He strolled to a knot of people gathered near the corner and began questioning them.

Face aflame, Russ retreated. He supposed these guys joked to avoid dwelling on the danger they faced every day. Plus, judging by that crazy bicycle contest at the party, cops must be risk-takers at heart. Nevertheless, if Rachel had any sense, she'd rethink her course once she weighed the impact on people who cared about her. Namely, him.

A second glass of Chardonnay and the news of her safety restored a measure of calm. Nearly an hour later, when Rachel sauntered into the kitchen as casually as if returning from the mall, he felt torn between a longing to hug this maddening women and an impulse to scold.

"What a zoo." At the counter, she poured herself a glass of wine. "Can you believe Chief Lyons showed up in the flesh? Guess he's got a standing order to be notified about anything involving Borrego."

"Department politics in the middle of a shooting?" That surprised him.

"Hey, everything's political these days. Too bad they didn't catch the perp. He must have stashed a car on Arches Avenue." She regaled Russ with the tale of the prowler, who'd apparently targeted a little girl's room.

"That's twice he's shown up in the same location," Russ noted. "Should we find another day care home for Lauren until this blows over?"

"Seems kind of hasty." Rachel fixed a peanut butter sandwich. Russ declined her offer to make him one. "Lauren's just settling in, and besides, if the guy has any sense, he'll find somewhere else to snoop. I wish I could have stopped him and neutralized the threat." She washed down a large bite with a swallow of Chardonnay.

He attempted to visualize the scene. "Was he armed?"

"Guess I left that out. Yeah, he was packing." Rachel wrinkled her nose at the flavors. "Wine and p.b.—not a great match."

Russ didn't understand how she could treat this situation so casually. "The suspect had a gun. And you're saying you should have put yourself in harm's way?"

"Depending on circumstances." A quizzical expression. "That's what cops do."

Russ moved on to the real issue. "When I heard the gunshot, I thought you'd been killed."

"Hey, I'm sorry. It didn't occur to me you'd be worried. Guess I'm used to being unattached." She reached to cover his hand. The contact felt so good Russ wanted to whisk her into the other room, remove these annoying clothes and hold her close until the chill of fear faded completely.

Except that he'd only be fooling himself. "If this were

a real engagement, if we were planning a future, I'd expect you to show more caution."

Confusion clouded her green eyes. "Got to use my best judgment, Russ. In the field, the worst thing you can do is second-guess yourself."

He held up his palms. "You're right. I didn't put that well." The thoughts that had been tumbling over each other came into focus. "What I mean is, making love changed our relationship."

Her expression brightened. "Yeah? I kind of thought so, but I wasn't sure you felt that way."

He cherished the simple statement. No fancy phrases, no demands for proof of his love, simply an honest acknowledgment that warmed him deep inside. He nearly stopped talking to enjoy the rosy hue of her cheeks and the inviting part of her lips.

But his adrenaline hadn't quit pumping from fear and anger. He couldn't live like this, and he couldn't ask his daughter to do so, either. "I care a great deal about you, Rachel. Maybe even…well, let's not go into that."

"Why not?" she asked hopefully.

He plowed on grimly. "Before tonight, I didn't mind your occupation, or maybe I hadn't thought about it enough. This is different. This was…wrenching."

She blinked. "I shoulda called. I'll be more careful in future."

"That's what we need to discuss—the future." He pressed on. "Tonight I had to face the possibility of losing you. That's what every officer's family endures, I guess, but it isn't normal to worry every time your fiancée or—" he wasn't quite ready to say *wife* "—partner walks out the door, that she may have to stop a bullet. That if a maniac blows into town, she's the first line of defense."

After finishing the sandwich, Rachel lifted the wine-glass, made a face at the contents and set it down again. A bit thickly she said, "Goes with the territory."

"There have to be other positions. Public information officer. Some kind of desk job. Even detective work, but not patrol."

She grimaced. "How about meter maid?"

Russ could see this conversation wasn't going well. "That's not what I meant."

"They might be hiring crosswalk guards down at the school district." Grumpily she went to the fridge. Milk sloshed into a glass and onto the counter. "How about a night watchman at the pickle factory?" She slammed the bottle into the fridge and shoved the door shut.

He yearned to argue. To fight for this woman who'd touched his heart, to make her understand how much he needed her. She'd awakened a side of him tonight that he'd never even suspected.

But between them lay a vast difference in personality and attitude. He couldn't reshape her, and he was unfair to try.

"You're right." He waited until she settled at the table. "I have no business demanding that you give up your life's work."

"It's who I am," Rachel confirmed. "I'd hate flying a desk. Derek Reed's the new P.I.O., and he's miserable. Man, I pity the poor schlub. Well, okay, he's got women beating down his door, so he's not *that* pathetic, but I wouldn't like to be in his shoes."

The next part hurt before he uttered it. Still, Russ went on despite the regret arrowing through him. "I can't claim that our sleeping together was a mistake. It meant a lot to me, and I think to you, too. But we can't do it again. We have to keep our distance. As for this engagement, when we've accomplished our goal, that has to end. Of course I hope we'll remain friends."

She sat stunned, a smear of peanut butter decorating the corner of her mouth and a milk mustache arching above. The sweetest, most down-to-earth woman he'd ever met, and a powerhouse in the bedroom. The longer he sat there, the more he wanted to withdraw his words.

But Russ had seen too many police funerals on television, too many grief-stricken widows walking beside caskets, too many motorcades of officers. Better to stop now. Better to set her free before he fell completely in love.

THE MAN HAD TO BE KIDDING, although Rachel knew he wasn't. People didn't abandon something so special because they got scared. Maybe they argued or indulged in a case of the sulks, but they worked it out of their systems.

Why turn himself inside out about her safety if he didn't care deeply? He'd practically declared he loved her. He ought to be grateful they'd found each other. *She* certainly was.

Finally Rachel dared to ask, disbelievingly, "No more sex?"

Russ looked glum but determined. "That's right."

"You can't be serious!"

His jaw twitched. "Let's not quarrel."

"Why not?" Every instinct demanded that she shake sense into this fellow. A short while ago in the bedroom, he'd launched her into the stratosphere. They couldn't stop now.

"As I said, I'd rather not fight." He averted his eyes.

Rachel certainly didn't want to provoke him into kicking her out. That gunshot had shaken him. She decided to give him some space and hope he'd recover his good judgment. "Then I should sleep in my own bed?"

"That's the idea." He carried his glass to the counter and, after rinsing it, disappeared into the interior of the house.

Rachel felt as if he'd just banished her from paradise. She hoped he changed his mind in a hurry, because she missed him already.

Chapter Fourteen

In the morning Russ remained pleasant but distant. Since Rachel had two more days off, thanks to the department's schedule, she swung by the condo complex. The workmen terracing the slope and compacting the soil were progressing much too quickly for her taste.

Once the condos reopened, Russ might send her back. Except for the matter of meeting with Janine, of course. Braced by that thought, she drove to the station to work out in the exercise room.

Hale poked his head in while she was on the treadmill. "Can't stay away on your day off?"

"Cheaper than joining a club." Stepping off, she wiped sweat from her forehead. "How about spotting me on weights?"

"Sorry. I gotta reinterview a witness about Baldy." The drugstore robber remained at large. "I'd keep a low profile, if I were you."

"Yeah?" What had she done? Oh, right, she'd initially failed to report the previous night's incident with the prowler. Although Rachel doubted calling it in would have made any difference in the events, still, she'd gotten mixed up with Borrego, whose return to town must irritate his successor. "You mean because of Vince?"

"The newspaper lady spent half an hour interviewing him," Hale explained. "She'll rehash that old scandal for all it's worth."

Last week, as expected, Tracy had portrayed Russ as a knight in shining armor and had run a photo of him atop the story about Nina's rescue. If she learned of his engagement to a cop involved in this latest mess…well, the *Villazon Voice* would hit the stands Thursday, which meant three uneasy days of waiting.

"Thanks for the heads-up." Rachel went to shower, and resolved to exercise elsewhere for a while.

In midafternoon, she dropped by the Villa Corazon homework center. Although her rotating schedule prevented her from arranging regular sessions, she provided spot tutoring in math.

She found Yolanda Rios, the retired teacher who'd co-founded Villa Corazon, helping a home-schooled youngster navigate an educational site on the Internet. As soon as she was free, Yolanda went to Rachel to congratulate her on her engagement, which she'd heard about from Marta.

"Kind of sudden, wasn't it?" The widow's eyebrows arched above her glasses. Coupled with the two white streaks in her black mane, the quizzical expression gave her an almost humorous air.

Rachel didn't answer, because she had a question of her own. "Your husband was a cop. Did that worry you?"

"Of course." The woman began distributing pencils, pens and paper on empty tables around the room, preparing for an influx of after-school students. "Although statistically, being a firefighter is more dangerous."

"Ever ask him to change careers?"

"No. He loved his work." Yolanda fixed her full attention on Rachel. "Does your fiancé have a problem with it?"

"A big one."

"Does he think it's unfeminine?" That sounded like a challenge. Yolanda didn't hold with stereotyping.

"He thinks I could get killed." Rachel outlined last night's events, including the gunshot.

"He'll get over it." Yolanda broke off as three young girls piled through the door. "Oh, would you help Sarah with her math? She got a D on a test last week."

"You bet."

By the end of the lesson, Connie had arrived, leaving her gift shop in an employee's hands to work with a five-year-old named Skip. In addition to needing help with the alphabet, he seemed hungry for contact, clinging to Connie's arm and seeking reassurance as he sounded out letters.

"His foster mother lets him spend far too much time alone. He roams all over the neighborhood by himself," her friend confided later while Skip was arranging alphabet blocks. For example, she said, the boy had walked several blocks from his home to the center without supervision. "I'd love to adopt him, but his foster mom has priority. I guess her child-rearing techniques pass muster, but if you ask me, he's just plain lonely."

Rachel decided not to bring up her problem with Russ. She had to collect Lauren for a haircut, which the little girl had requested.

On the way out, she scanned the roster of volunteers on the bulletin board and was relieved that Vince's name didn't appear. With luck, he'd forgotten about volunteering, thus sparing Elise an awkward situation.

At the day care, Keri seemed on edge after last night's disturbance, but expressed the hope that her father had scared off the prowler permanently. Since Rachel hadn't thought to make a hair appointment, she recommended a salon that took walk-ins.

The only thing that mattered to Lauren, Rachel discovered when their turn arrived, was that she have a cut like Rachel's—chin-length with bangs. It meant losing her lovely, long brown curls. "I want it!" she demanded from the large chair.

"We'd better ask your dad's permission first," Rachel said.

"No!" The little girl folded her arms stubbornly.

Rachel sought a diplomatic excuse to delay. "Let's wait till we see Janine, okay? Otherwise, she might get mad at me. She'll think this was *my* idea."

The stylist watched them with a strained smile, which reminded Rachel that others were waiting. She wished she'd thought to question Lauren earlier.

"No!" The girl waved a hand imperiously at the stylist and employed a phrase she'd probably heard on TV. "Make me look like Rachel."

"The kid knows her own mind," the stylist pointed out. "And it *would* be practical."

Rachel yielded. Guys didn't usually notice hairstyles. Anyway, in future, if he didn't change his mind about his relationship with her, Russ'd be the one escorting his daughter to the salon.

And everywhere else, she reflected unhappily as the scissors snipped off the long locks. How sad, when the three of them had started to form a family.

Her eyes misted as she remembered the feel of Russ against her. Inside her. She wished he were here right now, gazing at her with a glow on his face. Rachel wondered if she'd ever see that look again.

At last brown locks lay scattered across the salon's

linoleum floor. Freed of the weight, the curls bounced charmingly, unlike Rachel's straight bob. To her relief, the new do created a gamine effect that was uniquely Lauren's.

The stylist nodded approvingly. The little girl beamed.

They arrived home after Russ, who'd set out cans of soup for them to choose. Rachel braced for his reaction, but he went on tossing the salad.

"Dad!" Lauren piped up. "My hair!"

"You look beautiful, sweetie. Thanks for getting her a trim," he told Rachel distractedly.

End of story.

After Russ put the little girl to bed, he joined Rachel in the living room. She left the TV off, hoping he might discuss their estrangement, but instead he said, "I heard from Janine today."

The last step before he gives me the boot. "Did you schedule her visit?"

"In a manner of speaking." He took a chair, leaving Rachel alone on the couch. "Her beloved Byron wants her to settle what he terms 'this business with Lauren,' so she called from New York. I gather he's afraid I'll start insisting on child support or some such nonsense. In any case, she'd like to see us after she gets home."

Rachel tried to be pleased for Russ's sake that the process might end quickly. "When's she coming? I'll buy houseplants to frill the place up."

"Don't bother. Driving to Villazon doesn't fit into her schedule, so she asked if we could drive to L.A. this coming weekend."

Rachel stared at her hands. This weekend. *So soon.* "I have to work."

"I remembered that." He'd arranged the meeting for Sunday night, he told her. "Lord Byron—sorry for being sarcastic—Janine's future husband prefers not to run into us at his place, so she'll see us at the grandparents' house."

Following an estate sale to be held by a specialty firm on Friday and Saturday, Janine planned to inspect the premises Sunday. She had to make sure it was ready for the painters arriving the following day.

"Won't that upset Lauren, seeing the house empty and forlorn?" Surely the child should be spared that jolt.

Russ stretched wearily. "Perhaps it'll help her accept that this move is permanent." His daughter still occasionally spoke of returning to her grandparents' house.

Rachel remembered driving by the last house where she'd lived with her mother and insisting that Mrs. Byers stop. She'd scampered to the door and rung the bell, expecting her mother to appear, and been horrified when an unfamiliar man answered. Despite his kind face, she'd been horribly upset. The poor guy. He hadn't deserved to find a sobbing, hysterical little girl on his doorstep.

Rachel's thoughts skipped to the issue at hand. "Should I do anything to prepare for Sunday?"

"Janine's likely to ask how we met and how long we've been dating," Russ noted. "We'd better get our stories straight."

Rachel's brain was already spinning from trying to keep straight what she'd told her various friends. "We should stick as close to the truth as possible. That we met recently and that Lauren's circumstances influenced our decision to get engaged. Otherwise she might see through us and get mad. She could still change her mind." The prospect of Lauren's being handed over to strangers was too painful to consider.

"Well then, I guess we've got it covered." He seemed satisfied to leave the matter at that.

Nothing about what came afterward. No sign of any change in his attitude.

Rachel yearned to press the matter, to marshal her points and hash this out. But Russ stood and, with a brisk good-night, escaped to his bedroom.

She couldn't bear to lose him this way. Rachel needed advice, and in a flash she recognized where to get it.

LAUNDRY. THAT WAS THE FIRST THING she noticed in the Byers household. In the morning, there was always a basket or two awaiting the washer, and by afternoon a heap of clean clothes and linens stood ready for folding.

Rachel had driven ten miles to visit her mother on Tuesday afternoon because Susan Byers was the wisest woman she knew. After sharing a warm greeting, the two of them instinctively repaired to the living room sofa, where they sat folding garments of various sizes while they talked.

The big coveralls were for Rachel's dad, Tom, to wear to the garage he owned with twin sons Nick and Nate, who were five years older than she was. They'd bought the shop in Garden Grove seven years ago, at which point Tom and Susan had relocated from Villazon. Nick, who was single, lived with them, while Nate and his family rented a house nearby. The remaining laundry belonged to Rachel's sister Kathy and two foster siblings, Denzel and Alicia, who wouldn't return from school for several hours.

"I wondered why we'd heard so little from you these past couple of weeks." Susan unsnarled the Velcro fastenings on a blouse. The material made it easier for Kathy's palsy-stiffened hands to manipulate.

"Didn't want to lie," admitted Rachel, who'd just finished outlining her predicament.

To her relief, her mother refrained from pointing out that

she shouldn't have lied in the first place. She grasped that the consequences for Lauren would have been too dire.

"Are you sure this man shares your feelings?" At sixty-two, Susan's face showed remarkably few wrinkles, in part because of the weight she'd gained from heavy-duty cooking and baking. The local kids loved to hang out here, enjoying the cookies, jovial atmosphere and tolerant approach to mess.

"He's practically said so." Lint, plucked from a towel, flew into a small wastebasket on the floor.

"'Practically'? Pardon me for pointing out that you aren't the most objective person to make such an interpretation." Deftly, her mom rolled a pair of socks without even glancing at them. She must have dispatched thousands over the years.

"He's afraid I'll die. That shows he's not indifferent, right?" Rachel persisted.

"There's a big gap between 'not indifferent' and 'madly in love.'" Heading off an objection, Susan continued, "And that isn't the only issue. From what you've told me about his parents and his upbringing, you two make an odd couple."

The sleeves on a kid-size T-shirt resisted Rachel's attempt to pull them right side out. Taming them required three attempts, much to her annoyance. "That's why we're good for each other. With me, he can have fun and talk things over. And with him…" She hesitated before admitting, "I feel like a woman instead of his buddy."

"You *are* a woman, and a beautiful one," Susan returned. "I'd love to see you settled with the right guy."

After placing the T-shirt aside, Rachel leaned forward eagerly. "So how do I bring him around?"

"The only thing that can do that is time," her mother answered.

Not a helpful answer. "Time's against me. My condo'll be fixed anyday now. As soon as Russ gains custody, out I go. Except for visiting Lauren, I won't even have an excuse to drop by."

Gently Susan cupped one hand over the fists that had formed in her daughter's lap. "Listen to yourself, honey."

"Listen to myself how?" she demanded.

"If this man were in love, he'd find excuses to see *you*." Sympathy softened the conviction in her mother's words. "Obviously, you mean a lot to this doctor, but not the way you hope. He's made his position clear. You have to cut him loose, Rache. Mourn the loss and move on."

She'd sought encouragement, not an agonizing truth. Tears clouded Rachel's vision. Man, this hurt worse than getting dragged across the pavement while trying to stop a hit-and-run motorist, which had happened a couple of years ago. The abrasions had stung for weeks, though not as long as the guy's penalty had burned *him*.

A lump clogged Rachel's throat. She indulged in one last wistful fantasy: Russ, his slate-blue eyes shining, leaned above her on his bed, whispering how much she meant to him. He loved her. So did Lauren.

"She insisted on a haircut exactly like mine!" Rachel burst out.

"We're talking about his daughter?" Getting to her feet, Susan gripped the edge of a sheet. Automatically, Rachel located the other end and stood facing her mom as they brought the pieces together. "You'll have a better chance of staying close to her if you don't pressure her father."

She longed to argue. But she couldn't. Rachel probably *had* misconstrued Russ's behavior. She'd warned herself about the danger of jumping in, but nevertheless she had. Heart-first.

She'd dreamed for so long about falling in love. In her naiveté, she hadn't paid attention to those old songs about loving and losing, because she'd figured she'd never be fool enough to tumble for someone who didn't love her in return. But she had.

He'd asked to remain friends. That ought to be her goal, too. Friends for Lauren's sake.

"Guess I learned my lesson," Rachel said shakily.

"You're a terrific person. You deserve a man who's so crazy in love he'll consider himself lucky to be in the same room with you," her mom added loyally.

She'd been so certain that Russ cared. Rachel wondered if she'd ever develop enough judgment to tell the difference. "I think I'll wait awhile before I try again."

"I'm sorry, dear." Susan glanced up as a figure entered jerkily from the hallway. "Oh, hey, here's our scholar."

"Hi, big sis," came the familiar greeting.

At twenty-two, Kathy had defied predictions that she'd never learn to walk. Her movements might require the aid of a brace and a crutch, but her freckled face and welcoming smile made her instantly lovable.

Rachel went to hug her sister, careful not to upset her balance. The reminder of how hard Kathy worked for accomplishments that most people took for granted put other problems into perspective.

"I can't wait for graduation day!" Rachel took pride in Kathy's intelligence and hard work. "Four more months."

"With honors! Did I tell you?" The speech emerged slurred because of the stiffness in her jaw.

"That's better than I did," Rachel admitted.

She was glad to leave the subject of her ill-fated love life, and for the next few minutes the three women happily discussed plans for the Cal State Fullerton graduation ceremony and a big party afterward. This marked a true commencement rather than a conclusion, because Kathy intended to earn a master's degree in psychology and, ultimately, to counsel the handicapped.

When Rachel reluctantly excused herself to drive home, Kathy escorted her to the door while Susan answered a phone call. "Heard what you said earlier." Their discussion must have carried into the bedroom where she'd been studying. "Too bad. Doctor sounds nice."

More than nice. Special. Sexy. Afraid to mention those attributes, Rachel replied, "He's a good father."

"But stupid!" Kathy finished. They both laughed.

Outside, Rachel gazed longingly around at the working-class houses with patchy lawns, overgrown camellias, budding rosebushes and a scattering of toys. Maybe someday she'd share a place like those with a husband.

But not with Russ. The recognition that she'd lost him—or perhaps never really had him—twisted in her gut.

Right now, Rachel didn't feel at all like a tough cop. She felt like a woman who'd just had her heart broken.

Chapter Fifteen

Russ wasn't sure how to interpret Rachel's behavior. On Sunday night, she'd come on strong, yet ever since, she'd reverted to the casually friendly attitude of their first few days.

Once or twice he caught something he couldn't interpret in her body language. A kind of pulling away, a flash of hurt. But she recovered so smoothly that he figured he must be mistaken.

In many respects he welcomed the change. Dinner-table dialogue resumed its lighthearted tone, and on Thursday she sketched a humorous picture of the ruckus created by the local weekly. The chief had stomped around all day, furious at the way the paper treated Vince Borrego as front-page news and recapped his problems.

"He claims Villazon must be the most boring place on earth if the editor can't find anything more important to report than that," she relayed. "As if folks didn't always love a juicy scandal!"

Thank goodness there'd been no further sightings of the prowler. Russ's muscles still jerked at the memory of that gunshot. He tried not to think about the fact that, each day,

Rachel sallied forth in her patrol car on missions potentially just as dangerous.

Preparing for Sunday pushed everything else to the background. Lauren grew overly excited ever since he'd told her about the meeting. Despite his warning that her old house was empty and about to be leased, she chattered eagerly about seeing it again and insisted on carting most of her dolls and toys in the car.

He understood that she feared leaving them behind, because at some level she imagined she might resume her former life. However, he was about to put his foot down when Rachel suggested they arrange the toys inside the car and leave them there when they arrived.

"I'm sure they'll enjoy the view out the window, Lauren," she said, her tone serious. "They don't need to go indoors."

Lauren agreed, clearly desperate for his consent, so Russ yielded.

"I draw the line at holding Officer Bud on my lap while I drive," he teased, and was rewarded by his daughter's giggle.

On Sunday Rachel returned from work nearly two hours late. Although they didn't have to leave for another hour, Russ's blood pressure rose with the worry that she might be lying in the street or en route to a hospital.

He was fixing dinner shortly after five when she strolled in. He popped a plate of hot dogs into the microwave oven before asking, "What kept you?"

"Robbery attempt." Without missing a beat, she added a bottle of ketchup to the condiments on the table. "A customer recognized a robber we call Baldy outside a pharmacy and called in. He must have seen her, because he fled."

"Anyone hurt?" A salad and a bag of banana chips completed the meal.

"Nope," she said. "Can you believe three people saw him and nobody can describe his car, let alone recall a plate number? Frustrating!"

Russ hoped the sighting frightened the crook into leaving town. There'd be other crooks, though. And abusive husbands, gang members, drunk drivers with a grudge against cops…. Maybe he took the situation so hard because, as an intern, he'd worked a rotation in the emergency room and seen the damage. To him the possibilities weren't merely abstract.

He was about to call Lauren to dinner when Rachel added, "By the way, my condo association e-mailed."

Russ preferred that his daughter not hear this. He didn't dare reveal the cancellation of their engagement, not before the meeting with Janine. "About when you can move back?"

"Would you believe, the place is almost ready." Her tense body belied her casual tone. "If all goes well with your ex, we can…I can—" she breathed in and out deeply before concluding "—vacate next weekend."

A knot formed in his chest. The return to her condo hardly represented a shock, of course. And they'd already agreed that after her departure Rachel should continue to pick up Lauren from day care and join them for dinner several nights a week. If he were lucky, she might stick around for games as well. Friends, as he'd requested.

But the prospect of her absence churned in Russ's gut. He'd grown accustomed to discussing the day's events and sharing jokes. At night her presence filled the house with quiet comfort.

The pounding of little feet broke his trance. Lauren flew in, crying, "Rachel! Come see my toys! We loaded the car already."

"Okay, but then let's eat. I'm starving." She let the little girl whisk her out to the garage.

Russ busied himself pouring drinks. His daughter's future depended on making a good impression tonight, and walking around with a scowl on his face wasn't going to accomplish that.

After dinner, the drive to Los Angeles passed smoothly. The three of them sang camp songs to which he was surprised to find he remembered the words. The devastation of losing his grandfather's toy soldiers had overshadowed that summer so completely that, until now, he'd forgotten there'd been enjoyable experiences as well.

The former home of Joan and Jerome Holt sat on a block of 1920s and '30s-era homes west of downtown L.A. Russ had assumed that the senior couple owned a large house, perhaps because Janine gave the impression of hailing from the upper crust. However, her directions brought them to a modest white stucco structure. Its only distinctions were an arched doorway and two bird-of-paradise plants flanking the front steps.

Lauren unfastened her booster seat the moment the engine stopped. "Grandma! Grandpa!" She struggled to unlatch the door.

"Honey, they're not here." Rachel exited to help her out. "We're going to see Janine."

The child grabbed Officer Bud. "Please, can I bring my doll? Just this one?"

"All right." Russ eyed the expensive, late-model sedan parked in front of them. A safe guess it belonged to his ex-girlfriend.

The situation called for tact and charm, but at the moment he wasn't certain he could form a coherent sentence. And if Lauren started sobbing because her grandparents were missing, Janine might assume the child was miserable living with him.

He doubted she had any desire to go in search of an adoptive family as originally planned. Nevertheless, his brief encounter with her two weeks ago had reinforced his impression of his ex-girlfriend as high-strung and therefore unpredictable.

A For Rent sign in the yard drew a frown from Lauren, who clung to Russ's hand. He doubted she could read it, but the thing must strike her as out of place.

The door swung open as they ascended the steps. "Glad you found the place." Janine stepped aside to admit them.

Russ noticed how gaunt she appeared in her designer jeans and knit top. Perhaps she was stylishly thin, but compared to Rachel she seemed unhealthy and insubstantial.

He introduced his fiancée, who shook Janine's hand firmly. "Looks like you've been working hard."

She was referring to the living room, where a dim overhead fixture revealed a forlorn scene. Amid areas of wear on the carpet loomed the darker footprints of now-absent furniture. On the walls, patchy shapes revealed where the paint had been covered for decades.

Flustered, Janine brushed a wisp of hair off her face. "A charity picked up the stuff that didn't sell, but you wouldn't believe the trash! I filled two bags."

Clutching her doll, Lauren stared around wide-eyed. Clearly, this was nothing like what she'd expected.

Russ wished he could've softened the blow, but at least now his daughter might grasp the permanence of the change.

"The place'll look better after it's painted and recarpeted. Boy, I'm stiff!" Janine performed a twisting exercise in place.

"Who's going to live here?" Lauren asked wistfully.

"The rental agency's received several applications." She

must have realized that fact offered no comfort, because she added encouragingly, "Maybe they'll find a family with a little girl. I'm sure she'd love it here."

But this is my place! Lauren's expression proclaimed.

"Her bedroom furniture looks beautiful in her new room," Russ told Janine.

"Well, that's good." She sounded a bit uncertain. He understood why, when she added, "My friends can't believe I'm giving her up."

"Except Byron," he hastened to remind her.

"Sure. But…" She searched for words. "You wouldn't believe how many people consider this a second chance for me. Not many birth moms get such an opportunity."

"Not many birth fathers, either. I feel incredibly lucky." Russ had to persuade her that relinquishing custody was the best decision. For heaven's sake, she didn't really want the child; she was simply reacting to peer pressure. "The past couple of weeks has been a real adjustment, but everything's starting to gel. I think Lauren feels at home with us now."

Janine studied the child, whose lashes glistened with tears. "Yes, but this is obviously hard on her."

Impatience threatened to sharpen Russ's tone. He struggled for the right words, but conciliation came hard.

Rachel, who'd been observing them silently, knelt next to Lauren, heedless of the dirty carpet. "This feels weird, doesn't it, sweetie?"

"Uh-huh." The child seemed almost afraid to move, as if the walls—or her memories—might come crashing down.

"You wish things were like they used to be." The summation brought a brief nod.

"I miss Grandma and Grandpa." The little girl hid her face behind the doll.

"I lost my home when I was about your age." To Janine,

Rachel explained, "I used to be a foster child." She addressed Lauren again: "Even though I loved my new family, a piece of me belonged to my old life. But after a while, the bad feelings went away."

"I want mine to go away!" Lauren said.

"Did I tell you about my sister Kathy?" Rachel went on.

Officer Bud waggled from side to side, indicating no.

"She has a condition called cerebral palsy. It makes her walk and talk funny." The description interested Lauren enough for her to lower the doll. "Kathy lived with a bunch of different families until my new parents adopted her, just like they did me. We both started over, lucky for us, because we're really happy now."

Lauren chewed on her lip before asking, "Can I meet her?"

"You bet. She's going to adore you."

The promise met with approval. "Can we go see her now?"

"In a few days," Rachel said. "You can meet our new foster brother and sister, too. They're only a couple of years older than you, but they're sort of your aunt and uncle. Funny, huh?"

A smile at last. "What're their names?"

"Denzel and Alicia." Rachel straightened and dusted off her knees.

"If they're my aunt and uncle, don't they have to give me presents for my birthday?" Lauren asked.

"Honey, everybody's going to give you presents for your birthday!" was the cheerful response.

Janine watched with amusement. "I can see why she got her hair cut like yours. You're an inspiration." Startled, Russ realized that, despite the curlier locks, the style did mirror Rachel's.

"She's a great kid." Rachel draped an arm around Lauren.

Emboldened, the child asked to explore the house. Hand in hand, the pair disappeared into the interior, leaving the two parents alone in the front room. A moment of truth, Russ suspected, tautly awaiting Janine's next words.

"Rachel isn't the kind of lady I expected you to choose, but she's a good match. You needed someone down to earth," Janine said.

"Excuse me?" Despite the approval, he found the statement unsettling.

"You're wired the same way I am, so preoccupied with the noise inside your head that you can lose your bearings. Rachel's exactly the right counterbalance."

"I hadn't thought about our personalities that way, but you're right." Rachel's presence *did* ground him. "Then you'll let me take permanent custody?"

Janine chuckled. "You have a talent for closing the deal. You'd have made a great salesman."

"Used to be. I sold cutlery during med school, remember?" He regarded her questioningly. "Well?"

Janine stuck out her hand, and they shook. "I'll have my lawyer prepare the papers ASAP. That ought to thrill Byron."

"And me," he said.

"You're truly happy about being a father?" she probed. "I figured guilt might figure into your change of heart."

"I'd regretted my decision for years." When her shoulders tightened, he added, "I'm not trying to lay a guilt trip on you. At the time, we both did the best we could. I've changed, though, and Lauren means more to me than anything."

"She's obviously bonded with your fiancée." The sound of laughter from within the house reinforced Janine's observation. "I presume I'll be invited to the wedding?"

The answer nearly stuck in his throat. "Of course." Before Janine could quiz him for details, Rachel and

Lauren emerged, faces bright with merriment. Heaven knew what they'd found to joke about, but he was grateful for the interruption.

Lauren ran over and held out her arms, and Russ scooped her up. He didn't even mind that her doll's head whacked him in the ear. "Ready to go?"

"Yes!" His daughter had obviously seen enough of her old home.

Janine exited with them and locked the door. "I'm a little envious," she confessed. "You three form such a darling family."

"That's because Lauren's so cute," Rachel said.

"Must be," his ex agreed.

Russ wondered if Janine might be having second thoughts about her own forthcoming marriage, but he doubted domestic bliss would suit her nearly as well as the glamorous future Byron offered. Sure enough, she rebounded quickly. "Did I mention we're flying to the Bahamas for our honeymoon? I'm glad Lauren will be settled."

"As soon as the papers are ready, give me a call."

"Absolutely."

Russ tucked the child into her booster seat with a profound sense of relief. They'd passed the test. He and Lauren were on track.

Except for one huge glitch. He didn't see how he could bear to lose Rachel. Janine's comment had forced him to recognize how much he depended on her.

He wished they could stay together. Unfortunately, he had no idea how to accomplish that.

RACHEL WASN'T SURE how she survived the rest of the evening without acting like a complete fool. All week, since her conversation with her mother, she'd taken pride in her ability to stop clinging to Russ. Okay, she'd choked up a bit while informing him about the condo repairs, but their relationship had smoothed out, which confirmed her mom's assessment.

Letting go hurt worse than a stab wound. But driving him into complete estrangement was unthinkable.

Then Janine had described them as a family. For heaven's sake, that willowy, sophisticated woman envied them. As if a hypnotist had snapped her fingers and awakened Rachel from a trance, she'd suffered the same longings all over again. More strongly, if anything.

That night, thanks to soaring spirits, Russ exuded sexual energy. A desire to tackle the guy nearly overwhelmed her resolve.

While he was putting Lauren to bed, she retreated to the den with a book. Russ entered a few minutes later and sat beside her, fingering her hair and talking as if oblivious to the fact that he was driving her wild.

She finally focused on what he was asking. Specifically, had she ever fantasized about becoming anything other than a police officer?

Sure, she told him. She daydreamed about getting zapped by lightning and transformed into Superwoman. Flying around rescuing victims without requiring a bullet-proof vest sounded like heaven.

For some reason the answer seemed to annoy him. He turned grumpy and a short while later, left the room.

A stubborn part of Rachel longed to believe that he was seeking another career for her because police work alarmed him, and that his displeasure confirmed how much he cared. But heck, doctors and nurses got exposed to nasty illnesses, including potentially lethal ones, and she didn't let that bother *her*.

What an awkward position, with the rest of the world assuming they must be lovey-dovey. On Monday, after word spread about the mudslide repairs, a couple of officers inquired whether she intended to rent out her condo, and she muttered crossly that she'd post an ad when she planned to do so. It wasn't their fault high-quality vacancies were hard to find in Southern California. Nevertheless, Rachel wished they'd buzz off.

She'd feel better once the last of the uncertainty about Lauren ended, and with it the pretend engagement. Of course, she'd have to endure everyone's smart-aleck remarks or, more awkwardly, their sympathy. Thank goodness Connie and Marta knew the truth.

Except, they didn't. Not the whole truth. Not the fact that her entire body had quivered while Russ stroked her hair, and that she'd had to fight tears when she peeked in at his sleeping daughter and realized how much she was going to miss them both.

Everything Rachel longed for had been dangled in front of her and was about to be snatched away. Completely unfair. Although she would always treasure the photos from that day with Lauren and Russ and his parents, what she ached for most were the unexpected moments when he opened his soul to her. The connection between them that transcended the physical. The sense of belonging with him.

All wishful thinking. She'd created her own heartbreak.

The rest of Monday dragged on. Then, in the middle of the afternoon, the radio began spitting out codes and instructions.

Officer-involved shooting. Suspect hiding on premises. Office building under evacuation. Rachel could hear sirens wailing all the way to the far side of town, where she'd been patrolling.

Baldy had struck the pharmacy on the first floor of the Mesa View Doctors building. Stopping to pick up a prescription for a sinus infection, Patrolman Bill Norton had interrupted a robbery in progress and been forced to return fire. Mercifully, the robber's bullets failed to hit their target.

The suspect had vanished through a doorway into an interior hall and up a staircase. Guards immediately cut access to the adjacent hospital, but the perp could be anywhere in the office structure. Each floor was being systematically evacuated and searched.

Russ worked in that building. Perhaps he'd already been sent home for the day. Rachel refused to consider that he might be in jeopardy, because anxiety only detracted from her job.

Which, under the circumstances, extended past the end of her shift. Rachel had just turned west, answering a call for help with crowd control, when another report came in. An employee at the industrial park next to Amber View had spotted a trespasser, a man in his early thirties with shaggy ginger hair. The man had flashed what appeared to be a pistol and run toward nearby houses.

As the closest officer, Rachel hung a U-turn and responded. At the site, she located the witness, a fiftyish male who seemed eager to help.

He explained that the interloper had apparently been sleeping in an empty warehouse. When employees opened the docking doors to unload equipment, they'd flushed the guy. He'd left in a hurry, displaying the weapon to make sure they cleared the way. One significant detail: the subject's neck bore a tattoo of a skull and crossbones.

That brought to mind Noel Flanders, the prison escapee whose bulletin Rachel had read. She called up his image on the mobile data terminal.

"Yeah, that's the guy," the employee confirmed.

She radioed in the ID. Dispatch put out a call for backup, but with an armed felon heading into a residential neighborhood, Rachel couldn't wait. She turned onto Arches Avenue and burned rubber to the development entrance.

All senses roared to full alert. Convicted in a series of robberies, the perp had been given a lengthy sentence under California's Three Strikes Law and probably figured he had nothing to lose by shooting a cop. Worse, the guy was loose in a zone filled, at midafternoon, with women, children and retirees.

Even if he only wanted to hide, he might take hostages. A vehicle for sure, given half a chance.

Reluctant to activate her alarm and warn Flanders of her approach, Rachel cruised past the pool. On a crisp February day, it lay empty. So was the tot lot, at this hour.

She radioed to make sure dispatch alerted school bus drivers to keep a lookout before releasing their charges into the Amber View tract. Of course, the guy might be heading north into the old avocado grove or west toward the high school and shops.

Rachel surveyed houses and yards and scanned the occupants of the few passing cars. Spotting a woman walking her dog, she stopped to warn her and inquire if she'd seen anything. The answer was no, followed by a fast trot to get indoors.

Another bend, another street. No sign of the guy.

An elderly man knelt, pulling weeds in his yard. Cruising by, Rachel paused to alert him and ask for info. Hadn't seen anything, he said.

Well, that was a relief, she reflected as she turned onto Keri's block. It was too soon to make assumptions, but with luck the guy had simply been eager to get away.

Everything appeared normal. As she cruised past, however, she noticed Keri's front door ajar. That might indicate a parent had stopped by, perhaps Russ, since his office had been forced to close. But it was also possible one of the kids had opened it. Especially under the present circumstances, an unlatched door was a bad idea.

Rachel halted, notified dispatch and swung up the walkway, scanning the area for suspicious activity. She rapped on the door. "Hello?"

Abruptly the portal flew wide. There stood a red-haired man, his jaw twitching above a grim tattoo.

He held a gun aimed straight at her head.

Chapter Sixteen

Point-blank range. Not a chance of unholstering her weapon before he shot her, Rachel registered.

"Inside," commanded Noel Flanders, making a rapid survey of the street before reading Rachel's nametag. "Hand me your gun, Officer Byers, and don't try to be a hero. My quarrel isn't with you."

A quarrel. She didn't know what he was talking about and, right now, didn't care. A cop who surrendered her gun ran a high risk of becoming a dead cop, yet under the circumstances, she had no doubt he'd fire if she disobeyed.

Irked at herself for getting caught in this mess and at this jerk for creating it, Rachel complied. Although she wore a second, smaller weapon in an ankle holster, she'd save that until the suspect was distracted.

She didn't see anyone in the living room. When Flanders closed the door, however, he cleared her view of the family room on the left.

She went rigid. Russ stood with one arm around Lauren and the other around little Mary. Restrained fury heightened the angles of his face and emphasized a red mark across one cheek.

Their gazes met. She read tenderness, anguish and resolution. Pushed an inch, the guy might take action that could get him killed.

Rachel fought against fear for Russ and the girls and dismay at seeing them in this agonizing situation. She had to stay focused.

Discreetly she lifted one hand in a subtle calm-down gesture. Russ had to trust her to handle the situation and, if necessary, take the fall. She'd been trained to evaluate and react to situations like this. And she'd rather die than let anyone harm the man she loved.

Then she averted her eyes. She didn't want their captor to realize she had a special relationship with anyone present.

The rest of the room lay empty. Noting a cell phone on a table, Rachel surmised Keri had grabbed the other four children and hidden, relatively safe but with no means of summoning help. At least, she hoped that was the explanation. Certainly if Keri had escaped the house, she'd have notified the authorities by now.

Since the stairs lay in front and fully exposed, it seemed unlikely Keri had reached the second floor. The living and dining rooms were open to view, which left the kitchen at the rear of the house and an adjacent utility room.

Best guess: they were huddled in the utility room, awaiting an opportunity to flee through a connecting door to the garage but aware that the sound of a door opening and closing would draw the hostage-taker's immediate attention. Keri and her four little charges needed someone to sidetrack Flanders.

But before Rachel put her life or anyone else's on the line, she had to try reasoning. That wasn't going to be easy, since criminals didn't operate rationally, but their thoughts usually maintained an internal logic.

"You said you have a quarrel with someone," she noted

as the man gestured her to stand beside Russ. "Mind enlightening me about that?" She took a few steps in a semblance of obeying, but left maneuvering space.

"You know who I am?" he demanded. Receiving a nod, he continued, "Eight years ago, Vince Borrego investigated my case and railroaded me. I shoulda served a year or two, tops."

If he'd been the prowler, which seemed likely, that explained why he'd kept snooping around the same premises. Suspects often held a grudge against the cop who sent them to prison. That was a typical attitude among lowlifes; rather than take the blame for their own wrongful conduct, they sought vengeance against the person who'd protected their victims.

Rachel didn't intend to rile her captor by defending the old chief. Besides, she had no idea what had happened back then. "You want revenge?"

"Justice." The man's tattoo rippled with anger. "I ain't no killer. But the judge sent me away for twelve years when all I did was help my mother's no-good boyfriend. The heist was his idea, and he got most of the stuff. Borrego couldn't catch him, so he persuaded the D.A. I was running the show. "

"What are you going to do?" Rachel tried to keep her tone conversational. Although she could feel Russ's tension and the little girls' anxiety, she didn't dare let them affect her.

"Hold his daughter and grandkids until he confesses." The man's lip curled. "Maybe the press'll believe me then."

More likely, the press understood that some men would confess to anything to save their loved ones. No reason to say that, however.

"Have you moved for a retrial?" Rachel probed.

"Had a lousy lawyer, so I figured I'd better do this myself." The guy grew more agitated. "I had everything figured out, but then that witch—Keri—ran off. Maybe I should just shoot you and go find her."

Russ went rigid. Whimpering, Lauren buried her face in his jacket. Mary simply stared up in terror.

"But you aren't a killer," Rachel reminded the perp. "Besides, if your goal is to reduce your sentence, hurting people won't help." She didn't mention that breaking out of prison and taking hostages constituted serious crimes in their own right. Let him go on believing that a previous injustice—real or imagined—justified his actions. "Have you contacted Vince?"

"I made Keri call him before Daddy here popped in and threw me off. I told Borrego to come alone if he ever wanted to see the kids again." The man frowned at Rachel as another point occurred to him. "Did he send for you?"

"Absolutely not." Dealing with this guy was like tiptoeing through a minefield. "I got a call from the industrial park, and your description matched an APB. I was checking on the open door."

A brief reflection and then: "Okay."

She had to get Russ and the children out of danger before Vince showed up or Flanders decided events were taking too long. And before he realized Keri must still be on the premises.

"Listen, I used to work with Vince," Rachel improvised. "We were pretty good friends. *Very* good friends, if you follow my meaning."

He leered. "Yeah, I heard he had a taste for police babes."

"He'll be upset when he discovers you've got your hands on me." She deliberately used a phrase with sexual connotations, to reinforce the idea of her involvement with

Vince. "You can free these other people. They don't mean anything to him."

Russ, who'd been admirably controlled, spoke in a low tone. "You don't have to do this."

She refused to address him directly, keeping her gaze on Flanders. "I'm not crazy about Vince, either. He doesn't treat women too well—maybe you heard about that, too."

"Yeah, I read the news on the Internet. That police babe nailed him to a tree." He obviously exulted in his enemy's downfall.

Good. They were establishing rapport, as she'd been taught to do in Police Academy. *Gain his trust. Persuade him you're on his side.* "Vince still believes he can win me back. Sent me a nauseating e-mail just a few weeks ago about how much he misses me. I'm your ideal bargaining chip."

She could see the man feverishly reviewing the situation. "If I let these others go, they'll report me. The place'll be swarming with cops."

Rachel addressed Russ in an impersonal manner. "Sir, tell the dispatcher to keep the area clear. If Mr. Flanders so much as glimpses another uniform, it'll jeopardize my safety."

She meant what she'd said about keeping other cops out of sight. She'd radioed in her location, so it wouldn't take long for backup to reach them.

Russ shook his head. "You can't expect me to leave you here."

Rachel sidestepped the personal implication. "Sir, escort the children out the front door, like the man told you." Flanders had given no such order, of course, but with luck he'd forgotten that. "We'll both thank you not to interfere."

Sensing resistance in every fiber of Russ's body, she prayed for him to acquiesce. For everyone's sake, he had to put aside his instinct to defend her.

Lauren broke the deadlock. "Daddy, can we go home?"

Reminded of the children, he released a long breath. "Okay, sweetie."

Flanders stepped out of their way. "Remember, if I see another uniform, it'll look like a war zone in here."

Rachel willed Russ to hurry. She didn't want him or the girls anywhere near the place when Vince arrived, because the situation was almost certain to escalate.

Skirting the staircase, the threesome moved toward the exit far too slowly for Rachel's taste. Her fists clenched as Russ turned the knob.

His flinch told her he'd spotted someone outside. To keep Flanders occupied, she started chattering. "What shall I say to Vince when he gets here? We ought to have a plan. Or would you rather do all the talking?"

Could be almost anyone out there. A salesman with bad timing, a nosy neighbor—or Vince.

"I'll talk. You stick a sock in it." Flanders paid scant notice to Russ as he and the children hustled out.

"Gotcha," she answered with feigned nonchalance. "I'll just take my lead from you. So how do you think you'll deal with Borrego?"

During his rambling reply, a shadow filled the entrance. She couldn't ID the newcomer against the bright light, and didn't dare tip off Flanders by staring.

Behind him, the shadow jerked its head at her. She interpreted that to mean, *Get out of the line of fire.*

In a split-second move, Rachel hit the floor, curling to reach for her spare gun. Flanders swiveled. A shot roared, followed rapidly by two more. She wasn't sure who'd fired, but her captor collapsed, his gun skittering across the wood surface and blood spraying the furniture and walls. A few nasty bits hit Rachel, and her ears rang.

Despite the shock, she drew her gun and stayed in a crouch until she recognized the figure approaching from the entry as Vince.

"You okay?" he asked.

Holstering the weapon, she moved to the body on the floor. "Yes. You?" She collected both weapons and cuffed the suspect's hands before feeling for a pulse. Nothing.

"Right as rain." He called a quick remark out the door, presumably to Russ.

Rachel got to her feet, ignoring the shakiness in her knees. "Thank you." While the D.A. would undoubtedly investigate, she considered the shooting an obvious matter of self-defense.

"Glad I took him out," Vince answered briskly. "Where are Keri and my grandkids?"

"Hiding in the utility room, I think. Wait! We need to secure the premises." First priority was to search for anyone Flanders might have injured.

"Yeah, well, I'll start there."

Rachel phoned dispatch with an update and request for an ambulance, in case the perp could be revived. Then, gun in hand, she circled through the living room and kitchen. While it seemed unlikely Flanders had an accomplice, a cop should take nothing for granted. She was still furious with herself for getting caught off guard at the door.

From the utility room, Rachel heard happy cries that indicated a reunion. After confirming that Keri and the other kids were okay, and instructing them to exit via the garage, she and Vince cleared the upstairs. No problem there.

He went out to shepherd everyone away from the house. Rachel took a post at the doorway as sirens approached.

Producing a notepad from her pocket, she tried to write down every detail she remembered since arriving at the scene, but her hand shook so badly she had to stop. She'd never been involved in a fatal shooting before.

A few minutes ago, that pathetic figure on the floor had been a living, breathing man. She wondered whether he'd truly suffered an injustice eight years ago. Most likely he'd exaggerated his grievance. With Flanders dead, she doubted anyone would pursue the matter.

Outside, emergency vehicles swarmed onto the street. Amid the stir, Rachel caught sight of Russ waiting on the sidewalk with the girls. His eyes warmed as their gazes met, but she also read anger in the twist of his mouth.

Being placed in jeopardy played havoc with people's emotions. And while she'd trained physically and mentally for a confrontation like this, he'd stumbled into it blind. Rachel wished duty allowed her to commiserate, but they couldn't discuss their experiences until they'd been thoroughly debriefed.

She sank onto the porch steps, utterly weary. The brush with death made her long with all her soul to be surrounded by Russ's strength and gentleness, yet today must have confirmed his worst fears about how much danger she ran.

In spite of everything, she loved this job. Was grateful that she'd been able to gain a measure of the suspect's trust and secure the release of three hostages and that she'd retained her composure.

She wished that the man she loved could grasp how much this occupation suited her. And how desperately others, especially children, needed the protection that only people like her could provide.

RUSS STRUGGLED to contain his irritation as the evening dragged on. At the station, he had to endure both his own interview and Lauren's. For heaven's sake, the guilty party lay dead. Why did the innocent have to keep suffering?

He glimpsed Rachel a couple of times but wasn't allowed to speak to her. That infuriated him further. Technically, they were still engaged, and they'd gone through hell that afternoon. They should at least be allowed to comfort each other.

At last an officer drove him and Lauren home. How strange, he thought, that except for yellow tape on the Sommerses' front door, the neighborhood revealed no sign of trauma. But then, all the drama had taken place indoors.

A phone message from Keri alerted him that she'd arranged to supervise the children at Lisa's home the following day. She apologized for the disturbance and assured him—as she'd presumably done with the other parents—that she'd arranged for a psychologist to drop by in the afternoon to talk with the children.

Russ managed to calmly fix macaroni and cheese for his daughter and tuck her into bed. He assured her that the bad man would never bother anybody again.

Nestled against the pillow, she looked small and vulnerable. "Is Rachel okay?"

"Yes. She'll be home later." By then perhaps he'd sort out his turbulent reaction. "I'll make sure she peeks in on you."

"Okay. Don't forget! Even if I'm sleeping."

"I won't." The child clearly required further comforting. "Are you scared to go to day care? I can find a new place if you'd like. And you don't have to go to school tomorrow, either." He didn't like to postpone appointments, but his daughter's well-being came first.

Lauren issued a firm, "No, Daddy! I like Keri!"

"Okay, honey."

"And I *want* to go to school." She held up the action

figure she'd clutched through the whole experience. "Officer Bud is looking forward to Show and Tell. He was very brave. Just like Rachel."

He was very brave. Just like Rachel. As Russ kissed his daughter good-night and switched off the light, her words rang in his brain.

The stillness of the house yielded to vivid impressions, almost as sharp as when he'd first experienced them: the shock when, receiving no response at the door, he'd tried the handle and walked straight into the sights of a gunman; the anxiety as Keri fled with some of the children; and the sharp blow to his cheek when he blocked their captor's pursuit. The welt still ached, although he'd declined medical treatment.

The gunman had shouted curses, sending Russ's heart rate into hyperdrive as he braced for a volley of bullets. Their captor's agitation had barely subsided before he glanced out the window and went to confront Rachel.

Watching the man's finger hover near the trigger, Russ had realized that he himself was powerless to save the people he loved. *That* had been the most unnerving development of all.

The thought that Rachel ran this sort of risk for a living tore him apart. On any given day, she might deliberately tackle a situation any sensible person would shun. By wearing that uniform, she invited every nutcase, enraged ex-spouse or cop hater to turn his rage on her.

Russ didn't understand why this job appealed to her. Sure, he was glad that *somebody* was willing to serve the public, and Rachel had been free to choose while she was single. But not if she were his wife and Lauren's mother. How could she put her family through this?

He longed to hear her car halt in front of the house and

her footsteps approaching. To sweep her against him and bury his face in her hair. To know she was safe. The thought of enduring such fear again—let alone repeatedly—seemed intolerable.

She had to acknowledge both how much they meant to each other and how precious their future was. Far too precious for her to continue laying her life on the line for strangers.

SEVERAL DAYS OF PAID LEAVE and mandatory counseling were what had been prescribed to Rachel. She appreciated the department's response to her ordeal, but after hours of questioning, she'd have preferred a few throat lozenges.

To complicate matters, outside the station she ran a gauntlet of cameras, microphones and nosy news types from L.A., mostly seeking scandalous tidbits regarding the former chief. How did these hornets discover so quickly where to swarm? she wondered, when a group of them caught her departing through the station's rear exit.

They didn't seem the least interested in Baldy the drugstore robber, who'd been apprehended cowering behind a rack of wigs. On the second floor of the doctors' building, he'd taken refuge in a business that provided prostheses and head coverings for cancer patients. Except for the disruption of their afternoon, the structure's tenants had suffered no harm.

The story of the hour was former Chief Borrego's shooting of a man who'd taken hostages at his daughter's home. All evening, the station's TV set had rotated among channels blaring the latest reports. Some were wildly inaccurate. A claim that the gunman had interrupted Keri in a tryst with a lover had to be quickly retracted, as was a statement that he'd held a gun to a little girl's head.

Community Liaison Officer Derek Reed had helped Lyons prepare a statement. Earlier, the chief had read it on camera, grimacing once or twice as flashes went off in his face.

Pending the conclusion of ballistics tests, he'd said, preliminary information indicated that Vince Borrego had fired three times. Neither the suspect nor Officer Byers had discharged a weapon. Lyons credited Rachel with keeping Flanders calm and with arranging the release of three hostages.

Questioned about the intruder's purpose, he'd simply cited Vince's role in the original case. That seemed reason enough for revenge. Of course, Rachel had disclosed the entire story to Jorge Alvarez, the robbery-homicide detective investigating Flanders's death.

"What did Flanders tell you about his motives?" demanded a man with a microphone. "And why did Borrego arrive at the scene before your backup?"

"No comment." Rachel waved to Tracy, who'd once written a nice piece about the tutoring center. In the uneven glare of lights, the newswoman's brunette locks appeared auburn. "Did you dye your hair? Love the color!"

"Uh, thanks." During the momentary confusion that followed this remark, Rachel cut between the ranks and escaped to her car.

She was so tired she had to fight drowsiness on the drive home. But she snapped out of her stupor when Russ hurried out to her car and swept her against his soft V-neck sweater. He smelled wonderful, a blend of masculinity and—was that macaroni and cheese?

"Starving," Rachel announced when he released her.

"You missed dinner?" He touched the small of her back as they went into the house.

"Couple slices of cold pizza." That had been—when?—hours ago. In the kitchen, she found a pot of leftover pasta and dug in while standing. "Fabulous."

He set a plate for her at the table. "I promised you'd check on Lauren. Would you mind doing that and then joining me here?"

"No problem." She complied while scooping out the last of the macaroni with a fork. She found the girl sleeping peacefully.

When she returned, Russ had provided toast and butter along with a sliced apple. He poured them each a glass of milk and sat down to watch her eat, his slight smile revealing nothing.

Coming up for air, she noticed a lined pad on the table and recognized his jagged handwriting. "You journaling your thoughts? Good therapy."

"This is about you." He tapped the paper in front of him. "Here's what I came up with."

"For what?" She decided against fixing another round of toast. Overeating under stress was a cop's curse.

Russ cleared his throat. "You volunteer to tutor children. And you're great with kids."

"Thanks." Why was he mentioning those things now?

"You hate the idea of being tied to a desk," he continued. "Also, you want to help others."

Rachel was getting an uncomfortable suspicion about where this line of reasoning might lead. "So?"

"The community can always use gifted teachers." Russ didn't pause for a response. "The continuation high school provides an opportunity for teenagers who don't fit into the regular program. They need adults who can dish out tough love, who can discipline them without breaking a sweat. I checked on the Internet and, with your college degree, you could get temporary certification if you enrolled in the appropriate education courses."

Disappointment destroyed what remained of her appetite. "Russ, I'm not a teacher."

"Surely after today…"

If anything, today had reinforced her belief in her calling. "I had a chance to help save lives. At the very least, I spared the girls from witnessing a nasty scene."

"And nearly got killed. I heard those shots going off. You can't tell me you were perfectly safe."

That was true. "It got kind of hairy in there," she admitted.

He leaned forward eagerly. "Just think, no more rotating shifts. You'd have holidays and summers off to be with Lauren. And teachers save lives in their own way."

How tempting—for somebody else. Clearly, Russ had invested a lot of effort in trying to arrange their future as a family. But what cut like a knife was that he sought it with a person who wasn't really Rachel.

Tears smarted beneath her lids. "This isn't going to work, Russ."

"Sleep on it. Tomorrow…"

She waved him to silence. "I mean, the whole thing. Not just teaching, but you and me. Fundamentally, we're wrong for each other. Always were, but I didn't see it before. I'm sorry."

Her vision had gone so blurry she couldn't read his expression. Was he frustrated? Hurt? Furious?

His hand slammed onto the table, knocking the pad aside. "I'm trying to fix this and you won't even consider my ideas!"

"What if I demanded you give up medicine?" she retorted. "This is who I am."

"A woman who doesn't care about her loved ones?"

Anger hoarsened his voice. "Or maybe I'm assuming too much. You're pretty quick to throw us out the window."

"For Pete's sake!" As if he hadn't been the one who booted her out of bed in the first place! "You swore I was the type of woman who appealed to you. Except, now that push comes to shove, you expect me to change into something I'm not. What kind of woman *do* you want? Little Miss Compliant, who'll rework her personality to suit Dr. Wonderful?" She clamped her jaws shut before more hurtful words poured out.

Russ stared at her. Finally, stiffly, he said, "You're right. We *don't* suit each other, Rachel. Thank you for pointing it out."

He grabbed his wallet and keys and slammed out of the kitchen. She sat, stunned, listening to his car start in the garage and pull away.

He would return later, of course. This was his house and his daughter sleeping in the bedroom. But once he did, she'd head for her condo, yellow tag or not.

She'd known she was likely to lose him. But until now, she'd clung to her dreams like a fool.

Resting her head on her arms, Rachel surrendered to tears.

Chapter Seventeen

Russ wasn't certain how he reached the nearest shopping mall without getting a ticket.

He ran a yellow light just as it flipped to red, and exceeded the speed limit by at least ten miles an hour. Luckily, Monday-night traffic was light and he had good reflexes.

Going to the mall was what Southern Californians did when they chose to be alone, he remembered reading somewhere. Alone in a crowd.

Not much of a crowd tonight, he saw as he strode inside. With Valentine's Day past and Easter a month off, the mall lacked a festive atmosphere. That suited Russ. If hordes of shoppers had obstructed his path, he'd probably have bowled some of them over.

Fundamentally, we're wrong for each other. Absolutely. He must have lost his wits to believe he had anything in common with a woman who'd tried to arrest him the first time they met.

He paced past a gift shop and a boutique window filled with frothy pastel dresses and tiny tops and shorts. Rachel would sniff at nonsense like that. She was too vibrant for such paltry colors, and too active for skimpy garments.

She led a no-holds-barred existence. Like that insanity

with the bicycle and the swimming pool. That should have told him right there that the woman didn't suit his conservative temperament.

Still, he admired the way she'd acted at his parents' house. Straightforward and unpretentious, and not the least intimidated. And despite her openness, she guarded some areas of her heart. Only when she related the story about her abusive stepdad and alcoholic mother had Russ begun to grasp the whole picture.

A short while ago, he'd seen the pain glittering in her eyes as he stormed out of the house. Yet she was the one who refused to bend! She was the one who refused to make this relationship work!

Across the corridor, a toy store caught Russ's eye. Lauren's birthday was only a few weeks off. He might as well choose a gift while he had the chance.

Inside the store, stretching for a doll on a shelf, he noted a whiff of Rachel's residual scent from his sweater. For a few agonizing heartbeats, he missed her so much he could hardly breathe.

"Can I help you, sir?" A young salesman presented an impersonal smile.

"What's popular with five-year-old girls?"

"High-tech toys are big sellers." The fellow steered him to an array of gadgets. "We have phone-style walkie-talkies that she and her friends can use anywhere in the neighborhood. Or how about a digital camera?" He indicated a pink model with a daisy framing the lens.

"That isn't what I had in mind." None of this stuff inspired Russ. Too cold and impersonal.

"We just received a shipment of dolls that double as digital music players." The salesman went on talking and demonstrating his wares. What a relief when the fellow excused himself to wait on a young woman.

Russ escaped into the mall, aiming for a bookstore. Lauren loved reading, and he decided to select a new release for his own enjoyment, too.

Movement drew his attention to the window of a hobby shop, where a finely detailed small train whisked through a station. Lights flashed and guardrails lowered as the locomotive raced through a village.

Far too complex for Lauren, but the old-fashioned appeal of the scene drew Russ into the boutique. Miniature railroad equipment shared space with model rockets and planes. The sight of video equipment nearly sent him into retreat—until he spotted a fully furnished dollhouse.

Would Lauren enjoy it enough to justify the high price and significant amount of space it occupied? Much as he'd love to see her face when she unwrapped it, Russ doubted that.

A saleslady approached. Mercifully a phone summoned her to the counter.

Russ slipped around a corner, scanning smaller dollhouses and other play sets. A fire station. An airport. A police department.

He stared at the hand-painted officers with their cruisers and uniforms. Although smaller than Officer Bud, they incorporated movable limbs, and each face showed expressive features.

Almost reverently, Russ lifted one of the figures. The careful workmanship reminded him of the soldiers his grandfather had bequeathed him. Perhaps owning them would help Lauren feel close to Rachel even when they didn't see each other as often. He'd enjoy sharing them with his daughter, as well.

Joy rushed over him, as if he were being offered a

chance to reclaim those long-lost treasures. Yet, on the verge of calling the saleslady, Russ hesitated. These delicate figures would get lost or broken before long. If Lauren took them to day care, the boys would wrench off the arms. Why invest so much emotion in a set that clearly wasn't going to last?

He nearly abandoned the whole idea. And then shook his head at the awareness that he was standing in a store aisle obsessing about the impermanence of toys.

Or, more accurately, about the risks of loving and losing.

From an upper shelf, Russ grasped a boxed set of the police scene. He'd better hurry and pay for it, because he'd just realized he had another, much more important gift to buy.

RACHEL COULDN'T DECIDE what to do about the popcorn cart.

She'd packed her belongings, but she didn't see how this thing was going to fit in the car. Initially, the traffic sergeant had dropped it off, and until now she hadn't considered its fate.

Although she'd happily donate it to the household, when she announced the end of her engagement, Mark was probably going to inquire what happened to it. Maybe he'd even ask for it back.

Not that she cared about the darn machine. But right now her emotions were too wound-up for her to think straight.

Rachel was still stuck when a small sleepy girl emerged from the hall. "Where's Daddy?"

"Had to go out for a while." She left the matter at that. "Bad dream?"

A nod.

"Want to tell me about it?" Most likely related to the hostage situation. Any sane person would have nightmares about that.

"I was running and running and nobody helped." Tears streaked the child's cheeks as Rachel gathered her close. "Where were you?"

"On my way to rescue you," she replied calmly.

"You won't go away, will you?" Lauren asked.

A vise tightened around Rachel's heart. Children couldn't be expected to understand grown-up behavior, especially when the grown-ups didn't fully grasp it themselves. She saw no way to admit she was leaving without portraying either herself or Russ as a villain.

"I was about to pop corn but I didn't want to wake you," she responded instead. "You're welcome to join me, but you'll have to brush your teeth again afterward."

"That's okay." Clutching Officer Bud, Lauren plopped onto the couch while Rachel poured the corn. Soon an enticing scent filled the air, along with the rat-a-tat of the kernels.

"Bang bang." Lauren shivered.

Rachel hadn't considered the noise's associations. "Sounds like gunfire, huh?" Talking about their experience might be helpful.

"Guns are louder," the little girl replied. "Grandpa shot the bad man, didn't he?"

"Grandpa Vince did," Rachel confirmed.

"Grandma said angels watch over us." Lauren seemed to be wrestling with a rather large metaphysical issue for such a small person. "Grandpa isn't around but...but Grandpa Vince is. And Grandpa Max."

"You've got a lot of people watching over you." That seemed to satisfy the little girl, because she laid Officer Bud aside and ran to the popper. "Is it ready?"

"Almost."

Rachel was filling their cartons when a car pulled into

the garage. How awkward. She'd expected to leave as soon as Russ came home, but now that would upset Lauren.

A thump and a scrape warned that he was struggling to enter through the side door, probably with a package. Leaving Lauren on the couch, Rachel went to investigate.

The man had his arms around a large box, which he was unsuccessfully angling to fit through the narrow aperture. "I guess I'll have to bring this around the front," he told Rachel.

His efforts had scraped back the surrounding sack to reveal a picture of a play set on the box. "Lauren's awake," she warned.

"Oops." With a grateful glance, he retreated into the garage. "I'll leave this in the trunk."

Rachel stood rooted to the linoleum. A birthday present. How sweet and therefore how agonizing. Her tears threatened to return.

Russ entered a moment later, no longer encumbered. "Why is she awake?"

"Nightmare." Rachel found it amazing that she could stand here chatting normally despite the emotions jabbing her gut like a thousand glass shards.

"I'm glad you were here for her." He seemed in no hurry to move out of the kitchen.

"If I hadn't ticked you off, you'd have been here yourself," she noted.

"She's happier with both of us." At last, he went to join his daughter.

The reply puzzled Rachel. She felt the roller coaster starting all over again—the surge of hope that would inevitably lead to disillusionment. She couldn't handle any more of this. She needed to go home and lick her wounds until they healed.

No more insane optimism. No more agonizing falls.

Nevertheless, when she entered the living room, the touching picture lightened her mood. Russ and Lauren sat at opposite ends of the couch, each holding a carton of popcorn. He'd removed his shoes, and the two were pressing the soles of their feet together, bicycling slowly.

"This feels great when you've been walking around a mall," he announced. "Like a foot massage."

"It tickles!" Lauren giggled.

Rachel did her best to smile. How *was* a person supposed to act while being dragged in opposite directions simultaneously?

When she dug into her own pouch of popcorn, the stuff stuck to the roof of her mouth. She retreated to pour a glass of orange juice and hide out.

Soon she heard Russ give his daughter a horsie ride to the bathroom. She listened to the water running, mentally following the process as he brushed his little girl's teeth and returned her to bed.

Rachel was still standing in the kitchen when Russ entered. She set her glass on the counter. "I'd better go. My bags are packed. I'll collect the popper later." She'd decided to restore it to Mark.

"You can't leave yet," Russ answered.

"Why not?"

"I haven't given you your present."

Her brain labored to switch gears. "That toy set was for me?" It *did* involve a police station, she recalled.

"That isn't what I meant." In his expression she read amusement, hope and anxiety. But why? "It's for Lauren. I loved the set so much I nearly talked myself out of buying it."

That didn't sound encouraging. "Because it reminds you of me?"

"What? No!" Russ shook his head. "This gets complicated. Let's go sit in the den. We do some of our best talking there."

And some of our best cuddling. "No, thanks. Russ, I can't keep going through this. One minute I'm on top the world and the next I'm bungee jumping into an abyss. Except, I never know when the bungee cords are going to snap."

He didn't argue. "Let's go sit out front. That way you don't have to worry that I'll get sidetracked kissing you. I'm not a fan of necking in public."

Although Rachel supposed she ought to refuse, what was her rush? She didn't have to go to work tomorrow. "Okay."

After fetching a blanket from the linen closet, Russ escorted her out front. In the absence of porch furniture, they sat on the top step while he arranged the wrap around their shoulders.

Although the hour wasn't terribly late, many of the houses in the cul-de-sac had gone dark, yielding the night to a couple of streetlamps and an array of stars. On one lawn a cat rubbed its head against a forgotten tricycle.

Around the corner lay Keri's house. Although she couldn't see it, Rachel assumed the family had either gone to a motel for the evening or to Keri's mom's home.

Russ inched closer. "It's warmer like this."

Against her better judgment, Rachel relished this last bittersweet moment together. "I guess so."

He gazed over the neighborhood. "Ever notice how many circles there are?"

"Circles?"

He pointed to the moon, then indicated a sphere defined by the fronds of a pineapple-shaped palm tree. Lower, he gestured toward the tricycle wheels, a car's tires and a bush clipped into a globe. "Life's circular like that. Remember those soldiers I lost?"

His reflective tone carried her along. "Sure."

"I didn't know how much they'd affected me until I almost decided against buying my daughter something I knew she'd love," he explained. "I didn't want her to suffer the way I did if they were damaged."

"But that's the definition of a good toy," Rachel protested. "Stuff you play with till it falls apart."

"Exactly. That's when I had my epiphany."

Her forehead scrunched. "You had a religious experience?"

He chuckled. "I mean a sudden, blinding insight."

This made no sense to Rachel. "About toys?"

"About love," Russ said.

A cloud of fragrance drifted from a flowering vine that draped the porch railing. Under its influence, she struggled to hold fast to her skepticism. *Don't you dare imagine that he means you. He's referring to his love for Lauren.*

"So you bought them anyway." She hurried on. "She'll adore having a family for Officer Bud. Hey, how about if I invite her to spend a night at my condo once it's cleared?"

He caught her hands. His were warm; hers, icy. "Let me finish, sweetheart."

All desire to move vanished. "Shoot."

"Just as I gave away my gifts that Christmas when I was a kid, I've been denying myself things ever since. I haven't bought half the items I'd like for this house. Porch furniture, for example. I figured someone might steal or vandalize it, so why bother?"

"This was your epiphany?" She didn't get it.

Russ continued, unfazed. "I was doing unto myself before others could do unto me. How stupid is that?"

She began to see. "You were afraid to care too much."

"Yes. As if we can control who and what we love! And as if anyone can control fate." He rolled onward. "You terrified me today, Rachel. Here's the weird part—you made me proud, too. In that horrible situation, when all I could think of was fight or flight, you rolled into high gear. Inventing that story about you and Borrego, maneuvering the guy to release us. Not many people have that gift or that strength."

"Which is why I'm a cop." Rachel braced for the expected demurral. If he started outlining why she ought to follow some other profession, she was leaving.

"I know." The statement hung in the air.

Despite the chill on her cheeks, Rachel felt almost hot. "And you're okay with that?"

He considered before answering. "Am I thrilled? No. I hate the fact that you're a target for every loony who blows into town. But I'm not going to deprive both of us of the months and years we might share because someday, someone might take you away from me. And I'm hoping you feel the same, because speaking of circles…"

From his pocket, he withdrew a small object. The shadows obscured it until he laid a velvety jeweler's box in Rachel's palm.

"For me?" Guys didn't give Rachel jewelry. The most romantic gift she'd ever received had been a set of weights. Until now.

"It's not as fancy as Connie's, but we can pick out a better one later."

As fancy as Connie's what? she wondered.

"Aren't you going to open it?" Russ's eagerness made her realize he was nervous.

Gingerly Rachel pried open the lid. It budged slightly

before clamping shut on her fingertip. "Hey! Is this booby-trapped?"

"The hinges are stiff." He shifted position on the step. Definitely antsy. "Want me to do it?"

"Not necessary." Rachel tried again, afraid to exert too much pressure in case whatever lay inside flew out. Finally she got it open, and then had to turn the little box to catch the glow of a streetlamp.

A ring. Gold, with an array of sparkly chips. "Are those diamonds?" she asked in amazement.

"They'd better be."

All sorts of possibilities ran through Rachel's head. A friendship ring as a going-away present. Or perhaps he meant it as a birthday gift for Lauren and sought her opinion. But people didn't buy diamond rings for six-year-olds.

At the risk of sounding stupid, she asked, "What does this mean?"

Russ cleared his throat. "I prepared this whole speech in the car but I've forgotten it."

"A speech about what?"

"How much I love you." His eyes gleamed. "How scared I was of losing you. Will you forgive me, Rachel? Will you marry me?"

Those were the words she most yearned to hear, from the man she loved with all her heart. But she couldn't agree. Not yet.

"Are you sure?" she demanded. "Russ, we all suffered a shock today. Trauma does strange things to people."

"My decision didn't start this evening. I've been trying to figure out how to keep you," he protested. "My screwy method was to seek an alternate occupation, which you rightly pointed out was a boneheaded, arrogant idea."

"I didn't use those words!" She had a *little* more tact.

"Well, you should have used those words, because that's what it was. I'm sorry I lost my temper." The churning of a garage door down the street drew Russ's attention, and they both watched as a neighbor's car pulled inside. Another hum, and they were alone again with the stillness.

"Nevertheless, I'm not going to turn into the kind of woman your parents would approve of," Rachel warned. "I'll always be blunt and I'll probably embarrass you plenty in front of your friends."

"I don't want the sort of friends who find you embarrassing. Besides, my dad likes you," Russ retorted. "Here's the funny part. I moved to Villazon to take charge of my life. Part of the plan included meeting the right woman, some sweet, malleable type who yearned for a family and wouldn't threaten my peace of mind. You were right about that earlier."

"And who didn't pack a gun," Rachel observed wryly. This was exactly what she'd expected: that, given enough time, he'd talk himself out of the whole marriage business.

"Luckily, life didn't send me that woman. It sent me my soul mate," Russ said. "You."

She longed to say yes so much it was tearing her apart. But what if...what if...

What if you were offered everything you'd ever dreamed of, and you got cold feet? "I'm not as a brave as I like to think," Rachel admitted. "You might change your mind. I'm a real foul-up sometimes, and cops' marriages are notoriously difficult."

His arm slid around her. "The woman who dove from a bike into a swimming pool and faced down a gunman is afraid of taking the plunge?"

"Petrified."

"Put on the ring," Russ instructed.

She peered downward. "I have to remove this other one first."

"Need help?" he asked. "I've got spray lubricant and pliers in the garage."

"Naw." Rachel yanked Connie's band from her finger, scraping off a layer of skin cells over the knuckle. Ignoring the pain, she swapped it for the new one, which slid smoothly into place. "It's a little loose."

"We'll get it sized." Russ placed the old ring in the box for safekeeping. "You understand that putting it on constituted an acceptance of my proposal. Right?"

Rachel started to laugh. "Did you used to be a salesman?"

"During the summers in med school," he confirmed. "How does June sound for a wedding?"

She brushed a kiss across his mouth. "I could go for that."

Typical guy: he wasn't satisfied with one kiss. And never mind his qualms about necking in public.

When they parted, Rachel said, "I just thought of another problem."

"What is it this time?" he pretended to grumble.

"We can't shout to the world that we're engaged, because they think we already are! Well, most people do." How frustrating! "That kills half the fun."

"Then we'd better make the most of the fun that's left," Russ murmured. "Of course, we'd have to leave the shelter of this delightful blanket and remove our butts from this incredibly uncomfortable porch."

Rachel feigned shock. "Dr. McKenzie, did you just use the word *butt*?"

"It's a highly technical term. Mind moving yours?" As soon as she obeyed, he collected the wrap and reached for her hand.

As they crossed the threshold, she felt as if she'd

become a different person in the span of the last few minutes, a woman worthy of being loved. Maybe she'd always been that, but Russ had convinced her of it.

Rachel belonged here with him and Lauren. For always.

So the part where they raced each other to the bedroom, and everything that followed, was simply a bonus. But a really, really good one.

Chapter Eighteen

The first crisis of their engagement—the real one—occurred in connection with Lauren's birthday party. Lois insisted on an intimate gathering for her granddaughter and a couple of friends' grandchildren at her home. Neither her husband nor her son could sway her, and Rachel hesitated to play the bad guy.

So she handed the phone to Lauren, who'd been whining in her ear to *please* hold the party right here. "Tell Grandma what you want," she said. "Better speak up, kid. Assert yourself."

Russ frowned at her across the kitchen table. She shared his distaste at forcing their daughter to take a stand, but Lois had to hear the truth from the source. Besides, kids who feared to speak for themselves eventually got steamrollered.

"Grandma…" Lauren paused, listening to the voice on the other end. Finally, she jumped in. "Grandma! Please come to my party. If you don't, we'll miss you."

That ended the argument. Lois folded immediately.

And so, on a sunny Saturday in March, family and friends gathered at Russ and Rachel's house. Admittedly, they'd invited far too many people for a children's event, but the affair also served as an unofficial welcome to the family.

The entire Byers clan arrived early to help. In the living room, Lauren peppered Kathy with questions about her brace and crutch, then forgot the disability as they sang a silly song together. With her parents' help, Rachel attached streamers that fit the theme Lauren had chosen: Heroes.

They'd started with police, until they discovered heroes-theme decorations that also included firefighters, doctors and nurses. The prospect of including both her parents' occupations proved too appealing to resist, as did a child-size police costume Connie found.

Rachel enjoyed seeing how many little friends Lauren had made. Russ, too, clearly relished the good fellowship as he introduced his pal Mike to everyone.

Janine attended with her fiancé, who seemed ill at ease until he and Mary's father launched into a lengthy discussion of new computer technologies. Janine brought not only a gift but the excellent news that the legal papers would be ready to sign the following week.

Vince attended with his daughter and grandkids. His broad smile reflected his relief at the D.A.'s decision not to file charges in the Flanders shooting.

By the time the elder McKenzies navigated the freeway system and arrived, a group of adults had gathered on the front porch to watch the children whack at a police-car piñata. As Lois emerged from their expensive sedan, candies tumbled down amid shrieks of delight.

Wearing a silk pants suit, she stared with dismay at the rowdy goings-on. Russ had gone into the house to fetch some sodas, and Rachel was helping the kids collect the candy in small bags. Before she could break away, Susan Byers had reached the curb and introduced herself.

Rachel watched Lois's gaze sweep across the other woman's portly shape, loose blouse and long skirt. For a moment, she feared Russ's mother might spoil everyone's spirits with her critical attitude. But Max, bless him, responded with a hug, and when the threesome approached the porch, the two women were cheerfully coordinating what to wear to Rachel and Russ's wedding.

Amid greetings and introductions, the crowd filtered into the living room for refreshments. At Lauren's request, they were having fresh-popped corn, a big hit with the kids, and—in keeping with the police theme—doughnuts instead of cake. Ice cream cones completed the menu.

"The most nonnutritious food you'd ever want to eat," Rachel admitted to Lois.

"Well, it *is* a birthday party," her future mother-in-law responded gamely.

Everyone managed to find a seat for the grand opening of the presents. While Russ supervised the proceedings, Lauren oohed and ahhed over each one, making as big a fuss over Denzel's and Alicia's homemade cookies as about the big dollhouse from the McKenzies.

"You've done a good job with her," Janine said in a low voice. "She used to be kind of spoiled." They were standing near the hall door, slightly apart from the others.

"We had a little discussion about how to make everyone feel good. I told her how I stopped going to parties because I couldn't afford to buy expensive gifts," Rachel explained. "She said she wants heaps of friends, even if all they bring is a stick of gum."

"Russ knew what he was doing when he picked you." Janine nodded in approval as her daughter raved about a couple of picture books.

"Thanks for giving her to us."

"My parents couldn't have asked for a better home for her."

A short while later, a patrol car halted in front with dome light flashing. The driver was Bill Norton, who'd promised to drop by on his way back to the station at shift change. The winner of an informal draw for the right to rent Rachel's condo, he claimed he needed to stay on good terms with his landlady.

"Yep, a real cruiser, special for Lauren's party," he announced to everyone who piled onto the front lawn. "Sorry I can't give you kids rides, but remember to dial 911 if you need help." He distributed safety stickers before waving farewell.

At last the kids started drooping, and their parents carted them off, clutching goody bags filled with piñata candy and a miniature police car or ambulance. Max and Lois were among the last to depart.

"That was fun." Russ's father clapped his son on the shoulder.

"There's something to be said for allowing children to act like children." His wife regarded the streamers, cups and other odds and ends littering the porch. "I never could tolerate mess, but kids do seem to thrive on it."

"We're hoping for a tornado," joked Rachel.

Max burst out laughing. "That's a healthy attitude."

To Rachel, Lois said, "I'd like you and Lauren to join me for lunch one day soon. I'll introduce both of you to a few of my friends, if you're willing."

"I'd love it!" Being included in the invitation meant a lot.

"I'll give you a call."

After they left, they discovered the Byers clan inside,

stuffing paper into plastic trash bags. Rachel's brothers cleaned the kitchen, and her dad ran the vacuum cleaner.

"You guys are amazing," Russ told them. "Come back anytime. Especially after dinner."

They nearly overwhelmed him with hugs. Kathy got in the last word to Rachel. "Keep this one," she advised.

"Absolutely."

The house seemed too quiet after everyone left. To restore their spirits, the three of them watched a charming DVD Lauren had received, *The Wild Parrots of Telegraph Hill*, while eating ice cream and doughnuts. Rachel experienced a flicker of guilt at serving such an unhealthy dinner, but she vowed to make up for it the rest of the week.

Lauren went to bed without a squawk. Thank goodness she didn't suffer a tummy ache from all the sweets.

Russ fixed decaf in the kitchen and sat opposite Rachel at the table. He grimaced as his chair rocked. "Darn thing. I forgot to fix the legs."

"I can do it." Rachel recalled that, in their previous conversation, he'd basically warned her to leave his stuff alone.

"I'd appreciate that. Apparently it's one of those tasks I never get around to." He let the subject go. Didn't even bother to shift to another seat. "Today was special."

"For me, too." She inhaled the coffee aroma, and discovered she was almost too tired to drink it.

"I wish…" He hesitated, then pushed on. "I still worry about you, Rache. I want us to share a lifetime."

"I want that, too." Atop the table, she covered his hand with hers. On her finger, the ring sparkled. "Nobody gets a guarantee. Each day is a gift."

"The day I met you was a gift." Russ's eyes filled with love.

"Handcuffs and all?"

"The handcuffs were the best part," he teased, and leaned across the table to kiss her.

*****

Happily ever after is just the beginning...

Turn the page for a sneak preview of
A HEARTBEAT AWAY
by
Eleanor Jones

Harlequin Everlasting—Every great love
has a story to tell. ™
A brand-new series from Harlequin Books

Special? A prickle ran down my neck and my heart started to beat in my ears. Was today really special?

"Tuck in," he ordered.

I turned my attention to the feast that he had spread out on the ground. Thick, home-cooked-ham sandwiches, sausage rolls fresh from the oven and a huge variety of mouthwatering scones and pastries. Hunger pangs took over, and I closed my eyes and bit into soft homemade bread.

When we were finally finished, I lay back against the bluebells with a groan, clutching my stomach.

Daniel laughed. "Your eyes are bigger than your stomach," he told me.

I leaned across to deliver a punch to his arm, but he rolled away, and when my fist met fresh air I collapsed in a fit of giggles before relaxing on my back and staring up into the flawless blue sky. We lay like that for quite a while, Daniel and I, side by side in companionable silence, until he stretched out his hand in an arc that encompassed the whole area.

"Don't you think that this is the most beautiful place in the entire world?"

His voice held a passion that echoed my own feelings, and I rose onto my elbow and picked a buttercup to hide the emotion that clogged my throat.

"Roll over onto your back," I urged, prodding him with my forefinger. He obliged with a broad grin, and I reached across to place the yellow flower beneath his chin.

"Now, let us see if you like butter."

When a yellow light shone on the tanned skin below his jaw, I laughed.

"There…you do."

For an instant our eyes met, and I had the strangest sense that I was drowning in those honey-brown depths. The scent of bluebells engulfed me. A roaring filled my ears, and then, unexpectedly, in one smooth movement Daniel rolled me onto my back and plucked a buttercup of his own.

"And do *you* like butter, Lucy McTavish?" he asked. When he placed the flower against my skin, time stood still.

His long lean body was suspended over mine, pinning me against the grass. Daniel…dear, comfortable, familiar Daniel was suddenly bringing out in me the strangest sensations.

"Do you, Lucy McTavish?" he asked again, his voice low and vibrant.

My eyes flickered toward his, the whisper of a sigh escaped my lips and although a strange lethargy had crept into my limbs, I somehow felt as if all my nerve endings were on fire. He felt it, too—I could see it in his warm brown eyes. And when he lowered his face to mine, it seemed to me the most natural thing in the world.

None of the kisses I had ever experienced could have even begun to prepare me for the feel of Daniel's lips on mine. My entire body floated on a tide of ecstasy that shut out everything but his soft, warm mouth, and I knew that this was what I had been waiting for the whole of my life.

"Oh, Lucy." He pulled away to look into my eyes. "Why haven't we done this before?"

Holding his gaze, I gently touched his cheek, then I curled my fingers through the short thick hair at the base of his skull, overwhelmed by the longing to drown again in the sensations that flooded our bodies. And when his long tanned fingers crept across my tingling skin, I knew I could deny him nothing.

* * * * *

Be sure to look for A HEARTBEAT AWAY,
available February 27, 2007.

And look, too, for
THE DEPTH OF LOVE
by Margot Early,
the story of a couple who must learn that love
comes in many guises—and in the end
it's the only thing that counts.

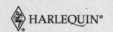
HARLEQUIN®

EVERLASTING LOVE™

Every great love has a story to tell™

Save $1.⁰⁰ off

the purchase of any Harlequin Everlasting Love novel

Coupon valid from January 1, 2007 until April 30, 2007.

Valid at retail outlets in the U.S. only. Limit one coupon per customer.

5 65373 00076 2 (8100) 0 11302

HEUSCPN0407

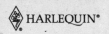

HARLEQUIN®

E V E R L A S T I N G   L O V E™

Every great love has a story to tell™

Save $1.⁰⁰ off

the purchase of any Harlequin Everlasting Love novel

Coupon valid from January 1, 2007 until April 30, 2007.

Valid at retail outlets in Canada only. Limit one coupon per customer.

52607370

HECDNCPN0407

REQUEST YOUR FREE BOOKS!
2 FREE NOVELS PLUS 2
FREE GIFTS!

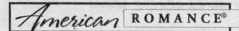

American ROMANCE®

Heart, Home & Happiness!

YES! Please send me 2 FREE Harlequin American Romance® novels and my 2 FREE gifts. After receiving them, if I don't wish to receive any more books, I can return the shipping statement marked "cancel." If I don't cancel, I will receive 4 brand-new novels every month and be billed just $4.24 per book in the U.S., or $4.99 per book in Canada, plus 25¢ shipping and handling per book and applicable taxes, if any*. That's a savings of close to 15% off the cover price! I understand that accepting the 2 free books and gifts places me under no obligation to buy anything. I can always return a shipment and cancel at any time. Even if I never buy another book from Harlequin, the two free books and gifts are mine to keep forever.

154 HDN EEZK 354 HDN EEZV

Name _____ (PLEASE PRINT)

Address _____ Apt. #

City _____ State/Prov. _____ Zip/Postal Code _____

Signature (if under 18, a parent or guardian must sign)

Mail to the **Harlequin Reader Service®**:
IN U.S.A.: P.O. Box 1867, Buffalo, NY 14240-1867
IN CANADA: P.O. Box 609, Fort Erie, Ontario L2A 5X3

Not valid to current Harlequin American Romance subscribers.

Want to try two free books from another line?
Call 1-800-873-8635 or visit www.morefreebooks.com.

* Terms and prices subject to change without notice. NY residents add applicable sales tax. Canadian residents will be charged applicable provincial taxes and GST. This offer is limited to one order per household. All orders subject to approval. Credit or debit balances in a customer's account(s) may be offset by any other outstanding balance owed by or to the customer. Please allow 4 to 6 weeks for delivery.

Your Privacy: Harlequin is committed to protecting your privacy. Our Privacy Policy is available online at www.eHarlequin.com or upon request from the Reader Service. From time to time we make our lists of customers available to reputable firms who may have a product or service of interest to you. If you would prefer we not share your name and address, please check here. ☐

HAR07

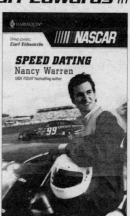

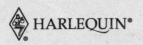

HARLEQUIN®

American ROMANCE®

COMING NEXT MONTH

#1153 HER SECRET SONS by Tina Leonard
The Tulips Saloon
Pepper Forrester has a secret—make that two secrets. Thirteen years ago she became pregnant with Luke McGarrett's twin boys and, knowing him as she did, didn't tell him he was a father. With both of them living in Tulips again, the time has come to confess. All looks to be well, until history begins to repeat itself....

#1154 AN HONORABLE MAN by Kara Lennox
Firehouse 59
Priscilla Garner doesn't want a man, nor does she need one. She's more interested in being accepted as the only female firefighter at Station 59. But when she needs a date—platonic, of course—for her cousin's wedding, she turns to one-time fling Roark Epperson. He knows she's not looking for long-term, but that doesn't mean he isn't planning on changing her mind!

#1155 SOMEWHERE DOWN IN TEXAS by Ann DeFee
Marci Hamilton loves her hometown of Port Serenity, but life's been a little dull lately. So she enters a barbecue sauce cook-off with events held all over Texas. Although it's sponsored by country music superstar J. W. Watson, Marci wouldn't recognize him—or any singer other than Willie Nelson. So when a handsome cowboy comes to her aid, she has no idea it's J.W. himself....

#1156 A SMALL-TOWN GIRL by Shelley Galloway
Still stung from her former partner's rejection, Genevieve Slate joins the police department in sleepy Lane's End hoping for a fresh start and a slower pace of life. But a sexy math teacher named Cary Hudson, a couple of crazed beagles and a town beset by basketball fever mean there's no rest in store for this small-town cop!

www.eHarlequin.com

HARCNM0207